FORREST REID was born in Be...
His father died when he was s...
ing therefore fell to his rather
As a youth he felt ill at ease w... ...piety of his
family's Presbyterian faith, and their solid middle-class values. After a local schooling, he was apprenticed at age eighteen to the tea trade. The work was not demanding, and Reid coped with the tedium of commercial life by retreating into a dream world of wonder and beauty, inspired by his reading of the Greek classics.

Reid later disowned his first two novels, *The Kingdom of Twilight* (1904) and *The Garden God* (1905). The latter risked controversy with its portrayal of romantic friendship between two boys; Reid dedicated it to his literary idol Henry James, who was outraged and never spoke to him again. After the death of Reid's mother, a small legacy enabled him to devote himself more fully to his writing, and in the 1910s he published a string of excellent, though not commercially successful, novels including *The Bracknels* (1911), *Following Darkness* (1912) (said to have been an influence on Joyce's *A Portrait of the Artist as a Young Man*), *At the Door of the Gate* (1915), *The Spring Song* (1916), and *Pirates of the Spring* (1919).

The best of Reid's works, though, came later in life, beginning with *Uncle Stephen* (1931), which, with *The Retreat* (1936) and *Young Tom* (1944), made up the *Tom Barber* trilogy, regarded by many as his masterpiece; the final book in the trilogy won the James Tait Black Memorial Prize as the best novel published in 1944. Reid's other mature work includes *Brian Westby* (1934), inspired by his friendship with nineteen-year-old Stephen Gilbert, who also went on to become a novelist, and *Peter Waring* (1937) and *Denis Bracknel* (1947), rewritten versions of *Following Darkness* and *The Bracknels*, respectively. Forrest Reid died in 1947, well regarded by critics, but never having achieved the widespread popular recognition he deserved. When Valancourt Books reprinted *The Garden God* in 2007, all of Reid's books were out of print. Valancourt is now in the process of restoring his best works to print.

ANDREW DOYLE is a playwright and stand-up comedian. His plays include *Borderland* (national tour for 7:84 Theatre Company, Scotland), *Jimmy Murphy Makes Amends* (BBC Radio 4) and *The Second Mr. Bailey* (BBC Radio 4). His most recent solo stand-up show was *Whatever It Takes* at the Soho Theatre, London. He has a doctorate in English Renaissance Literature from the University of Oxford where he also worked as a lecturer.

By Forrest Reid

FICTION

The Kingdom of Twilight (1904)
The Garden God (1905)*
The Bracknels: A Family Chronicle (1911)
Following Darkness (1912)*
The Gentle Lover (1913)
At the Door of the Gate (1915)*
The Spring Song (1916)*
A Garden by the Sea (1918)
Pirates of the Spring (1919)
Pender Among the Residents (1922)
Demophon: A Traveller's Tale (1927)
Uncle Stephen (1931)*
Brian Westby (1934)*
The Retreat (1936)*
Peter Waring (1937)
Young Tom (1944)*
Denis Bracknel (1947)*

NON-FICTION

W. B. Yeats: A Critical Study (1915)
Apostate (1926)
Illustrators of the Sixties (1928)
Walter de la Mare: A Critical Study (1929)
Private Road (1940)
Retrospective Adventures (1941)
Notes and Impressions (1942)
Poems from the Greek Anthology (1943)
The Milk of Paradise: Some Thoughts on Poetry (1946)

* Available or forthcoming from Valancourt Books

DENIS BRACKNEL

by

FORREST REID

With a new introduction by
ANDREW DOYLE

VALANCOURT BOOKS

Denis Bracknel by Forrest Reid
First published London: Faber & Faber, 1947
First Valancourt Books edition 2014

Copyright © 1947, 2014 by the Estate of Forrest Reid
Introduction © 2014 by Andrew Doyle

Previously unpublished materials are copyright © 2014 by the Estates of Forrest Reid and Stephen Gilbert and are reprinted here with the permission of Queen's University Belfast.

Published by Valancourt Books, Richmond, Virginia
Publisher & Editor: JAMES D. JENKINS
20th Century Series Editor: SIMON STERN, University of Toronto
http://www.valancourtbooks.com

All rights reserved. The use of any part of this publication reproduced, transmitted in any form or by any means, electronic, mechanical, photocopying, recording, or otherwise, or stored in a retrieval system, without prior written consent of the publisher, constitutes an infringement of the copyright law.

ISBN 978-1-939140-97-5
Also available as an electronic book.

All Valancourt Books publications are printed on acid free paper that meets all ANSI standards for archival quality paper.

Set in Dante MT 11/13.5
Cover by M. S. Corley

CONTENTS

Introduction • vii
Denis Bracknel • 1
Appendix • 196

INTRODUCTION

The pivotal moment of *Denis Bracknel* occurs in Chapter 19, and is as surprising as it is inevitable. The scene takes place late at night, in the woods near the Bracknels' home in County Down, Ireland. Hiding in the brushwood by an open glade, Hubert Rusk observes his pupil Denis as he performs his secret ritual:

> Denis advanced into the middle of the grove, and there was something in his movements, a kind of rhythmic precision and alacrity that was yet not haste, which gave Rusk a momentary impression that he might be walking in his sleep. The possibility brought him a sudden hope, but of this hope he was doomed to swift disappointment, when he watched the boy uncover the altar and place a moon-shaped object upon it. This object, Rusk saw, was decked with white tapers—tapers Denis was now lighting. When all were ablaze he bowed low before them as to some unseen presence, and then proceeded to go through the most amazing ceremony Rusk was ever likely to behold.

Rusk is observing something atavistic, a practice long dead stirring headily to life. This is theatre: the full moon works as a spotlight, deepening shadows and washing away colours to a pallid sheen. The skin of the naked boy is sharply illuminated like the transfiguration of Christ on Mount Tabor. Rusk watches, numb with incomprehension, as Denis enacts his nocturnal rites. He is awake but the scene is oneiric, the cold night air thick with unreality.

Rusk is a rationalist, but having eliminated the possibility of somnambulance what else remains? This is no private whimsy; Denis is no Mr. Bumble, counting teaspoons and dancing when he thinks himself alone. He is a high priest of his own religion, guided by elemental forces, bearing an ancient burden that only he can understand. By daylight he is an embarrassment to his father, denigrated as a "freak" and a "facetious little beast" by his peers. For the first time Rusk has seen the boy on his own terms, not as the youngest son of an upper-middle-class family, but as the "moon-worshipper" finding solace in his private ceremony. "What, then," considers Rusk, "was the relation of this naked pagan boy, with body bared to the whiteness of the moon, to the young Presbyterian who sat Sunday by Sunday in his father's pew?" The disparity is seemingly irreconcilable.

Mr. and Mrs. Bracknel have appointed Rusk as Denis's tutor on the advice of local physician Doctor Birch, who hopes that this young Englishman's pragmatic outlook might temper their fifteen-year-old son's eccentricities. It soon becomes apparent that there are other problems in this family, characterized as it is by competing personalities and closely guarded secrets. The head of the household is Mr. James Bracknel, a fusty and conservative businessman whose attempts to assert his authority are frequently met with derision. Only his downtrodden wife is susceptible to his bullying, a woman of forty-six who appears much older. Their daughters are May and Amy. Passionate and sentimental, Amy soon becomes infatuated with Rusk, and begins to see her sister as a rival for his affections. May, by contrast, is a level-headed young woman who does her best to avoid being drawn into Amy's self-constructed melodrama. Their elder brother, Alfred, continually frustrates his father with his indolence and incompetence, unbefitting characteristics for an heir to the family business. Rather than devoting himself to the trade and to self-improvement, he spends his time gambling, drinking and philandering, whilst Mr. Bracknel's illegitimate son John Brooke works diligently for the firm, unaware of his own parentage. It is not long before Rusk, as the outsider, has unwittingly assumed the role of confidant to various members of the family. As intrafamilial tensions escalate Denis becomes increasingly marginalized, and Rusk soon learns that the boy's personal demons are threatening to engulf him completely.

At the core of Denis's story is the timeworn theme of the struggle between good and evil. In this sense, *Denis Bracknel* bears comparison with Reid's novel *The Spring Song* (1916), in which the hero Grif Weston is caught between the influences of the sinister organist Clement Bradley and the benevolent Nancy and Narcissus Batt. But whereas Bradley represents a single embodiment of these malevolent forces, Denis's demons are nebulous and seemingly omnipresent. He suffers from "a fear of something that was there and yet not there", a nameless "horror", "something malign though very indefinite—floating in the air". One night Denis asks to sleep next to Rusk having heard "a kind of ticking . . . somewhere at the head of the bed". This is the death-watch beetle which, for Denis, carries the same ominous significance as it does for Tom Sawyer, one of Reid's favourite literary creations: "the ghastly ticking of a death-watch in the wall at the bed's head made Tom shudder—it meant that somebody's days were numbered".[1]

Yet these are not the mere superstitions of Denis's overactive adolescent mind. His visions can, on occasion, be remarkably pronounced. At times he senses predatory creatures lurking in the shadows: early on, a "huge sprawling sphinx" with "curved cruel claws dug into the ground, and half-raised head, expectant, listening"; later, a pale face hovering at the window, some terrifying entity that intends to "follow him to the ends of the earth". Denis tells Rusk that a previous occupant of the house had committed suicide in one of the bedrooms, and we are invited to consider that this might be the ghost that Denis saw repeatedly as a child. "It used to stand at the foot of the bed," he tells Rusk, "very tall, and with a long, white, smiling face. It was its smile that was the worst—its teeth." This apparition is no doubt a reconstruction of the ghost of Reid's own childhood, described in his autobiography *Apostate* (1926) as a "tall smiling figure with long, pointed, yellow teeth" towering over his bed. According to Reid this was no optical illusion. "If I had the requisite skill I could draw that face now," he writes, "as I still half-believe I could have photographed it then."[2] His was a mind "swarming with ghosts" that eventually he "learned to elude".[3] In *Denis Bracknel*, this spectral figure is recast as the unseen antagonist, a distillation of all of Denis's worst fears.

Denis Bracknel is a reworking of Reid's breakthrough novel *The Bracknels*, which was published in 1911. Of the two versions, *Denis Bracknel* is the superior work. Published posthumously in 1947, it was Reid's last effort, and shows him at the height of his powers. It had been a similar endeavour to his revision of *Following Darkness* (1912) as *Peter Waring* (1937), and had he lived he would have done the same for *The Spring Song*.[4] Reid's goal was to leave a body of work true to his authorial voice, one developed and perfected over a career spanning more than four decades. As he explains in a letter to his friend Knox Cunningham: "I intend now to have a look at *The Spring Song* and see how I fare with it before definitely scrapping all the tales (F. D. excepted) prior to *Pirates*. If the seven remaining are kept in print, that is all I want."[5] The sentiment is unsurprising given that Reid's earliest work shows a writer struggling to develop an individual style. Of *The Kingdom of Twilight* (1904) Reid wrote that the "pretentious title points to d'Annunzio, the opening sentence is pure Henry James".[6] Likewise, *The Garden God* (1905) is heavily indebted to the rich aesthetic tone of Walter Pater. As Reid notes in his second autobiography *Private Road* (1940), such influences "were bound to be transitory, because they did not really suit me".[7] In the interim he had discovered Anatole France, described by Reid as the person "to whom, so far as writing is concerned, I owe everything".[8] Without having recourse to imitation, Reid sought to emulate what France described as the three greatest qualities of French prose: "d'abord la clarté, puis encore la clarté et enfin la clarté".[9]

In his review of *Denis Bracknel*, Tangye Lean misinterprets this emphasis on clarity in Reid's later work as an example of what might today be called "dumbing down".[10] Lean's verdict is that Reid has been "chiselling away his masterpiece rather as cabinet-makers in the past three decades undertook the removal of Victorian flourishes from furniture". This is largely a matter of taste, of course, and Lean is entitled to prefer the more florid quality of *The Bracknels*. However, where he falters is in his insinuation that Reid has made these alterations in an effort to appeal to popular trends, that he was "preoccupied . . . by the changing standards of the audience". In an effort to explain the revisions Lean has hit upon an untruth. Reid strove to realize a singular artistic vision, mediated through a simple and lucid style, one wholly unrelated to public perception.

Moreover, the relative weakness of his earlier prose is difficult to deny, particularly when compared directly with its later incarnation. Here, for instance, is the opening paragraph of *The Bracknels*:

> Amy Bracknel, the morning sunlight picking out threads of gold from the loose mass of her dark-red hair, and accentuating the delightful purity and freshness of her complexion, watched her father for a moment of meditative silence. A faint smile passed across her face, a smile which became more pronounced as her glance encountered her sister's rather small brown eyes expectantly fixed upon her from the other side of the table. "What is he like, papa?" she asked. "Is he good-looking?"[11]

And here is the revised passage in *Denis Bracknel*:

> Amy Bracknel, the morning sunshine gilding her red hair and lighting up the delicate purity of her complexion, watched her father for a moment. A faint smile passed across her face, a smile which became more pronounced as she saw her sister's rather small brown eyes fixed anxiously upon her from the other side of the breakfast-table. "What is he like, papa?" she asked. "Is he good-looking?"

Note how the mild tautology of "purity and freshness" is remedied, and the "gilding" effect of the sunshine replaces the needlessly elaborate Petrarchan metaphor of the "threads of gold". Nothing is lost in the substitution of "she saw" for "her glance encountered", a phrase which lends an unwarranted sense of gravitas to a relatively inconsequential moment. The adverb "expectantly" is intended to denote May's complicity in the teasing of their father, whereas the implication of disapproval in "anxiously" is far more in keeping with her character. Similarly, Amy's "meditative silence" seems to belie the inherent mischief in her question, and so is rightly excised. In short, the passage from *Denis Bracknel* is tauter, more elegant, and free from affectation, far closer in tone to the narrative style of Reid's masterful Tom Barber trilogy.

A collection of correspondence, recently uncovered amongst the possessions of the late Stephen Gilbert, reveals that Reid had never intended the novel to be called *Denis Bracknel*.[12] Although Reid had considered adopting a new title, he eventually decided against it.[13] He had entertained the possibility of *The Pupil*, which he felt would have worked "beautifully", but for some reason felt that Henry James's short story of the same name, published in 1891, precluded the option.[14] The title *Denis Bracknel* was the invention of the book's publisher Geoffrey Faber, and was met with approval by Gilbert, whose only reservations were due to his feeling that Reid had "intended to let the original title stand" (see Appendix III).[15] This point was seized upon by the poet George Buchanan, who strongly objected to the change (see Appendix IV).

In addition to the modified title and the painstakingly redrafted prose, Reid removed five chapters in their entirety when it came to reworking his novel. Chapter XIV of *The Bracknels* relates a heated argument in which Amy's sexual jealousy provokes her into rashly accusing May of attempting to seduce Rusk.[16] In Chapter XIX, Amy pays a visit to Rebecca, the toothless old woman who lives in the lodge, to procure a love potion which she later mixes into Rusk's cup of tea in order to bewitch him.[17] Amy's nerves fail her; she shakes and drops the cup, spilling its contents on the carpet.[18] Chapters XXXIX to XLI form a coda set one year and nine months after the novel's climax, in which Rusk returns to Northern Ireland to visit the family before leaving for Australia where he plans to start a new career as a farmer.[19] Again, Reid's revisions for *Denis Bracknel* prove judicious. These final three chapters had been added at the insistence of Reid's publisher, Edward Arnold. When it came to the rewritten version Geoffrey Faber felt much the same way and tried to persuade Reid to retain them.[20] Reid wrote of the matter to Stephen Gilbert just ten weeks before his death: "I think all his objection amounts to is that he wants a happy ending."[21] The book's commercial performance was, of course, the least of Reid's priorities. In a unique annotated copy of *The Bracknels* presented to Gilbert on 22 July 1932, Reid has defiantly written "The End" after the last line of Chapter XXXVIII.[22]

In spite of Reid's various dissatisfactions with the published version, *The Bracknels* was an important artistic turning point. It was the work that brought Reid to the attention of E. M. Forster, whose letter of admiration initiated a close friendship that was to last for the rest of Reid's life. "The book has moved me a good deal," Forster wrote, "it is what a friend ought to be but isn't; I suppose I am saying in a very round about and clumsy way that it is art" (See Appendix II).[23] Yet it was only through dogged determina-

Forrest Reid (left) with his friend James Rutherford and their dogs Pan and Nyx in Ormeau Park, Belfast. Reid was living with Rutherford while he was writing *The Bracknels*.

tion that the novel was written at all, as Reid had considered giving up entirely. His first two novels—*The Kingdom of Twilight* and *The Garden God*—were published before he went up to Cambridge, and he felt strongly that during his three years as a mature student he had been back-pedalling as an artist. "I think I shall give up writing," he wrote to his friend Theodore Bartholomew, "as it is more bother than anything else & by dropping out for 3 years I have lost all the ground I had ever gained."[24]

Reid's letters from the years directly following his university career contain allusions to a number of projects. Eventually he had completed a full draft of a new work, provisionally entitled *A Romantic Experiment*, which Reid described as an "ordinary novel with the ordinary love interest" written to please his friend and housemate James Rutherford.[25] In attempting such a work, Reid was delving into experiences that were entirely alien to him, and was bound to fail. He had little empathy for heterosexual desire, a shortcoming only because he persisted in writing on the subject. As he later wrote to Knox Cunningham: "My range is very narrow, and the moment I try to pass beyond it, as I have done on several occasions in the past, the result is deplorable."[26] Reid was his own harshest critic, but it is true that the most successful elements of *The Kingdom of Twilight* are those dealing with the passionate friendship between Willie Trevelyan and Nick Grayson. Willie's subsequent marriage to Hester Urquhart is a misstep from which the narrative never quite recovers, a point noted by Henry James in a letter to Reid composed shortly after the novel's publication.[27] Reid was later to destroy copies of the novel wherever he could find them, including Belfast's Linen Hall Library, but was unable to suppress it entirely. *A Romantic Experiment*, however, was consigned to the flames at the hands of its author.

It would appear that *The Bracknels* rose from the ashes of *A Romantic Experiment*. Having had his manuscript returned with a rejection letter from the publisher, Reid started on this new work as "an act of defiance" immediately after the bonfire was over. This account of the novel's origins appears in Stephen Gilbert's annotated copy, in which Reid explicitly identifies the inspiration for his boy hero:

> The story was suggested by a boy called Denis Sinclair. I only met him once, but he gave me the idea of Denis. I tried to imagine a story for him and wrote *The Moon Story*—about 12 to 20 thousand words. In this Denis & his tutor were isolated figures. When I had finished it I thought I ought to give Denis a family and expand the whole thing into a realistic novel.

According to his autobiography, Reid met Denis Sinclair at the Newcastle tennis club where he was playing against James Rutherford.[28] Two schoolboys had joined them to make up teams for doubles, and Denis (known as "Skinny") had partnered Reid. They barely spoke, but something about the boy inspired him, and that evening *The Moon Story* was conceived. Later, he incorporated elements of this tale into a projected "family history", one that reawakened his desire to be a novelist. His excitement is evident in the extant letters from that period to Theodore Bartholomew. "I have got what seems a ripping thing on [my] hands", one letter reports. "It is my moon tale but transformed beyond recognition. I feel that it is

Pages from Stephen Gilbert's unique annotated copy of *The Bracknels*. Forrest Reid presented the book to Gilbert on 22 July 1932. Image courtesy of Special Collections, Queen's University Belfast.

excellently strong if I can only do it" (see Appendix I).²⁹

In *Apostate* Reid writes of the "two worlds" of his childhood, one of which is located in a "dream-land" and the other in the reality of everyday existence. Apparently it did not occur to him at any point to ask himself "whether one were less real than the other".³⁰ When not fulfilling society's expectations in his own stumbling way, Denis too occupies a "dream-land"; Rusk observes his tendency to indulge in reverie, that after waking "the boy's mind would still seem to be filled with reflections and images from his dream; as if, indeed, he were hardly capable of distinguishing between it and reality". According to Reid, *The Bracknels* was his first novel to emerge from this other "mysterious region". Denis was "not consciously invented, certainly not observed" but rather "created by a collaborator working beneath consciousness".³¹ His encounter with "Skinny" at the tennis club in Newcastle was merely a catalyst; as far as the visionary Reid was concerned, he was drawing on other forces, those same forces that haunt the

Malone House in Belfast, the model for the Bracknels' home, drawn by Joseph Molloy in 1832 and engraved by Edward K. Proctor. Image courtesy of the Deputy Keeper of Records, Public Record Office of Northern Ireland (ref. T3553).

minds of his boy heroes. In *The Bracknels*, then, Reid's "dreamland" was not only his inspiration for the story, but became the story itself. Just as Lavinia in *Titus Andronicus* brings onto the stage a copy of Ovid's *Metamorphoses*, the very source text upon which Shakespeare based her terrible experiences, Reid presents the reader with a fictive recreation of his own artistic wellspring.

This is not to say that Reid's novels are entirely fantastical. Brian Taylor has persuasively argued that these dream-landscapes "are not idealisations of the real but glimpses of an ideal seen *through* the real".[32] Reid's work represents a sensitive counterpoising act by which the lost domain of his childhood is presented through a realistic and recognizable Ulster landscape. Those familiar with Reid's favoured locations will have little trouble identifying the specific buildings, streets, and rural landmarks in his novels. The Bracknels' home, for instance, is closely modelled on Malone House near Shaw's Bridge in Belfast.[33] For the purposes of the narrative Reid moves the house to County Down, but the architectural features are faithfully replicated.

Other incidents in the novel are also drawn from life. Mrs. Bracknel's naïve criticisms of Henry James's *The Princess Casamassima* (1886) are based on those once made by Reid's mother.[34] May's "Confession Album" once belonged to Reid's eldest sister Adelaide, a book to which the young Reid had "a passionate longing to contribute, but was never allowed".[35] Although Reid had claimed that the characters were products of his imagination, "gathered from the four winds", the annotations in Stephen Gilbert's copy of *The Bracknels* reveal that Mr. Bracknel and Amy are "done from life, though I was only in the Bracknel house once".[36] According to Reid, the altercation in Chapter 15 over Amy's treatment of the servant Dixon "actually took place", and the details of her father's life had been provided by the real Mr. Bracknel's nephew.

Rebecca, the "small bent old woman" who lives in the lodge and for whom Rusk feels an immediate animosity, is a recreation of Anna, the woman who lived in the cottage by the back gate of Reid's Uncle George's house in Ballinderry. Rusk's dismissal of Rebecca as a "villainous-looking old hag" is quite distinct from the young Reid's attitude towards her real-life counterpart. In *Apostate*, Reid recalls how his Aunt Sarah warned him not to approach this "undesirable person".[37] His determination not to obey leads to a bizarrely erotic encounter:

> She smelt nice; she smelt of the bread she had been baking; and her brown and ruddy skin was smooth yet not too smooth, but velvety, like the skin of a peach or an apricot . . . And when she caressed me exactly the way one would caress an animal, her hand drawing in a slow rhythmic sweep down my side from shoulder to knee, I felt strange little electric thrills passing through my body, and queer little noises rising in my throat—noises which I only half suppressed, so that she laughed and said I was a fox and knew how to get what I wanted.[38]

Given Anna's inherent sensuality, it is perhaps fitting that in the original version of the novel Rebecca creates a love-potion for Amy. But whatever else this peculiar anecdote might reveal, it suggests strongly that Rusk's temperaments and prejudices are not those of his creator.

It is of course Denis, not Rusk, with whom Reid most closely identifies. Yet in spite of his acknowledgement that his heroes can be seen as "mere pretexts for the author to live again through the years of his boyhood", this explanation fails to do justice to the scale of Reid's achievement.[39] The semi-autobiographical elements of his novels are not so significant as the actualization of a specific and unique artistic vision, a process that began with *The Kingdom of Twilight* and culminated in *Denis Bracknel*. Émile Zola's definition of art as "un coin de la création vu à travers un tempérament"— paraphrased by Reid in *Brian Westby* (1934) as "life seen through a temperament"—is a principle that lies at the heart of all of Reid's best work.[40] It was in *The Bracknels* that he first found an effective means of expression for his pantheistic faith in an immanent reality, one which proved to be the driving force behind his art. For this reason the book has been rightly described as "the foundation stone of his literary career".[41] It is, to use E. M. Forster's phrase, a "delicate and disturbing novel", one in which visions of evil are offset by moments of tremendous beauty and pathos.[42] It took Reid another thirty-five years of honing his craft before he was in a position to add *Denis Bracknel* to his already considerable legacy. As discerning readers of the novel will agree, it was time well spent.

ANDREW DOYLE

January 11, 2014

NOTES

1. Mark Twain, *The Adventures of Tom Sawyer* (Hartford: American Publishing Company, 1876), p. 86.
2. Forrest Reid, *Apostate* (London: Constable, 1926), p. 48.
3. Ibid., p. 7 and p. 72 respectively.
4. A letter from Reid to his acquaintance William McCready dated 2 November 1945 reveals how arduous he had found the process. "It's an awful job," he writes. "1000 times worse than revising *Following Darkness* which really was easy." This letter is held by the Linen Hall Library, Belfast.
5. Letter from Reid to Knox Cunningham dated 21 September 1945 (Public Record Office of Northern Ireland, Belfast, MIC/45/1).

"F.D." is a reference to Reid's novel *Following Darkness* (1912), and "Pirates" an abbreviation of *Pirates of the Spring* (1919).

6   Forrest Reid, *Private Road* (London, Faber and Faber, 1940), p. 21.
7   Ibid., p. 73.
8   This quotation is taken from a note on the back of p. 9 of the original manuscript of *Private Road*, handwritten by Reid, held by Libraries NI.
9   Anatole France, *La Vie Littéraire* (Paris: Calmann Lévy, 1888), première série, pp. 54-55. It was precisely this lack of clarity in Walter de la Mare's introduction to his anthology *Love* (1943) that prompted Reid to criticize the writing as "mannered to the point of jargon". The remark appears in a letter from Reid to J. N. Hart in which he makes clear his own views on prose style: "I have tried more than once to persuade him that simplicity and lucidity are very important qualities in style—to my own mind you can't have a good style without them—but evidently he doesn't agree with me." See letter from Reid to J. N. Hart dated 1 November 1943 (Public Record Office of Northern Ireland, Belfast, T2121/1).
10 Tangye Lean, "'Progress' & Fiction", *Sunday Times* (12 October 1947).
11 Forrest Reid, *The Bracknels* (London: Edward Arnold, 1911), p. 1.
12 These letters are currently in the possession of Tom Gilbert, the younger son of Stephen Gilbert.
13 In a letter to Stephen Gilbert dated 26 October 1946 Reid wrote that he could not see "any point in changing the title" (Special Collections, Queen's University Belfast, MS45/1/14/58). Indeed, he continued to refer to the novel as *The Bracknels* right up until his death. See, for instance, letters from Reid to Knox Cunningham dated 18 November 1945 ("I took *The Bracknels* with me to Warrenpoint") and 26 April 1946 ("Finished *Bracknels* this evening"). Public Record Office of Northern Ireland, Belfast, MIC/45/1.
14 See letter from Reid to Stephen Gilbert dated 30 October 1946: "I don't think I'll change the title. I can't hit on a good one, so may as well stick to the old. In spite of what you say, the new version is nearer to the original one, which I called *The Bracknells* [sic], than the intermediate, published version. Of course if I could get a better title I'd use it. *The Pupil* has been used by Henry James or it would do beautifully" (Special Collections, Queen's University Belfast, MS45/1/14/59).
15 That the title was Geoffrey Faber's idea is made apparent in a letter to Stephen Gilbert dated 13 February 1947 in which Faber refers to *Denis Bracknel* as "the title I have suggested". Gilbert had evidently

consulted Reid's closest friends to gauge their feelings on the matter. Faber's letter notes John Sparrow's approval, and in a letter to Gilbert dated 25 March 1947, Doreen Sheridan argues that *Denis Bracknel* is an "unobjectionable" title, and one "that FR might have accepted", citing the precedent of the change from *Following Darkness* to *Peter Waring*. John Sparrow and John Bryson subsequently urged Faber to change the title to *Denis*, a move rightly resisted by Gilbert, who ultimately saw *Denis Bracknel* as a safe compromise which would ensure avoiding "doing anything of which Forrest could possibly disapprove" (See Appendix III). All letters cited in this endnote are in the possession of Tom Gilbert.

16 *The Bracknels*, op. cit., pp. 109-113. This excision makes sense given Reid's general modifications of May's character in *Denis Bracknel*. The dissimilarities of the sisters' temperaments are accentuated, and May is represented as the far more mature of the two. Note also the contrast between May's outburst at Denis reading from her "Confession Album" in *The Bracknels* (pp. 177-178) and her relatively placid response in *Denis Bracknel* (pp. 122-123 of the present edition).

17 *The Bracknels*, op. cit., pp. 142-147. For the spilling of the tea, see pp. 190-191.

18 Ibid., pp. 190-191.

19 Ibid., pp. 290-304.

20 Reid had asked his closest friends for their opinions on the matter. At the time of his death, Doreen Sheridan was in possession of a typescript of the last three chapters of *The Bracknels* to which was attached "a record of his friends' voting on their inclusion or omission". This was displayed in an exhibition of Forrest Reid's work held at Belfast Central Library in 1953, but its whereabouts are currently unknown. See the catalogue *Forrest Reid: An Exhibition of Books and Manuscripts* (Belfast: City of Belfast Pubic Libraries, 1953).

21 Letter from Reid to Stephen Gilbert dated 30 October 1946 (Special Collections, Queen's University Belfast, MS45/1/14/59).

22 Underneath, Reid has written: "This is where the book really ends. The three following chapters were written against my will and only because the publishers insisted on them. E.M.F. says the publishers were right, but they weren't, they never are" (p. 289). This unique copy of *The Bracknels* is held in Special Collections, Queen's University Belfast, but is currently uncatalogued.

23 Letter from E. M. Forster to Reid dated 31 January 1912 (Special Collections, Queen's University Belfast, MS44/1/22/1).

24 Letter from Reid to Theodore Bartholomew dated 10 March 1909 (Special Collections, Queen's University Belfast, MS44/1/6/33).

25 *Private Road*, op. cit., p. 83. See also Reid's handwritten note on a letter from Theodore Bartholomew dated 16 Feb. 1909, in which he writes that the "wretched novel" was "written to please James" (Special Collections, Queen's University Belfast, MS44/1/6/30).

26 Letter from Reid to Knox Cunningham dated 19 March 1943 (Public Record Office of Northern Ireland, Belfast, MIC/45/1).

27 Of *The Kingdom of Twilight* Henry James writes: "The very commendable source of its interest seems to me to be that, up to the middle at least, you see your subject where it *is*—in the character and situation of your young man—that is, in the development and spectacle of these; and that, so seeing it, you stick to it with artistic fidelity and consistency. I confess, however, that *after* the middle, you strike me as *losing* your subject—or, at any rate, I, as your reader, did so. After the meeting with the woman by the sea—certainly after the parting from her—I felt the reality of the thing deviate, felt the subject lose its conditions, so to speak, its *observed* character and its logic." The letter is quoted in full in *Private Road*, op. cit., pp. 26-27. Copies of the four surviving letters from James to Reid are held in the archives at Balliol College, Oxford, amongst the papers of John Norman Bryson (1896-1976), a friend of Reid's and Fellow of Balliol from 1940.

28 *Private Road*, op. cit., p. 84. Elsewhere, Reid's notes indicate that he intended to use the surname "Sinclair" for a character called Derek in his unwritten novel *Nina Westby* (Special Collections, Queen's University Belfast MS44/3/12).

29 Letter from Reid to Theodore Bartholomew dated April 1909 (Special Collections, Queen's University Belfast, MS44/1/6/34).

30 *Apostate*, op. cit., p. 72.

31 *Private Road*, op. cit., pp. 85-86.

32 Brian Taylor, "A strangely familiar scene: a note on landscape and locality in Forrest Reid", *Irish University Review* vol. 7, no. 2 (Autumn 1977), pp. 213-218. See p. 216.

33 This is confirmed by Reid's handwritten notes on p. 1 of Stephen Gilbert's copy of *The Bracknels*. See image on p. xv of this edition.

34 Ibid., p. 141. Mrs. Bracknel says: "Madame Grandoni. A most peculiar character, and not at all natural. She says that she is a hundred and twenty. It seems so off, for she appears to be quite active and intelligent." In the margin Reid has written: "A remark of my mother's".

35 Ibid., p. 177.

36 Ibid., p. 128. For Reid's claim that the characters were wholly invented, see *Private Road*, op. cit., p. 85.

37 *Apostate*, op. cit., p. 140.
38 Ibid., p. 153.
39 Ibid., p. 4.
40 Forrest Reid, *Brian Westby* (London: Faber & Faber, 1934), pp. 165-166. See also Émile Zola, *Mes Haines: Causeries Littéraires et Artistiques* (Paris: Achille Faure, 1866), p. 25.
41 Stewart Marsh Ellis, "Forrest Reid", *The Bookman Gallery* (May 1920). This article has been pasted into one of Reid's scrapbooks with a signed note by Ellis "in sincere appreciation" (Special Collections, Queen's University Belfast, MS44/4/2). See pp. 55-57 of scrapbook.
42 E. M. Forster, audio recording as part of *A Portrait of Forrest Reid*, BBC radio broadcast on 25 January 1952 (British Library, T6001R).

ACKNOWLEDGEMENTS

I am grateful to the following individuals and organizations for their support with my research: Deidre Wildy and her team at Special Collections, Queen's University Belfast; John Killen and the staff at the Linen Hall Library, Belfast; Deputy Keeper of Records, Public Record Office of Northern Ireland; Anthony Kirby at the Historic Monuments Unit, Northern Ireland Environment Agency; Catherine Morrow at Libraries NI. I would also like to thank Will Bordell, Philip Doherty, Tom Gilbert, Brian Taylor, and James D. Jenkins at Valancourt Books.

DENIS BRACKNEL

To
DOREEN SHERIDAN

NOTE

The Bracknels was originally published in 1911. *Denis Bracknel* is more than a revision. The theme remains, but from first to last it has been so completely rewritten that the result is practically a new book.

F.R.

I

Amy Bracknel, the morning sunshine gilding her red hair and lighting up the delicate purity of her complexion, watched her father for a moment. A faint smile passed across her face, a smile which became more pronounced as she saw her sister's rather small brown eyes fixed anxiously upon her from the other side of the breakfast-table. "What is he like, papa?" she asked. "Is he good-looking?"

Her voice was firm, and its extreme clearness somehow lent an effect of boldness to the question, even a suggestion of cynicism. May at any rate, sitting opposite, knew that it would annoy their father, and to divert his attention hastily put a question of her own. "He's only a beginner, isn't he, papa? I mean, Denis will be his first pupil?"

Mr. Bracknel looked up from his newspaper. He drank a mouthful of tea and sucked the ends of his moustache, while his dark eyes rested discontentedly on Amy. But it was to May he replied. "He told me he had coached his young brother for an examination—so I suppose we may count that as something."

He spoke quietly if dryly, nevertheless May cast a glance at her sister, warning her not to pursue the subject, which indeed had occupied them ever since the beginning of the meal. Amy, however, ignored the warning. "How old is he, papa?" she continued, with a half-defiant smile.

"Twenty-three." This time Mr. Bracknel did not look up.

"A year older than May! How interesting! Is he dark or fair?"

"He's fair," her father snapped. "And now, if you've asked all your questions, be so good as not to mention his name again."

Amy raised her eyebrows, but it was the only tribute she paid to this little outburst, which apparently left her unperturbed.

"Don't worry your father, dear," Mrs. Bracknel murmured timidly from behind the tea-things. She watched every movement of her husband with dark, lustrous, melancholy eyes, that seemed very large in the thin sallow face with its hollow cheeks and bloodless lips. She was forty-six, and her eldest child, Alfred, was twenty-five. Her thin smooth hair was already turning grey about her temples, so often racked by headaches. The eyes, in fact, were all that appeared to live in a discoloured, dried, emaciated countenance. When she met her husband's glance her expression was of a mingled nervousness and fascination. She was painfully fragile. Her body seemed like a slender husk, hardly capable of retaining the life burning quickly away within it, as if without intervals of rest or sleep.

The boys, the two sons, the eldest and youngest members of the family, were neither of them at the breakfast-table, a fact upon which Mr. Bracknel presently commented.

"Where is Alfred? Where is Denis?" he asked peevishly, looking at his wife as if he suspected her of having persuaded them to stay away. A maid, who had just then entered the room bringing the morning's post, ventured to reply to the latter question:

"Master Denis went out this morning early. He'll have forgotten the time."

Mr. Bracknel again looked at his wife, who had made some little murmuring ejaculation. "It seems to me that that boy is allowed to grow up exactly as he likes, and to do exactly as he likes. I hope when his new tutor comes there'll be no more of this."

"Dear Hubert will hardly be able to prevent him from getting up early," said Amy carelessly.

"Be silent, miss . . . ! And Alfred!—where is Alfred? I suppose he'll stroll down about twelve! I insist on their breakfast not being kept hot for them. Remember—I insist on it." His voice took a higher pitch and his brown eyes opened wider in his fat dark face, as they always did in moments of excitement. "This is the result of their training in childhood—or I should say of their lack of training. Just what might have been expected."

"Why weren't we trained, papa?" asked Amy pertly.

"Amy dear!" her mother remonstrated.

Mr. Bracknel wiped his mouth, leaving a greasy stain on the napkin. He rose from the table. His right hand, large and white with thick fingers on one of which was a signet ring, rested for a moment on the back of his chair. The throbbing of the big car drawn up before the hall-door beat into the room. "I'll drive Rusk home with me to-night," he said, ignoring his daughter's impertinence. "He'll be here for dinner."

He left the room. They could hear him for a minute or two moving about in the hall; then the front-door banged; he was gone for the day. With that an unconscious sigh of relief was breathed into the air, and almost at the same moment Alfred appeared in his dressing-gown.

"Governor away?" he asked softly, crossing the room and peering out of the window from behind the curtain. "Looks rather peeved about something—as usual." He turned to the others with a little laugh.

"Don't you think, Alfred," Mrs. Bracknel murmured, "that you could manage to come down a little earlier in the mornings? You know how it annoys your father when you're late."

"I never saw him when he wasn't annoyed," Alfred returned calmly. "At any rate he likes having something to jaw about. Chuck over the paper, Amy, and ring the bell."

He began to read the sporting news while his mother poured out his tea. She had almost finished doing so when he happened to glance up. "Oh I say, I'm not going to drink that, you know! How long has it been in?"

"It came in with the rest of the breakfast, naturally."

"Ah well, you'd better keep it for Denis, then. I'll have some fresh." He turned again to his newspaper, over which he bent a heavy unintelligent face that somehow did not inspire confidence.

His mother and May had risen from the table, leaving Amy to look after him, but from the door Mrs. Bracknel turned back to say: "I suppose you'll be home for dinner to-night?"

"I don't think so," Alfred mumbled, with a slight frown. He always mumbled when asked questions he did not wish to answer. It was his way of intimating that if other people would only mind their own business he could be counted upon to mind his.

"Mr. Hubert Rusk is to be here," said Amy irrepressibly. "Don't you want to see him? We're all dying to."

"Who's Mr. Hubert Rusk? What a name!"

But Amy was accustomed to her brother's manner, which merely amused her. "What's wrong with his name? He's a most superior young man at any rate. . . . Cambridge. . . . Doctor Birch knows all about him. He's Denis's new tutor."

Alfred grunted. "He'll have a fat time of it then. I thought Denis's education was supposed to be complete."

"Complete at fifteen? Still, dearest boy, it *is* a good deal more complete than yours is ever likely to be." She patted him on the head.

Alfred pushed away her hand. His thick, carefully-parted hair was slightly ruffled by the contact, and he growled out something unintelligible. In an adjoining room May could be heard trying over a new waltz on the piano.

Amy stood watching her brother, and smiling half-derisively, half-affectionately. For some obscure reason she preferred him to the other members of her family. She felt there was a bond of sympathy uniting them, though exactly what constituted it she could not have told. Still, his very brutality appealed to her, and she could understand him, understand the kind of life he led, his deliberate pursuit of the particular pleasures he cared for, in perfect disregard of what other people felt, or said, or thought. She threw him over a cigarette from a box on the chimney-piece and he accepted it with another grunt. Alfred's communications with his fellow-creatures very often took this simple form. "What's the matter with him, anyway?" he asked brusquely, flinging away his newspaper.

"The matter with Mr. Rusk? There's——"

"Oh, hang Mr. Rusk. What's the matter with Denis? Why can't he go to school? What's wrong with him?"

"There's nothing wrong with him," Amy replied.

"I'll swear there is," said Alfred simply.

His sister watched him for a moment in silence. Then she said: "I don't know what you mean."

Alfred leaned back in his chair, his hands in his pockets, a half contemptuous expression on his face. "Denis'll never be a man," he said. "And at any rate he's mad."

"He's only clever," answered Amy carelessly, for her own view of her younger brother was not much more sympathetic. "May thinks he's a genius." She was leaning with one elbow on the chimney-piece, and as she stood there, with her large limbs and golden-red hair, she gave the impression of an inexhaustible fund of vigorous animal life.

"What does Birch say?" Alfred went on. "Does *he* think Denis is all right?"

Amy continued to regard him with clear, slightly derisive eyes. "*All right?*" she repeated, emphasizing the words. "What extraordinary—not to say horrid—ideas you get hold of!"

"Well, it was Birch who was responsible for bringing this new man, Rusk, wasn't it?—so he must have said something."

"Whatever he said he didn't say it to me," Amy returned. "As a matter of fact he takes a great interest in Denis. Not in the way *you* mean of course: he thinks a lot of him."

Alfred looked sceptical.

"Also," Amy went on, "if I might change the subject and drop a hint, I'd advise you to be a little more careful about your *own* behaviour: papa is furious."

This last remark had the effect of making her brother glance at the clock. "By Jove! I suppose I'd better be getting along." For all that, he still remained seated. "What's this chap Rusk like, d'you think? I hope he won't be a nuisance. I mean, I hope he isn't one of those highbrow fellows, supposed to be tremendously cultured and all that."

"Nobody but papa has seen him yet," Amy said good-humouredly. "Of course, he's English."

"English and public-school, I expect, with side sticking out in all directions. What sort of screw is he knocking out of the governor, I wonder? Not that I grudge him anything he can get in *that* way."

"I haven't the least idea," Amy replied. "It was Doctor Birch who arranged everything." She paused for a moment, and then suddenly added: "You'd better come home this evening."

Alfred frowned impatiently. "I can't possibly. I've an engagement."

"Don't keep it then. What's the use of irritating papa more than is necessary?"

Alfred stared, but he looked more doubtful. "He's got it badly, you think?"

Amy gave a little shrug. "We didn't see you all last week, you know. And papa is worried about something. As a matter of fact he *has* been, for some time; though I don't think even mamma knows what it is. He wasn't in the sweetest of tempers this morning."

Her brother pondered this: then he looked at her once more. "I suppose he's backed the wrong horse somewhere?" he murmured interrogatively.

Amy again shrugged her shoulders. "Like me," she rejoined.

These words, for some reason, had the effect of amusing Alfred. His countenance for the first time expanded in a broad grin. "Well, dash it all, it wasn't *my* fault," he chuckled. "You'd think I'd made the brute lose on purpose. All I told you was that it was *practically* a certainty. Anyhow, I dropped a good deal more over it than you did."

But Amy was not impressed. "You can make it up in other ways," she said. "I can't. I had to borrow the money from May to begin with. However, I forgive you."

"And I'd better come home to-night, you think?"

"I do." Then she turned away impatiently. "You can please yourself, of course, but it seems to me stupid to be perpetually having rows."

Alfred threw the end of his cigarette into the grate as he yawned and rose slowly to his feet. For a minute or two he regarded himself complacently in the mirror over the mantelpiece. "Well, I'll see," he murmured, as if he were conferring a special favour. "I'll see what can be done."

2

As Mr. Bracknel drove along he caught a glimpse of a slight, bareheaded figure scudding across the fields in the direction of the house, and recognized his younger son. The recognition apparently was unaccompanied by any feeling of pleasure, for his face immediately grew darker, though it had not been shining with benevolence before. Mr. Bracknel was not satisfied with his family. Each individual member of it, to his present sense, appeared to vie with all the others in a persistent endeavour to give him the greatest possible annoyance. The girls first of all, with their silly questions about a young man they had never seen. Probably they would spend all morning chattering about him in the foolish idleness they had been brought up to, and idleness was a thing Mr. Bracknel detested. It loomed gigantically before his eyes now, swelling up in a sinister way till it became something like the source of all vice. Yet the chief result of his own abhorrence of it had been to put it within easy reach of every other member of the family. They accepted his years of constant labour as giving them the right to live in luxurious ease, and he doubted if, in their hearts, they even thanked him for the privilege. The despondency of his expression grew more profound. . . .

What use was Alfred in the business? More of an anxiety than anything else; and so far as the work he did went, not worth a pound a week. Denis, too, was growing up. There rose before him again a vision of that slight, bare-headed figure scudding across the fields towards home. What could he possibly do with Denis? Mr. Bracknel suddenly felt a violent grudge against his wife; a woman not capable of bringing up her children properly; in the end not even capable of bringing a properly normal child into the world. He had an obscure sense that she ought to have known all this before she got married; that she must have known it. She mightn't exactly have been able to foresee the illness that had so greatly changed her, but she must always have been delicate. He felt that he had a grievance, and unfortunately it was one for which there was no redress. . . .

He drove on, his face set in an expression of gloom. He was now fifty-seven years old, and, as regarded his life's work, an exceptionally successful man. That work nevertheless had told upon him. In contrast with his stoutness and commonplace coarseness there was something strange about his eyes—strange because it did not harmonize with what would otherwise have been the perfect animalism of his appearance—a kind of fretfulness and evasiveness, as if beneath its outer covering of heavy flesh the spirit were uneasy, troubled, possibly afraid. He wore a moustache and a short beard, and his dark skin had a greasy and unhealthy appearance, producing the impression that he was not too fastidious in the care of his person.

He was a self-made man, and the struggle for wealth, despite an amazing share of luck, had been not only hard but hardening. His energy, his mind, his entire life had been devoted to his business. It was almost as if he had come to look upon it as a huge game of skill, which had for its end the making of a fortune he would never have either the time or the desire to spend. During business hours he had rarely left the office except to attend a commercial meeting. He had even had a room fitted up there, where he could sleep when it did not suit him to go home, and where he had taken, and still took, his meals during the day. . . .

Twenty-six years ago, after a brief courtship, he had married a charming girl, without fortune, but extremely pretty—pretty, indeed, with a kind of soft radiance that was too delicate to last. It had not been his only amorous experience, but neither it nor any of the others had been able to divert his life from the fixed narrow groove in which it ran. Looking back on that life indeed, there had been singularly little in it to tempt him to sentimental retrospect. He had soon grown indifferent to his wife; his children had been born; he had bought and largely rebuilt an old house with a fine stretch of land attached to it; and he had occasionally asked his acquaintances and their wives to dinner. Also he had attended a Presbyterian church where Sunday after Sunday he had sat with his family, listening, or possibly not listening, to a theory of life he would never for a moment have dreamed of putting into practice.

And now, at the end of all his labours, he felt that Providence instead of rewarding had somehow cheated him. If his health were threatened, that might be partly his own fault, the result of over-work; but it certainly was not his fault that his sons were failures, that his wife was a semi-invalid, and his younger daughter, ever since the discovery of her far too great familiarity with an undergardener, much more a cause for anxiety than parental complacence. True, the gardener, a simple country youth, had been easy to deal with; he had been dismissed on the spot. But the matter went deeper than that; much deeper; since the mortified father knew only too well from whom the first advances must have come.

3

On reaching the office Mr. Bracknel got out of the car and went straight to his private room without saying a word to anyone. There he began at once to go through the early morning mail. The fifth letter he glanced at drew an exclamation from him. Some goods had not been delivered on the date promised, and this note now was to cancel the order. Alfred again, he thought; and put it aside to be dealt with later. The next letter was in a rough unformed hand, but he read its contents through carefully before tearing the white, smooth sheet into minute fragments. It ran as follows:

16, Medway Street.

DEAR MR. BRACKNEL,

I would be favoured if you would call here as I have something to say I don't want to write. If you would come to-morrow morning I would be glad, and it will be better than me going to the office which I do not wish to do.

Yours respectfully,
MARY BROOKE.

To-morrow—that meant to-day.... What did she want? he wondered, his eyes turning to a faded fly-soiled map that hung on the opposite wall. He began to consider several possibilities, but dismissed them one after another as unlikely. Yet curiously enough the letter did not seem to add to his annoyance—rather, his brow cleared a little, till presently the ghost of a smile passed across his face. Certain memories came back to him—memories in which Mary Brooke played the leading part. He saw her as she had been in her youth—the handsome shop-girl, a little sullen-looking, with dark hair and pouting lips. Well, all that was over now, and the secret of it had remained between them, but he was sure he had never cared for anybody else as he had cared for her then. If he had not been married already probably he would have married her. At least he had never deceived her, had never hidden from her his exact position. It had all been perfectly straightforward on both sides: she had not loved him and had not pretended that she did. Later she had become the wife of Brooke, an anaemic clerk with a pale face and weak eyes—Brooke, dead now for six or seven years—perhaps more. She could never have cared for Brooke: she must have married him for the sake of John; and when John was twelve years old they had even adopted a little girl, the orphan child of the clerk's brother. As he meditated, a strange regret overshadowed Mr. Bracknel's mind. John was worth a hundred of Alfred and Denis, yet he could not acknowledge him, could only help him more or less indirectly; and the thought that at his death so much would pass into the squandering hands of his wife's children, and away from the only child he felt really in sympathy with, filled him with bitterness. . . .

The day's work began, but Mr. Bracknel's thoughts kept hovering around Mary Brooke's letter, and at a quarter to eleven—for there was a Council meeting at twelve which he could not possibly miss—he went out, with the intention of calling first at Medway Street. He hailed a cab and gave the man the address, telling him to drive quickly.

Their way led through the most populous district of the city—most of the streets they traversed being lined by ugly little shops displaying stale-looking fruit and vegetables, groceries and butcher's meat, with a public-house at every corner. By and by, however, they emerged into a more open quarter, where the houses, though still small, were clean, and each could boast a dingy little plot of scanty grass and dusty shrubs before its door. At number 16 the cab drew up, and Mr. Bracknel stepped out on to the pavement, telling the man to come back in half an hour. He walked up the cinder path, but Mrs. Brooke, who must have been watching out for him, opened the hall-door before he had time to ring the bell, and after the briefest of greetings stood to one side to allow him to pass her in the narrow hall and enter the little parlour, where he seated himself in a hard, black, slippery armchair draped with a lace antimacassar. She herself sat on a sofa near the window, beside a table on which were arranged a few books that looked like school prizes.

Mr. Bracknel glanced round the room, which obviously was used only on special occasions. White muslin curtains hung before the window, and a large fat bluebottle was buzzing about them, every now and again banging into the pane. Two vases of artificial flowers under glass shades stood on the chimneypiece on either side of a chromo-lithograph portrait of Queen Victoria, who gazed down placidly and yellowly upon the visitor. On the opposite wall hung a coloured print of the Duke of Wellington when a schoolboy, and a few framed photographs represented, he supposed, the absent friends of the family. To add to the cheerfulness there was an enlarged portrait of the late Mr. Brooke himself, taken evidently towards the end of his life, when he was already in an advanced state of consumption.

Between the door and the fireplace, now filled with pink and green tissue paper, a sideboard too large for the room projected awkwardly; and a piano was wedged between the sofa and the window, shutting out a good deal of the light. Mr. Bracknel, quite impervious to their hideousness, had time to take in all these details while he sat waiting for the somewhat dour-looking woman opposite him to tell him what she had to say. Every now and then he gave her a quick sidelong glance not altogether free from suspicion, and at such moments he became aware of something hard and unyielding in her expression, that was far from reassuring.

He had laid his hat down on the table, but now he took it up again. Mrs. Brooke noticed the involuntary movement, and possibly it had the effect of bringing her at once to the point. She spoke simply, without hesitation, but in a rather ominous tone. "I've been thinking Rhoda had better look for another place," she said, "and I wanted to tell you first."

Mr. Bracknel immediately scented trouble, though he betrayed no sign of it. "What's the matter with her present place?" he asked.

Mrs. Brooke folded her hands in her lap and waited a moment before replying. "It's Mr. Alfred," she said, "not the place. He seems to have taken a fancy to her. He's been getting altogether too friendly—wanting to take her to theatres and such."

Mr. Bracknel frowned. "Why doesn't she send him about his business?"

"She says she's tried to, that she's never encouraged him. But I can see it flatters her to think a fine gentleman like Mr. Alfred admires her, and I don't wish things to go any further.... So I thought I'd better tell you."

Mr. Bracknel gave her a quick glance, but he said nothing.

The woman also remained silent for a minute or two, as if to give her words their full effect. "Rhoda's flighty," she then went on. "She's very quick and bright, but she's very little sense, and thinks of nothing but having a good time. John is always kind to her; it was he who hired that piano for her; but I don't know that they get on particularly well together, or that they're much company for each other. John and I are too serious for Rhoda—that's what it comes to. She finds the house dull, so she's always looking for pleasure outside. I've said nothing to her as yet, but I've thought it over and decided that she'd better leave. Only, if she does, I can't have Mr. Alfred meeting her after hours, which I know he's done more than once already, though Rhoda pretends it was an accident."

"He's met her—outside the office, do you mean?"

"It wasn't her fault: she made no appointment with him."

Mr. Bracknel rose to his feet. He stood with his back against the chimneypiece, lost in frowning contemplation of the youthful Duke of Wellington. "You can let Rhoda keep her place," he at last pronounced grimly. "I can see I'll have to get Alfred away from his present surroundings and companions in any case. I've thought of it before; it's the only thing to be done—quite apart from what you've just told me. He's got in with a bad set—drinking, betting, playing cards. I'll send him out to the house in Switzerland."

Mrs. Brooke's countenance relaxed a little. Her eyes followed the movements of the restless bluebottle, who was now wandering over the portrait of her late husband. Presently he came to a pause in the middle of Mr. Brooke's high white forehead, while she watched him with such apparent earnestness that Mr. Bracknel's gaze also turned in that direction. "How soon will it be?" she suddenly asked.

"At once—at once. You needn't be afraid. I'll see about it to-day. I suppose you've warned Rhoda?"

Mrs. Brooke rose and flicked her handkerchief at the fly, who set up a loud protesting buzz, but almost immediately returned to his former position. "What good does warning do?" she asked impatiently. "I can't trust Rhoda. I don't want to be hard on her, but there's none of my blood in her, and I never know how she'll act or how much she tells me. She wouldn't have told me this if I hadn't got a hint from somebody who saw her and Mr. Alfred together."

There followed a silence, during which Mr. Bracknel slowly twirled his hat: then replaced it on the table. "I've been thinking," he began, but for the moment got no further. . . . "I mean—sometimes I've regretted how things—— Sometimes I think John ought to be told."

"To be told what?" Mary Brooke asked sharply.

"The truth. I think perhaps I ought to—to acknowledge him. . . . Privately of course," he added hastily.

"Privately?"

"Yes, of course: that would be necessary. But I haven't quite made up my mind what would be best. It's very difficult—but I feel that I can trust him, and—and—I've a very high opinion of him."

His last words had not been really what he wanted to say, but there was something in the woman's face that discouraged him. He had been going to tell her that it was his intention some day to offer a share in the business to John; just as by his own old employers one had been offered to him. He felt, in fact, a most unusual impulse urging him to make even further confidences, to draw a comparison between John's prospects and his own as they had been at John's age; to evoke a sympathetic atmosphere in which his youth and that of his unacknowledged son should be mingled; but before beginning he required some slight encouragement, and her manner gave him none.

Possibly, however, he misjudged her, for after a brief silence she rose and said simply: "Come and see his room."

He followed her, half regretting now that he had spoken at all, for her reticence still left him at a loss. He had only once before been in the house, and he looked about him with a sort of awkward curiosity, trying to imagine it as his own home. It is true, that if he had married her it would not have been his home, any more than it would have been hers—only somehow he could not picture her in other surroundings.

She opened a door, and he passed before her into John's bedroom. It was a cheerful sunny room, but he would have liked to know what her object had been in bringing him up to see it. The walls were bright with coloured pictures from old Christmas Numbers, and in one corner was a bookshelf. Mr. Bracknel read the titles of the books, which were mostly concerned with economics. Three bird-cages depended from hooks in the woodwork above the window: a small looking-glass was nailed to the wall. A low stretcher, a chest of drawers—serving also as a dressing-table—a washstand and a couple of chairs—one of them an armchair—completed the furniture of the room.

Mr. Bracknel gazed all round, pleased with what he saw. He had the odd delusion that the austere simplicity was reminiscent of his own youth, and he thought of Alfred's sporting prints and photographs of actresses.

"John's a fine fellow," he sighed. "He's going to do well—particularly well. He's going to be a success."

But he got no further; an instinctive caution holding him back. Through the open window came the shouts of children playing in the street below.

Mr. Bracknel descended the steep narrow staircase and took up his hat for the third time from the parlour table. "Well," he said, "I must be going. I've a meeting at twelve. I'll remember what you told me. You needn't worry."

"I wouldn't have troubled you to come, only I thought I could explain better if I saw you than if I wrote."

"Yes. . . . Well—I don't think there's anything more." He opened the hall-door and she watched him drive off.

Yet before he had gone very far his mood, which had temporarily mellowed under the influence of his visit, began to alter, and his earlier annoyance to gain ground. Especially when he thought of Alfred's conduct was he indignant. Somehow, while they had been talking of John, it had slid into the background, but it now resumed the foremost place.

Nor did matters at the meeting go well either. Mr. Bracknel's views on all points differed from those of his colleagues, and were apparently of a nature that did not easily admit of amicable discussion, much less of contradiction. They were, too, expressed with a pertinacity, a warmth, and above all a personal note, which in the end, though it failed to triumph, led to an animated climax wherein action threatened to supersede argument. Mr. Bracknel wanted the tramway to be brought out as far as a certain tract of land in his own possession, which at present was of no use to him, though it had long been advertised to let for building purposes. Surely that was reasonable enough, yet the scheme met with unexpected, and in the end bitter, opposition. Therefore, when he returned to the office he was in a thoroughly bad temper, and by no means inclined to overlook anything that might have gone amiss during his absence. The first person he saw was Rhoda Brooke, typing a letter. He could not deny that she was strikingly pretty, and in addition there was a brightness and animation about her, which he could imagine might be attractive. But at present its only effect was to remind him of Alfred, and he at once asked for that young man, merely to be informed that he had not yet returned from lunch. Mr. Bracknel inquired at what time he had gone out, and learned that it had been shortly after twelve. He looked at his watch. It was now two o'clock. He sent for John Brooke and spoke to him of one or two trivial matters before finally saying: "Send Mr. Alfred to me as soon as he comes in."

"Yes sir," Brooke replied, and with strangely mingled feelings Mr. Bracknel watched him leave the office—feelings which, oddly enough, had less to do with Alfred than with Brooke himself. He began to wonder what John thought of him, to wonder if he liked or disliked him. His manner was invariably respectful, but nothing more. Mr. Bracknel would have preferred to see him less independent; he would have liked him to come now and then of his own accord to consult him about things, to ask his advice, perhaps his help; but this never happened.

Three—four o'clock came round, and still no Alfred. At twenty minutes to five he strolled in, feeling in distinctly good form, and diffusing an odour of the various refreshments he had partaken of during a highly successful game of poker. Naturally he was in a mood when it bored him to have to listen to accumulated indignation, though to do him justice he listened with considerable patience, for he had not forgotten Amy's warning. Unfortunately, towards the end of a long tirade, he was thoughtless enough to yawn. It was only half a yawn, being quickly suppressed, but his father's mouth drew in ominously at the corners. "I've had enough of this," he said with repressed fury. "To give a kind of completeness to your conduct, I understand that you've been making yourself objectionable to one of the girls in the office; that you've taken advantage of her position here in order to force your company upon her. The thing is odious, disgusting. I had a letter from her aunt this morning suggesting that in the circumstances she'd better leave; but I'm not going to allow her to be victimized because of *your* behaviour."

Alfred coloured, and for the first time since his entrance looked genuinely taken aback. "What does she say I've done?" he asked with a certain naïveté. "I saw her once outside the theatre door, I think, and paid for her ticket."

"I don't intend to discuss the matter with you. There are some things you're evidently dead to, and a sense of decency is one of them. I intend to write to the Swiss house to-night, telling them you leave here as soon as possible, and that they're to find a position for you."

Alfred shrugged his shoulders. He knew his father sufficiently well to avoid an argument when he was in this mood. He simply turned on his heel and left the office.

4

The car which met Rusk at the train brought him to the office at half-past six in order that they might all drive home together. Before they started he was introduced to Alfred, but Alfred was sullen and silent, and during the drive sat staring into vacancy and an imaginary Switzerland, while Mr. Bracknel himself seemed scarcely more talkative. Between them the new tutor's attempts at conversation were allowed to pass practically unheeded, or at most to receive a curt word or two in reply. "What awful manners they have!" he thought, wondering what the other members of the family would be like; for a visit to the South of Ireland, where he had been staying for a few days with a college friend and had met a good many people, left him quite unprepared for anyone resembling either Mr. Bracknel or Alfred. So he leaned back, and decided not to trouble further in an obviously hopeless attempt to make himself agreeable.

All the same, he felt disheartened. He was among strangers in a strange country, and for the first time in his life in a dependent position. He began to speculate dubiously as to how he should get on with his future pupil, picturing some surly, stolid boy of rude speech and uncouth ways. Then he remembered that Denis was delicate, and wondered if this would make a difference, make things easier. Alfred, even more than Mr. Bracknel, struck him as singularly unprepossessing, as belonging to a type with which hitherto he had never been obliged to associate, and Alfred's brother might very possibly resemble him. He hoped not, of course; but the welcome he had received had not been encouraging, and he began to think that he might have done better to have remained in his own country, among people more civilized.

Rusk was tall, well-built, and fair-haired, with blue eyes and an honest, kind expression in them. At school and at the university he had been fairly good at games and fairly good at work, though not brilliant in either department. On the other hand, he had been decidedly popular. Fortunately his forebodings in regard to his pupil were instantaneously relieved on an introduction to that youngster, which took place as soon as they reached the house. Denis, whatever else he might be, was obviously not in the least like either Alfred or his father. The boy's share of personal beauty might be meagre, but there was something pleasant about him, a kind of shy friendliness. He was thin and sallow, with straight coarse black hair tumbling untidily over a broad forehead. His grey eyes, beneath thinly-pencilled eyebrows, were dark and very peculiar, being set wide apart and slightly obliquely in his face, giving him, in Rusk's opinion, an almost Oriental look. His features—ears, mouth, nose—were not at all aristocratic; nevertheless Rusk came at once to the conclusion that he looked attractive. His second impression was that, though slight, he did not seem to be particularly delicate. He had been playing tennis and was dressed in white flannels, with a loose red-and-black striped blazer and a crimson tie, which happened to go exceptionally well with his dark complexion. Then, as Rusk shook the thin brown hand the boy held out, he noticed that his narrow, slanting eyes had the deep grey of an autumn sky, and that he had a singularly pleasant smile. "There's something nice about him," he decided. "I don't know exactly what it is, but it's there."

He had a further opportunity to study his pupil a little later, for he found himself sitting opposite him at dinner. Denis was very quiet, never addressing him directly, but now and then, when he glanced across the table, he smiled shyly, as if he were prepared to be very friendly. Rusk thought him strangely different from the other members of the family, yet could not make up his mind just what it was that produced this impression. For really the difference lay not so much in his outward appearance as in something more difficult to seize. Then it occurred to him that it must be because, by an effect of association, he could not help seeing the others in relation to their father, whereas his pupil sat there in a kind of odd detachment, as complete in its own way as that of the cat asleep upon the window-seat.

Watching him closely, he presently saw the boy's expression alter. His eyes were lowered, and he seemed to be gazing fixedly into a tumbler of water beside him. Meanwhile Mr. Bracknel, possibly with a desire to make amends for the surliness he had shown during the drive, was in the midst of a ponderous anecdote of the kind that develops slowly. He told it well, nevertheless, with a boisterous sort of humour one would hardly have expected. Rusk, both puzzled and curious, was still observing his pupil when May, next whom he sat, warned him in a rapid undertone: "Don't take any notice." It was hardly more than a whisper, yet her father must have overheard it, for after one rapid glance round the table he came to an abrupt pause. His brow contracted; for a few moments he continued silent as if gathering breath: then, "Denis!" he suddenly shouted, and the boy jumped.

"How often have I to tell you that I won't have these tricks? If you can't behave like a gentleman your meals will be served to you in the kitchen. . . . D'you hear me? What are you doing with that tumbler?"

Denis met his tutor's eyes for a second, and a quick deep flush spread over his face.

"What are you doing with that tumbler?" his father repeated.

"Nothing."

Rusk looked away. Exhibitions of violence never appealed to him, and this one struck him as particularly uncalled for. The man, he decided, must be a bully.

"Put it away, dear," Mrs. Bracknel softly interposed, and Denis at once pushed the glass away, while the blush died slowly from his cheeks.

To Rusk it was all as strange as it was disconcerting. He observed, too, that Alfred now for the first time showed signs of mental animation: his small dull eyes were wide open and he was watching the scene with a broad grin. The brief storm over, Mr. Bracknel immediately proceeded with his story as if nothing had happened, though Rusk had only just sufficient presence of mind to laugh when the point was reached.

"Papa hates anything of that sort," May explained to him later on in the drawing-room, speaking in a half-apologetic tone.

"Of what sort?" Rusk inquired. He was again seated beside her, this time near an open window, through which they could have stepped out into the cool, evening garden.

"Anything—well, I can't exactly explain—but anything that he would call superstitious. You know what Denis was doing, don't you? He and Amy are for ever putting their foot in it. Amy, I sometimes think, does it on purpose, but Denis is quite different; he forgets. . . . I hope you won't be too hard on him, Mr. Rusk."

"On your brother? But why should I be? Do you think I look

hard?" He liked her now: it was clear from the way she had spoken that she was very fond of Denis.

"Oh no," May said quickly, "I think just the opposite. Only he——" She paused, and they both looked across the room at the object of their remarks, who was seated in a corner, with his hands in his pockets and his head sunk a little forward on his breast. "Oh well, you know, Denis is rather odd."

"Odd?" echoed Rusk. "In what way?"

"I mean unusual; but you'll see for yourself; I'm very bad at explaining. He's—I don't know the right word exactly—very unworldly. I dare say it sounds rather silly to talk like that about a boy: however, you'll find out what I mean later on."

"Shall I? I've an idea that I'm rather unworldly myself."

"Then you'll understand him."

"You're very fond of him, aren't you?" Rusk asked.

"Yes I am, and I hope you will be."

He watched her, his face expressing the sympathy he had begun to feel. He could see her better now than he had been able to during dinner, and he corrected his earlier impression. There was an almost boyish quality about her, though she was not in the least masculine. Still, Rusk imagined, had she been playing in an Elizabethan comedy, she would have made up excellently as a boy. He was pleased to find himself getting on so well with her. He stretched his legs and leaned back more comfortably in his chair. Amy, who was winding a skein of wool for her mother, glanced at him with approval.

"Is there anything in it?" Rusk pursued. "In the crystal-gazing, I mean. It *was* crystal-gazing, wasn't it?"

"I dare say it was supposed to be. He probably found some book about it in the Birches' library. He brings home the most extraordinary books."

"And does he see anything—any pictures or visions or whatever it is one is supposed to see?"

"He says he does. He described the most wonderful thing to us the other day, but I'm sure he made it all up."

"And have *you* tried?"

"I've tried, but I've never seen anything. We've all tried, for that matter—all, that is, except papa and Alfred. But you'd better not mention it: you saw how angry papa got at dinner. I don't know why Denis should have begun experimenting just then—though it was very like him."

"And he really does see things?" Rusk persisted.

"No, I'm sure he doesn't." She hesitated. "I'm sure it's only a kind of game. You can never tell with Denis whether he's pretending or not, and I don't think he always knows himself. Anyhow, it doesn't do to take everything he says too seriously. . . . Look! he knows we're talking about him."

Denis's eyes were in fact fixed on them, and as Rusk looked over he got up and walked across the room to where they sat.

"Well, it's very interesting," Rusk murmured.

"What's very interesting? What has May been telling you?" The boy stood before them, smiling a little, his hands in his trouser pockets, his manner an odd mixture of shyness and friendliness.

"She's been telling me about you," Rusk replied.

"I knew that," Denis said. "She's been warning you, I expect; but you ought to judge for yourself."

"I'll be delighted to, if you'll help me."

Denis laughed. "Oh, I'll help you. I'll do anything." His bright intelligent eyes met Rusk's frankly. "In the meantime I think I'll go and have a look at the garden."

These last words were added as Mr. Bracknel appeared in the doorway, and a moment later the boy had stepped through the open window. Rusk looked after him: then broke into a sudden laugh, which, however, he immediately checked.

Mr. Bracknel had approached his wife and was talking to her in a carefully lowered voice so that his words should be inaudible to anyone else. Rusk noticed how she seemed to hang upon what he was saying, how her eyes were fixed on him, and how she once made a slight movement as if to caress his hand. The sight somehow struck him as unpleasant and he turned away. It had made him feel uncomfortable, for he had the impression that she was distinctly refined, and he was quite sure her husband was very much the opposite. That indeed was obvious, even from his table-manners, and to imagine her caring for him in the particular way that everything in her attitude just now suggested, jarred upon the young Englishman, offended in him a kind of fastidiousness which an experience of life had not yet had time to blunt. He told himself that he must be getting morbid, and turned again to the girl beside him.

May meanwhile chattered on, quite unconscious of the little shadow her parents had cast upon the scene; and very soon, indeed, that shadow was removed, for Mr. Bracknel, having finished what he had to say, took up a position before the fire-place, from which he surveyed his drawing-room, his wife and his daughters. His attitude was one of conscious proprietorship, as if he owned everything in the room, both animate and inanimate, including the new tutor.

"Do you play or sing, Mr. Rusk?" Amy suddenly asked.

Rusk made a slight grimace. "I sing a little—very badly—so badly that I suppose it would be kinder to say I don't."

"Oh, it's too late now!" Amy cried, and both girls at once became interested.

"I wonder if I know any of your songs," May said, "but perhaps you play your own accompaniments?"

"I'm afraid I don't—not even with one finger. Shall I get my songs and let you see them?—it won't take a minute. The people I was staying with in Waterford made me sing now and then. I ought to tell you, however, that they weren't good critics."

"Oh, do get them: you must," the girls cried.

"I dare say I can manage an accompaniment if it's not frightfully difficult," May added. "At any rate we can try how we get on."

So Rusk departed, and presently returned with half a dozen songs. Amy would have grabbed them, but May was too quick for her, and having gained possession began to turn them over, making various comments and asking questions. Eventually she chose Tosti's *My Dreams*, and seated herself at the piano, while Rusk made the usual excuses and apologies. He had a tenor voice, not very strong, and with an incurable tendency to flatness; but he sang the sentimental words with a certain amount of feeling which the girls appreciated, and which Denis and Mrs. Bracknel too enjoyed. For at the first note the boy had come in again, and stood now by the window, half hidden behind a curtain.

> *"I dream of the day I met you,*
> *I dream of the light divine*
> *That shone in your tender eyes, love,*
> *When first they looked into mine.*
> *I dream of the flowers that made me*
> *A path for my longing feet,*
> *I dream of the star that led me*
> *To your chamber window, sweet. . . ."*

And so on, through the inevitable three verses that were a feature of the songs of those days.

When he had finished, Rusk knew he had pleased them. They thanked him enthusiastically, and the girls were loud in their praises, begging him to sing again. They thought his voice delightful, and Mrs. Bracknel was reminded of an Italian tenor she had once heard—extremely well-known, if one could but recall his name. It was all quite genuine, and Rusk of course was flattered, though naturally he insisted on the girls doing their share. May did not sing, but she would play something if he liked. Chopin's second Nocturne—it was a thing she loved. So she played it, and then Amy stood up to sing. At this point Mr. Bracknel left the room.

Amy had chosen the Flower Song from *Faust*, but it did not go very well—partly because May, when turning the page, turned the music on to the floor. It had to be begun all over again, and this time May played several wrong notes, lost her place, and the song once more came to a standstill. The effect was sudden and amazing. Snatching the music up, Amy flung it across the room.

"Amy!" her mother expostulated, but Amy was in a towering rage.

"She did it on purpose! I know she did it on purpose!" And she rushed from the room before anyone could intervene.

Poor Rusk had turned very red. He didn't quite know what to do, and tried hard to look as if he had noticed nothing. Meanwhile May had picked up the music, and now stood holding it in her hand.

"Hadn't you better go after her, dear?" Mrs. Bracknel suggested meekly.

"I'm sure I'll do nothing of the sort," May replied. "If she chooses to behave like that she can look after herself. *I'm* not going to bother about her."

It was Denis who came to the rescue. He left his position by the window. "Well, I think I'll go to bed," he murmured. "I expect it's time we all went, and I dare say Mr. Rusk is tired."

Rusk glanced at the clock hypocritically. "I suppose it *is* getting rather late," he made answer, though he felt it better to linger for a few minutes longer before he said good-night and left the room in company with his pupil.

Denis conducted him in silence. After they had reached the bedroom he still loitered there. "It's not a bad room," he said quietly. "There's a rather nice view, though of course you can't see anything now. I hope you'll be comfortable. If you think of anything you want, just give a thump on the wall. No one will hear you but me. I'm next door to you." He walked over to the window and back again, as if hesitating about something, as if there were something weighing on his mind. But if that were so, apparently he decided to leave it unspoken, for he simply held out his hand. "Well, good-night," he said. "Be sure to let me know if you want anything."

5

Left to himself, Rusk of course made a closer survey of his room. It appeared to him to be extremely comfortable, giving on to a lawn at the side of the house, and having a couple of large casement windows, which might prove draughty in winter, but were very delightful now. He opened them wide, leaning out into a night as soft as velvet, and breathing the coolness of the air, as he considered the rather startling climax to this, his first evening. Rusk detested scenes; emotional outbursts of any kind always made him feel uncomfortable; and this one had been so especially crude, and he himself, through his mere presence as a spectator, so unpleasantly at the centre of it. He had a premonition that it behoved him to be extremely careful in his dealings with the Bracknel family, though at the moment he saw no more than this, since, with the exception of May perhaps, he felt that he did not understand any of them. He was still at the window, gazing out into the brilliantly moonlit garden, and still engaged with these thoughts, when he heard someone tapping at his door. Instantly he drew in his head and called: "Come in," expecting to see Denis; but to his surprise, when the door opened, it was to admit Mrs. Bracknel.

She entered softly, and begged his pardon for disturbing him. "I came to make sure you have everything you want," she said in her low sweet voice. "You must tell me if there is anything I can do to make you more comfortable."

"Thank you very much, I'm sure I shall be perfectly comfortable," Rusk replied, feeling slightly embarrassed. "It all seems very nice," he went on, as she still stood there. "I was just looking out into the garden."

"It's very quiet in the moonlight," Mrs. Bracknel murmured. "But I'm disturbing you, Mr. Rusk."

"No, no, not at all," Rusk said hastily, though a somewhat lengthy pause followed his words.

It was Mrs. Bracknel who broke it. "I thought I'd like to talk to you for a minute or two if you didn't mind, and it occurred to me that this might be a good time; but of course it will do perfectly well in the morning. I'm afraid my not being a very good sleeper myself sometimes makes me inconsiderate of other people. Do tell me if you're too tired."

"I'm not in the least tired," Rusk answered, half laughing. "Besides, it's really quite early, isn't it? As a matter of fact I usually read for an hour or so before turning in."

"Then, if I'm not keeping you from bed, I'm keeping you from your book, which is just as bad. However, I shan't be very long. . . . I wanted to speak to you about Denis."

Rusk felt relieved, he didn't quite know why. But he recognized now from whom his pupil had got the sweetness of his smile. Mrs. Bracknel, indeed, seemed quite different when her husband

and Amy and Alfred were not present. "Won't you sit down?" he asked, pushing forward the armchair, while he himself took a less comfortable seat at the foot of the bed.

"It's very good of you to be so patient," she said. "It makes it so much easier for me to say what I'm going to say. I was half afraid you might snub me for interfering."

"Oh, I don't think you need fear that," Rusk answered. He felt still a little shy, a little nervous, as he waited for her next words.

"I know my husband must already have spoken to you about Denis," she went on softly, "and I expect he told you that he had been at a boarding-school, and had had several tutors, and was hard to manage—didn't he? And he told you that you must be very strict?"

"He did say something of the sort," Rusk admitted artlessly.

"Yes; I know he looked at it in that way, and I suppose it's natural that he should. But there are some things, Mr. Rusk, a boy's father doesn't understand so well as his mother."

"A good many, I should say," Rusk replied. He could see that she was anxious about something, but he did not quite know how to reassure her. "I think it will be all right," he went on at a venture. "I mean to say, I don't think you need be afraid." He paused for a moment, and then added with a heightened colour: "I'm fairly decent, you know; and at any rate I like him. That is perfectly sincere, perfectly genuine, not just a polite speech. One has these— these intuitions. At all events I have."

Mrs. Bracknel's slender hands were crossed on her lap, and as her dark, gentle eyes rested upon him, Rusk felt a sudden sympathy with her.

"It is really because I thought I saw that you liked him, Mr. Rusk, that I wanted to talk to you about him: it would have been useless otherwise. You see—we have not been very successful up to the present in finding anyone for him. He was at school, as I say; but only for a few months—at a school in the south of England. It was near the sea, and we thought this might be good for him; but he was most unhappy there. He got ill, very ill—in fact for a day or two the doctors thought he might not recover. But he did: and after that we tried having him taught at home, though somehow that was not successful either. His tutors did not seem to understand him, and he did not like them. Of course, I dare say he was often rather trying, and I shouldn't have been surprised if they had lost patience with him now and then; but I really think they did not understand him. He is a good boy; very affectionate and sweet-tempered; but now and again he does rather odd things. You saw an example at dinner to-night."

"We all do odd things now and again," Rusk broke in reassuringly.

"Yes; but his father gets impatient with him; and that, I'm afraid, does more harm than good. Denis has taken a liking to you, Mr. Rusk. I could see it at dinner, though he did not open his lips. But that was only because he was shy."

"I'm sure we'll get on famously," Rusk declared, his voice giving almost the effect of a promise to the words. "I don't see why in the world we shouldn't."

Mrs. Bracknel smiled. "I just thought it might be better to tell you a little about him—that it might make things easier for both of you."

"So it will. Thanks very much."

"I don't want to make excuses for him; but sometimes there are such things as good excuses. Don't you think so, Mr. Rusk?"

"Of course there are," Rusk laughed. "Personally I find even bad ones better than nothing."

Mrs. Bracknel regarded him gravely, with gentle serious eyes before which his small joke faded away.

"At school for instance, and here at home too, he was always getting into trouble—about his lessons, about not working harder, about other things. I dare say he is inclined to be a little idle, and I know he is often absent-minded—careless about being in time for meals, and things of that sort—but there is something, I think, at the back of it all. When he was a child, I remember, I was dreadfully frightened and unhappy about him, because he was so different from what my other children had been. There were times when he would sit perfectly still, and I couldn't get him to play, or to take notice of anything. It seemed so unnatural for a young child to be quiet like that, and I didn't know what was the matter. I thought, too, he would never learn to read. Then one day, when he was about eight years old, Miss Anna Birch showed him a Bible with queer ornamental letters that somehow caught his fancy, and he learned to read almost at once. It is just the same now: there are some things he doesn't seem able to learn; but I don't believe it's because he is stupid or careless or obstinate. It is simply a mental peculiarity he has."

"It's a fairly common one," Rusk rejoined, without any ironical intention. Then, since Mrs. Bracknel said nothing: "I'm inclined to think myself there's not much use trying to learn things that merely bore you to death."

"Yes, don't you think so, Mr. Rusk? I've always thought so. But his father wishes him to have a sound commercial education as well as—as the ordinary thing, you know."

Rusk looked somewhat puzzled though he tried not to. "Ah yes—a sound commercial education," he repeated vaguely. And then, after a pause: "What exactly does he mean by that?"

"By a sound commercial education? I'm afraid I don't know. I thought *you* would know. It's the expression Mr. Bracknel always uses. I suppose it has something to do with the office."

"I see."

"Now and then he puts Denis through a sort of examination, and it is always after this that things reach a crisis. Denis is never able to give the kind of answer his father seems to want."

"I see—I see," Rusk repeated, but this time rather blankly. "I don't think he mentioned anything about *that* to me," he went on. "In fact I'm sure he didn't. I'm afraid——"

"Ah well, don't bother," Mrs. Bracknel murmured. "I'm sure it will be all right."

Rusk certainly hoped it would, but he felt doubtful. Mrs. Bracknel, however, rose and held out her hand. "And now you must forgive me for having kept you up so long." Her eyes rested upon him, her half-timid smile. "Good-night, Mr. Rusk; I hope it isn't even yet too late for your book."

Left for the second time to himself, Rusk went over to the armchair she had vacated. He wheeled it close to the window, and making himself comfortable, began to turn over in his mind what she had told him. He felt that his position was becoming complicated; but at the same time there was dawning in him a determination, even a desire, to cope with it. He thought for a little of Mrs. Bracknel; then of Amy; then of his pupil. Finally he thought of his own home—so utterly different from this—of Cambridge and his friends there, of the men who had gone down at the same time as he had, and those who were still up. There were several letters he must get off his hands soon, but not to-night; it was too late; and anyhow he was not in the mood. He looked out across the moonlit lawn and sank into a reverie. He sat there for a long time. At a little distance the trees were dimly massed, black and motionless against the sky. The air was warm and soft, and full of a fragrance of hidden leaf and flower. Everything was extraordinarily quiet. He supposed that all the rest of the household had gone to sleep, and he had just decided that it was time that he too should turn in, when he fancied he saw a figure moving below him, but keeping in the shadow of the house. Rusk's drowsiness slipped from him in a flash, and he became at once very wide awake indeed. He leaned out of the window as far as he could without toppling over. Yes, someone was there!—a slight, dark form, skirting now the edge of the lawn and making for the shrubbery beyond. A moment or two later it was lost to view, but Rusk had time to believe that he had recognized Denis. After all, who else *could* it be? Not a burglar, at all events: it was a boy's figure, and he was going from the house, not trying to enter it. To make quite sure he softly opened his door and tapped lightly on that of the room his pupil had told him was his. There was no answer, and Rusk turned the handle. The moonlight streamed in through the unblinded window, pale and radiant, and he did not need to strike a match to see that the room was unoccupied. He advanced a few steps. The bed bore the signs of someone having lain upon it, but the clothes had not been turned down. Rusk retraced his steps and re-entered his own room. This time he undressed and went to bed.

6

Next morning, after breakfast, Rusk and his pupil retired to a room called indifferently the study or the library, because it contained perhaps a couple of hundred musty volumes which Mr. Bracknel in a moment of intellectual expansion had bought at an auction where things were going cheap. To this collection a few novels had been added from time to time by the girls, but the room was rarely used, and latterly had been set apart for Denis's studies. Master and pupil sat down now at the table, and the former, by a few general questions, endeavoured to gain some idea of the boy's scholastic acquirements. He found these to be on the whole more striking than encouraging, though after his conversation of the night before he had not expected much. If Mrs. Bracknel had represented her younger son as possessing somewhat wayward and peculiar tastes, her description seemed fully justified by the manner in which his studies had been pursued. In the garden of learning it was clear that he had wandered at his own sweet will, and some of the flowers he had plucked there were a trifle bewildering to a young preceptor whose own studies had been conducted on strictly orthodox lines. Denis might have been late in learning to read, but it struck Rusk that since then he must have made up abundantly for lost time. On the other hand, it had all been so desultory, so unpractical, so undirected, that it had left him in many respects childishly ignorant. Rusk began to see how his predecessors might have found their pupil difficult, for after an hour's investigation he himself was still extremely hazy as to where they ought to begin.

"I can't quite get at exactly *how* you've been working," he was driven at last to confess. "What is your own idea in the matter? You've followed your own ideas pretty exclusively, haven't you? so you ought to be able to tell me. If you were left to yourself, I mean, what would you do?"

"I don't know, I don't expect I'd do anything," Denis replied.

Rusk frowned. "That, of course, is nonsense. You *have* done things: you haven't just taken the line of least resistance. What is it you were looking for in the books you read? You seem to have read some unusual ones, and it can't have been altogether by chance."

Denis, without answering, leaned back in his chair, his hands in his pockets, a slightly bored expression on his face.

To most persons there would have been something distinctly irritating both in his silence and in his attitude, but Rusk was not easily irritated, though possibly a certain dissatisfaction was visible in his countenance, for the boy abruptly sat up and his air of indifference vanished. "I'm sorry," he apologized. "I *will* try to work properly."

Rusk broke into a laugh. He could not help it. There was something in Denis's expression which told him that the apology had been genuine, and that it was his own method of approach which was at fault. He had started on his duties with a vague notion of pedagogic dignity to be kept up, but all such ideas now melted away in a sense of amused companionship. This odd friendly boy was altogether too different from the pupil he had pictured in his mind to allow him to make use of any preconceived methods and plans. He felt that their relation would either have to be one of simple friendship or else that it would fail. "By the way, how old are you?" he asked.

"Fifteen. . . . I know I'm frightfully ignorant for my age."

"Oh, you're not particularly old," Rusk said good-humouredly.

There followed a pause, during which he became conscious that Denis was regarding him with a doubtful, half-questioning look in his eyes. "I think you're disappointed," he said.

Rusk's mouth twitched at the corners. "If you'll only keep your promise and do a little work I'll not be disappointed," he replied.

"I'm going to: I'm going to work like anything."

"That's all right, then," Rusk said. "I think we might work a little at cricket too, if we can get a net fixed up."

These last words had been prompted by a glance out of the window into the green and gold summer morning, but the response they elicited was dubious. "I'm absolutely rotten at games," Denis said frankly. "I've never had any practice either."

"Then we'll begin as soon as possible. You play tennis, I know. You'd been playing yesterday before I arrived."

"I suppose so—after a fashion. . . . Honestly, it will be no fun for you playing with me."

"We can try at all events," Rusk persisted. "I'm not such a tremendous blood myself."

He next set him a few rudimentary questions in mathematics, only to discover that here at all events his pupil's mind was virgin soil. He remembered what Mrs. Bracknel had told him, and decided that he must have hit upon one of the subjects which hadn't proved interesting. But at this juncture there came a quick tap at the door, followed immediately by the turning of the handle.

"May I come in?" Amy asked, leaning her head, with its nimbus of red-gold hair, into the room, while she held the door ajar and smiled at Rusk, who had looked up on hearing the sound. "I want to get a book." Her smile persisted, but she made no movement to come any further till Rusk rose from his chair. Then she advanced, looking him straight in the eyes, and it was he who first averted his gaze. "Oh, please don't bother about me, or I'll think I'm disturbing you." She went over to the shelves, still smiling.

"It would be a pity to give you such a wrong impression!" Denis murmured.

Amy's smile vanished. "Don't be impertinent," she answered sharply. "I can't say I envy you, Mr. Rusk, having to teach my brother."

"If that——" Denis was beginning, when his sister interrupted him. "Now he's going to be clever," she said.

Rusk, with the memory of last night's scene still vivid in his mind, felt shy and uncomfortable. He did not quite know what to do, for he was not inclined, while Amy was still in the room, to proceed with the explanation he had been in the midst of when she had entered. On the other hand, to wait in silence made him feel foolish, and to feel foolish naturally annoyed him. He had a strong suspicion, moreover, that her book was an imaginary one, and that she had come in merely out of curiosity. He hoped she wouldn't make a habit of doing so, and perhaps it would be as well to let her know at once that he didn't care for interruptions. But his courage failed him, and he contented himself with the thought that he would certainly do so next time, if the thing should ever occur again.

Meanwhile Amy had seated herself in an armchair, with all the appearance of settling down for a chat. "Alfred is going to Switzerland to-morrow," she began. "Papa is sending him. He's to go into the business there, and he doesn't want to. He's been grumbling at mamma and May and me for the last half-hour; as if *we* could do anything! Before papa, of course, he's as quiet as a lamb."

"He doesn't care for the idea, then?" Rusk murmured politely.

Amy laughed. "Care for it! If you only heard him! Of course it means leaving all his friends here, and I must say I can understand his not liking that part of it. . . . Besides he says he hates foreigners."

"He knows so many!" Denis put in.

Amy ignored the interruption. "*You* have been to Switzerland, Mr. Rusk, haven't you?" she asked.

"Only for a week or two."

"To climb the mountains, I suppose?"

"I did do a little climbing while I was there."

"I'm sure you did. I expect you're awfully good at anything of that sort!" This last remark was accompanied by a glance of frank appreciation.

"I say, you know," Denis began, "we're supposed to be——"

"Oh, do hold your tongue. Of all the odious little prigs! *You'll* never climb a mountain, at any rate." And once more she turned to Rusk, who, to his annoyance, felt the blood mounting to his cheeks.

"Well, I suppose I must see if my book is here," she laughed, yet still without getting up.

"Can I help you?" Rusk asked, stepping forward.

"No, thanks: I'd be ashamed to tell you the title. You're far too learned and I'm afraid this is only a love story."

Rusk said nothing, but he had an uneasy feeling now that his shyness was amusing her.

"The hero comes from Norway," Amy pursued deliberately. "He's tall, with fair hair and blue eyes."

She kept her own eyes on Rusk's face as she enumerated these attractions, and again the young man felt himself colouring. Decidedly he did not like the freedom of Miss Amy Bracknel's manner, and to escape from it he turned to Denis. "Well, I think we'd better be getting on with our algebra," he said, seating himself at the table beside the boy. But he still felt that Amy's gaze was fixed upon him, and he grew more and more nervous as he endeavoured to bring some light to his pupil's extremely hazy ideas on the subject before them.

"How *can* you be so stupid, Denis!" Amy broke in suddenly. "I wonder Mr. Rusk has any patience left!"

"You might have seen he has a good deal," her brother replied.

Rather to Rusk's surprise, Amy at this did at last get up. "Thank you," she returned with dignity, and moved slowly across the room, while the tutor remained carefully absorbed in Denis's sum.

Only after he had heard the door closing behind her did he glance up, to find his pupil's narrow grey eyes studying him with an unfathomable expression. As he encountered Rusk's gaze, however, Denis immediately lowered his own, and neither of them spoke a word till the boy asked some question regarding his work.

7

The advent of the new tutor was followed a few days later by a period of cold wet weather during which, except for afternoon walks along heavy muddy roads under grey skies and dripping trees, master and pupil were confined pretty closely within doors. But when this was past the summer renewed itself, and a golden sleepy July followed on a rainy June. Rusk had dropped by now completely into the ways of his new life. The strangeness had worn off; he had had time to look about him; and he had already formed the basis of the friendship which was henceforward to bind him more and more closely to his pupil. Yet Denis often puzzled him. At times the boy seemed even younger than his actual years, while at other times the things he said, or perhaps more his manner of expressing himself, were quite grown-up. Rusk decided that it was because, except for that brief and unfortunate experience of school, Denis had mixed far too little with companions of his own age.

He was somewhat surprised to learn that the Bracknels, as a family, never went away for the summer, but he was not, in his present surroundings, greatly dismayed by the prospect. For these surroundings he thought extremely pleasing. The house itself, no doubt, could boast more of comfort than of beauty, but it had at least been erected on an admirably-chosen site. It stood upon an eminence just high enough to give a charming view from certain spots, whence one could see between fine old trees a distant chain of blue-grey hills, with dark lines of hedges lining the lower slopes.

On hot summer days a bluish haze hung perpetually about these hills, while the middle distance swam in a sea of floating light. All around was a singularly beautiful country. On the right was the river, winding between richly wooded banks: on the left, a broad tract of pasture-land, intersected by ancient lanes and brambled ditches. The slope up to the house from the road was dotted with clumps of gorse-bushes, among which, ever since Alfred's departure for Switzerland, rabbits flashed their white scuts in happy security; and on this slope, in the shadow of a horse-chestnut tree, one afternoon Rusk and his pupil lay basking in the heat. They had just come out from lunch, and were wearing loose flannel suits. Rusk had put on a panama hat, which half hid his sunburnt face, but the boy as usual was bare-headed. He was sitting up playing with Rex the spaniel, while his tutor lay stretched at full length on the grass.

"What are we going to do?" Denis asked for the third time, giving his companion a slight poke, as if to prevent him from falling asleep. "Shall we go out in the punt?"

"My dear boy, it's much too hot and much too soon after lunch for violent exercise. Why can't we stay where we are?"

"It would be nice on the river under the trees," Denis said, stroking the spaniel's long, silky ears.

"Possibly; but we'd have to get there first; and I've an idea there would be flies."

"Flies!" echoed Denis disgustedly. "What matter about flies? Would you like to play croquet?"

"Certainly not."

"Tennis?"

"Later on, perhaps. But why this sudden passion for activity?"

"Oh well, you know; you're lazy."

Rusk yawned, and felt in his pocket for his pipe. "Very likely. I shouldn't mind a bathe.... By the way, I saw you last night. I thought I'd better tell you."

Denis raised his eyebrows and gave a slight shrug, but he said nothing. He clasped his lean brown hands about his knees and looked away towards the hills. The trees at the end of the plantation were dark and compact, though faintly veiled by a thin quivering haze which indicated the full heat of the day, while those closer at hand stood out clear and vivid, showing in relief against the remoter landscape with the freshness and brightness of a child's transfer-picture. A few swallows were skimming over the grass in low curves of flight, and in the hedgerow at the foot of the incline, the purple of a mass of foxgloves caught the sunlight. On the right, higher up, one had a glimpse of a corner of the house itself—with a thin wreath of smoke from one of the chimneys floating up into the still air. The grey stone spire of a church peeped between the trees on the left, and the distant crowing of a cock came faintly across the fields from the same direction, mingled with the low sounds of summer.

"I only mentioned it," Rusk went on, "because I think I saw you once before—on the night of my arrival. Is it indiscreet to ask what you were doing?"

"Supposing it is?"

"Oh then you needn't tell me, and no harm will be done."

Denis hesitated. "Where did you see me?" he asked.

"I saw you going into the shrubbery, and I kept a look-out for nearly half an hour, but you didn't come back."

The boy for a minute or two sat silent. He looked at Rusk, who had kept his eyes closed all the time he was speaking. "I don't sleep very well," he said at length.

"Not much wonder, if you wander about half the night."

"But I don't really—at least, not always."

"You don't what?"

"I don't sleep well. It's when the moon is full."

Rusk at this partly unclosed his eyes to give his pupil a glance: then he closed them again. "What has the moon got to do with it?" he asked.

The boy shrugged his shoulders. "How do I know? I was born under it, I suppose. 'My mother bore me 'neath the streaming moon, and all the enchanted light is in my soul. . . .' I'm talking nonsense: don't bother about me."

He made a movement as if to get up, but Rusk stretched out a large detaining hand in whose grasp he was helpless.

"Seriously," Denis went on, surveying his own limbs rather ruefully, "do you think I'll ever be any good for anything?"

"It depends on what you want to be good for," Rusk replied. "I don't think you'll ever be a champion heavyweight, if that's what you mean; though you've wonderfully improved even in that direction since I've known you: that is, in the last two months."

"In the direction of champion heavy-weights?" Denis sighed sceptically. "I'm only seven stone something. . . . When I was at school I used to be ashamed to undress before the other boys because I was so thin. I'm ashamed still, when there's anybody to see me—at a bathing-place, for instance. You've seen me yourself, but I don't mind so much about you." Again he made an attempt to escape. "I say, do let me go."

"I'll let you go when you promise not to talk in a stupid way about yourself: not till then."

"I wish it *was* stupid," Denis rejoined, with a half-comical grimace.

"It is."

"But why?"

"For one thing, because it isn't true."

"Why isn't it true? You must know as well as I do that it has taken all kinds of manœuvring even to keep me alive."

"That's a thing of the past," Rusk said quietly.

"It'll have to be a thing of the future too, unless the trouble is all to be wasted."

Rusk said nothing, but he still retained his grasp of the boy, who every now and again gave a futile wriggle towards escape.

"In Sparta I'd probably have been exposed immediately after I was born. Papa, don't you think? would have been all for exposure, but not mamma."

Rusk got on to his feet and brushed the little particles of stick and grass from his clothes. "You're an amazing kid," he murmured. "I don't know what to make of you." His eyes rested in a sort of grave, doubtful amusement on the boy, who smiled up at him gaily.

But presently Denis frowned. "By the way, you didn't say anything to anyone else about seeing me, did you?"

"No."

Denis coloured. "I'm sorry," he said. "I don't know why I asked you that." He passed his arm beneath his tutor's, and they sauntered slowly over the grass, the dog running on ahead and every now and then darting off in wild, fruitless pursuit of a rabbit. They reached the bottom of the hill, where the grass grew lush and green in the shadow of a hedge of twisted oak and beech and bramble. The honeysuckle was faintly fragrant, and on a half-unfolded wild rose a dragon-fly hung, gleaming in the sunshine like some highly-polished jewel. The water in the ditch had dried up, but the weeds and grasses were still fresh and cool and moist. The hedge was full of birds, flying in and out, dipping over the tops of sorrel and plantain to catch darting flies.

Abruptly, through the low music of this summer world, there came the noise of an approaching car. "It's Doctor Birch," said Denis, turning to look; and as the car came opposite them the driver drew up, opened the door, and stepped out. He was a middle-aged man, with very keen eyes, clear-cut features, and hair already grey at the temples. He greeted the pedestrians from the other side of the hedge, and Denis introduced his companion.

"I've been intending to call on you for weeks," the doctor declared. "But I was away from home when you arrived, and I've been extremely busy ever since I got back. . . . I hope this young man is behaving himself."

"Oh yes, fairly well."

"As well as can be expected, I suppose. . . . Bring Mr. Rusk over to tea this afternoon, Denis. I'll tell my sisters to expect you." And he got into the car again.

"He's clever," said Denis, watching him drive off. "He was doctor at the Asylum for a while, but he gave it up a year or two ago. I wonder if he felt he was beginning to get a bit queer himself."

"Is he queer?"

"No, of course not: I was only making fun. I like him."

They walked on, keeping close to the hedge, till they reached the fringe of a little wood lying in a triangular-shaped valley which stretched from the road up past the house and gradually widened in that direction.

"By the way, you haven't *yet* answered the question I asked you under the chestnut-tree," Rusk observed. "Don't you want to?"

Denis for a moment looked uncertain. "It isn't that," he said. "I mean, it isn't that I want to keep anything from you. I don't. . . . Come and I'll show you my temple," he added impulsively. "I'll tell you all about it as we go along. I've never spoken of it to anyone else."

Rusk laid his hand on the boy's shoulder. "I think you like mystifying people," he said.

"No, no; it isn't that," Denis answered. "It isn't really. I don't want to mystify *you*, for instance. I'd like to tell you everything. . . . It's only that I'm afraid you mightn't understand."

Rusk laughed. "You think I haven't sufficient imagination? But even supposing I don't understand?"

"Well, then—it would be all wrong, don't you see? But I'm going to risk it. . . . It was to come here—to this place I'm taking you to now—that I went out last night, and that other night you saw me."

"You mean, to come to your temple?"

Denis nodded. "You mustn't look like that," he went on. "I can't tell you if you do. It's real; it's true. . . . It isn't a temple," he added: "it's only an altar. I found it by accident—or perhaps not quite by accident—just a big stone beside a well: but I thought it was an altar, because I knew the ancient Druids used to look upon wells as sacred. Beside the well there is a hawthorn."

"And do you connect it with anything—the altar, I mean? Is it dedicated to anything in particular?"

"To the moon-spirit," Denis said.

Rusk was curious, for the boy seemed to be speaking quite seriously. "You mean you have a secret place where you come to worship the moon?"

Denis nodded.

"You really mean it?"

"Yes."

The tutor looked only half convinced. Nevertheless, there was an odd note in Denis's voice which deepened his attention, for he had never heard it there before. At that moment, happening to glance at him, he even fancied that he had grown paler, though probably this was only an effect of the light, for they were passing under thickly-leaved boughs, which stretched almost like a green, trellised roof above them. "And for how long has this been going on?" he asked.

"Oh, for ages. . . . I don't know for how long. . . . Not always in this place, of course. This place I found in a dream."

"In a dream?" Rusk thought of the crystal-gazing, and May's comments upon it.

"I dreamt of it one night, and when I went there next morning I found the stone and all, just as it had been in my dream—except that the stone was nearly hidden by creepers which I had to clear away. . . . What I'm telling you is true," he went on, turning his grey eyes—now a little clouded—on his companion, as if in some way he divined the instinctive incredulity Rusk had been careful not to express. "I swear that it's true, but if still you don't believe me I can't tell you anything more. . . . And I know you don't believe me," he added next moment. "We'd better go back."

Rusk hesitated. He felt that the whole thing might become rather queer. But possibly his curiosity got the better of his common sense, or of his conscience, for he said: "Of course I believe you: only I'm a little surprised, naturally."

Denis still appeared to waver between mistrust and a strong desire to unburden himself.

"But don't tell me if you don't want to," Rusk added good-humouredly, and these words for some reason had a reassuring effect upon the boy.

He went on more confidently. "I've had this feeling all my

life. . . . I told you that the moon affected my sleep. It affects me in other ways too. I can feel something wakening in me as it grows fuller—a kind of excitement—something moving in my blood. My mind seems to waken up: I feel freer——"

Rusk glanced at him searchingly. "I suppose you haven't been reading anything to give you such ideas?" he questioned, but Denis shook his head. "I've always had them. . . . I've read things, of course—what I could find—but it wasn't much."

"There was the worship of Artemis among the Greeks," said Rusk vaguely. "But I don't know a great deal about Greek religion, and Artemis, I dare say, may not have been entirely a moon-goddess. . . . There was Selene, too, the moon that fell in love with Endymion; and Hecate——"

"I don't think of any particular god or goddess," Denis said. "I mean I don't think of names. There is something behind them all."

"Something——" Rusk began; but the remark he had been about to make he left unspoken. "The old religions, then, don't interest you?"

"Oh yes, they do, but—— Oh yes, they interest me very much." The last words, however, were spoken in a different tone, as if he felt that possibly he had said too much, and were trying now to cover it up. "It was principally by agricultural races like the ancient Babylonians that the moon was worshipped," he went on, with an erudition sufficiently quaint to have amused Rusk at any other time. "Among them the moon was a god, not a goddess. With the Persians it was one of the seven archangels. . . ." Then his voice dropped again into its former dreamy cadence. "Do you remember the verse in the Bible? 'If I beheld the moon walking in brightness; and my heart hath been secretly enticed or my mouth hath kissed my hand; this also were an iniquity; for I should have denied the God that is above.'"

"I'm afraid I don't," Rusk confessed.

"It's an allusion to moon-worship, I suppose."

"No doubt. . . . Of course you come across references to the moon in lots of old writers." He vainly tried to remember one or two. "They thought it had an effect on the—eh—growth of things, didn't they? and that it sometimes caused madness—lunatics, you know?"

He was not much impressed by his own learning, but it appeared to have made Denis thoughtful. "Madness?" He paused on the word, and when he went on again there was a vague disquiet in his voice. He spoke slowly, as if with a certain difficulty. Rusk, looking at him, felt for the first time a faint shadow of uneasiness creeping across his mind.

"You begin your work when the moon is growing—and the full moon brings it to perfection. . . . If you fill a silver basin with water and hold it so that the full moon is reflected in it, and if you drink the water, then the power of the moon——"

"But my dear boy, I hope you don't *believe* in all these old superstitions?" Rusk interrupted sharply.

"No; I don't." Again a troubled look came into his face. "I—I don't know what I believe." His voice shook, and he turned away. Rusk could see that he had suddenly become very much agitated; that he was even trembling. And this perception brought him up at once with a quick, unpleasant shock.

"Never mind, Denis," he said firmly yet gently. "We'll talk about it another time."

"It's just here," Denis murmured, parting the bushes with his hands. "You may as well see it now you've come so far." And Rusk followed him into a kind of glade.

The well was there, and the old hawthorn, but he did not see the altar till the boy removed a heap of branches which hid it from view. He then saw a large flat stone, oblong in shape, and hollowed in the middle. It seemed to be about four feet in length and eighteen inches thick, but it was partially buried in the ground.

Rusk examined it curiously. He was no antiquary, however, and could make nothing of it. "How was the—the ritual conducted?" he asked. "I suppose there was some kind of ceremony."

"You mean in the old time?" said Denis dejectedly.

"Yes."

"I don't know. I could never find anything definite. Sometimes there was dancing. There were libations and incense, and moon-shaped cakes that were covered with lights."

All at once Rusk's expression changed and he gave the boy a quick keen glance. He bent lower, then lower still, over the hollow stone, as if he had detected something. "Was there ever more than that?" he asked slowly, and without looking up; but Denis made no reply. "There seems to be a——" He paused. For a moment it appeared as if he were not going to finish his sentence: then he brought it out in spite of himself. "Has anything been killed here?" he asked, trying to speak quite naturally. "Has there been any living sacrifice—any blood spilled?"

Denis drew back. His face was white and scared, and his eyes had grown darker, as if with an awakened memory. "Yes," he whispered.

There followed a silence, during which Rusk was conscious of feeling rather sick. In spite of himself a sense of repulsion made him draw away from the boy beside him. "So it was that!" he said, and for all his effort he could not keep an instinctive note of aversion out of his voice.

Denis looked at him a moment; then dropped on to the grass and hid his face in his arms. The whole thing had come so quickly, so unexpectedly, that Rusk stood there dumbfounded, not knowing what to do. The mere sight of the boy lying there had changed his feeling of repugnance to compassion. He felt, indeed, horribly ashamed of himself. It seemed to him that he had urged Denis to confide in him, and then had turned on him for having done so. He bent down over him. "Denis!" he said.

But the boy did not stir for a minute or two, and when he got up he showed Rusk a white and troubled face. "I couldn't help it," he said in a low voice. "I've been trying to realize it. I'll never do it again. I'm not cruel really. I never hurt anything before. Something made me do it; I don't know what. . . . I did it twice, but the other times there was never anything living—I just brought flowers, and the things I told you of." His words came out a little jerkily, and he did not look at Rusk while he was speaking.

"Oh, it's all right," the latter said rather lamely. "It was only that for a moment I—didn't understand, didn't see."

"It isn't all right," Denis answered miserably. "I—I can't understand it myself. . . . It is as if it—was something from outside. But

—you know—if it is in your mind—— It's like trying to struggle against a dream when you're dreaming."

"Don't bother about it," Rusk said. "I was stupid. I've no imagination. I can never grasp anything until it has been drummed into me for years."

"No, no: it was quite natural—what you felt. But—— I didn't think of any of this when I began to tell you."

"I think you're making a great deal too much of it now," Rusk said quietly. "We'll talk it all over some other time."

Denis shook his head. "I don't want to talk of it another time: I've nothing more to say: you've seen now for yourself."

"I haven't seen anything that makes the least difference," Rusk replied.

"Haven't you?"

"No." His mouth closed determinedly, and they moved slowly on, retracing their path. Presently he placed a large hand firmly on the boy's shoulder. "By the way, before we leave all this, there's something—— I mean I hope you won't be afraid to ask me if there's ever anything I can do.... You understand? ... What I want to say is that I hope you won't, on account of what happened this afternoon, be afraid to tell me about things—*anything*—even if you think it something bad—really bad, that is—wicked.... I behaved like a fool to-day, but I won't be so stupid again. I dare say it's unnecessary for me to talk like this, but still—— If you should ever feel inclined, for instance, to do something you've an idea you might afterwards be ashamed of having done.... It seems a rotten notion to suggest—but you know what I mean.... You'll promise, won't you?"

"Yes," said Denis.

They had by this time issued forth again into the sunshine, and Rusk wondered what he could do to put all that had taken place out of the boy's mind. For that matter, he himself felt that the sunlight was very welcome, and unconsciously he breathed a sigh of relief. But it was Denis who solved his problem by reminding him that they had promised to call on the Miss Birches, an engagement which must be kept at once if it were to be kept at all.

"You don't mind going, do you?" Denis asked.

"No; I should like to."

So they started off, walking quickly, as if eager to leave behind them the wood, which to Rusk still seemed to cast a disquieting shadow along their path.

8

They approached the long, low house by a path that led through a sweetly-smelling, trim and brilliant garden. A gardener was mowing the grass at the side of the house, and the hum of the machine rose sleepily through the heat of the cloudless afternoon. There was for Rusk an old-fashioned charm about the place —about the house with its drapery of creepers, about the garden, even about the mellow sunlight on the grass and on the flowerbeds—which seemed to make it an ideal spot wherein two elderly maiden ladies might pass their quiet lives. It all reminded him— with an odd jump back to other days—of the illustrations to certain mid-Victorian poems and tales which in his childhood, on wet afternoons, he had now and then been allowed to colour— pictures found in old magazines, wood-engravings by Millais or Pinwell or Fred Walker. The ladies too were there, sitting in comfortable chairs, with a small table before them, prepared for the tea a capped and aproned maid-servant was at this moment bringing from the house. The maid deposited her tray while Rusk was being introduced by Denis to Miss Birch, and then to Miss Anna Birch, before they all sat down. It appeared that their brother had not, after all, told them visitors were coming.

Miss Birch was prim, and even a little shy. She looked half a dozen years older than her sister, and it was evident that the Doctor was the youngest of the family. Her face was pleasant, in spite of a somewhat vague and wandering expression which reminded Rusk of the Sheep in *Alice*; her conversation was limited to small general remarks of an unexacting nature; and he found both ladies charming. They certainly formed a striking contrast to the Bracknel family, and he felt himself at once perfectly at home in their garden, with its red brick wall—against which the orange lilies just now were somewhat garishly brilliant—its closely-clipped hedges and dark gravel paths. It was a relief, too, not to have to set himself psychological conundrums; the Miss Birches were the kind of people he had lived among and understood; and he even saw himself cultivating their acquaintance rather assiduously. Miss Anna, in particular, struck him as being extremely kind. Before he had talked to her for ten minutes he found himself wondering why she had never married. Her manner was sympathetic; she was intelligent; and even in her slight air of primness—which after all was but the feeblest reflection of her sister's—he discovered a distinct charm. Moreover, she was still very nice-looking, her complexion was still fresh, though her loose black hair was half turned to silver. Both ladies seemed very pleased to make his acquaintance, and talked to him of Cambridge, which they had visited on two occasions while their brother was an undergraduate there. They perfectly remembered Rusk's college—one of the smallest: they had paid a visit to its library and had seen the Pepys manuscript.

After tea the younger of the two visitors asked permission to go indoors and choose a book. He had nothing to read at home, he said, a remark which caused Miss Birch to express the hope that Rusk also would make use of her brother's library. She had resumed the embroidery she had laid down while they were having tea, and for some reason merely to watch her gave Rusk a sense of peacefulness he enjoyed immensely. He took up a volume which was lying open on the grass and glanced at the title.

"Harriet makes me read aloud to her when she's working," Miss Anna said. "At present we're in the middle of *Mansfield Park*."

"Do you like it?" Rusk tilted back his chair and stretched his legs, a proceeding which secretly alarmed both the Miss Birches, but which signified that he himself was feeling very comfortable.

"I should like it better, perhaps, if it didn't so often send Harriet to sleep," Miss Anna said. "As it is, I not only have to read, but next day I have to tell most of it all over again."

"It's so very long," Miss Harriet interposed mildly, "and you know, you yourself, Anna, can't always find your place when the marker comes out."

Rusk laughed. "I must be careful not to lose it, then." And he laid the book down on the table.

He could not help feeling that the Miss Birches had accepted him, were pleased with him. They wondered how he was getting on in the bosom of the Bracknel family, and he told them that he liked his pupil extremely. He also said that he liked Mrs. Bracknel and May, but was silent in regard to the others. At this point they were joined by the Doctor.

The Doctor greeted Rusk anew, while his sisters remonstrated with him for not having told them that Mr. Rusk and Denis were coming. They might have gone out, and what would Mr. Rusk have thought then? The Doctor only laughed.

"He's a perfect egotist," Miss Anna suddenly and surprisingly declared.

"Are you alluding to me?" her brother asked; "or are you perhaps returning to an earlier topic?"

"I'm alluding to Mr. Bracknel. I remember once, shortly before Denis was born, he wanted something which he had left upstairs—at the very top of the house; and he sent his wife up for it. She said something about ringing for a servant, but he told her he didn't care for servants rummaging among his things."

"All the same, she's devoted to him," Rusk replied, lighting a cigarette.

"That only makes it worse."

"Of course, he isn't a gentleman," Miss Harriet observed, as if this explained much.

"Do you think she's really fond of him, Mr. Rusk?" Miss Anna pursued doubtfully. "Don't you think she only tries to be, because she herself is so sweet-tempered; and perhaps in order to make him more—more passable?"

"Oh, it's real enough," Rusk returned, and paused.

Miss Anna waited a moment as if she expected something more. Then, since Rusk remained silent, she continued: "She's very nice, you know; and she was one of the most beautiful young girls I've ever seen—much better-looking than either of her daughters. I must show you her photograph some day. Such a sweet face."

"You remember her, then, when she was young?"

"But she isn't very old now, Mr. Rusk. She's several years younger than I am."

"I should never have thought so," Rusk confessed.

"She had a dreadful illness a year or two before Denis was born; that is what altered her."

Doctor Birch, who had been listening somewhat abstractedly to all this, now rose to his feet. "You haven't seen the garden yet," he said to Rusk. "Come and I'll show it to you."

"He can see it from here I dare say," Miss Anna murmured, but her brother led the young man off.

They had strolled for a few minutes among the flower-beds, pausing every now and again before a finer specimen, and making desultory remarks of a more or less horticultural nature, when abruptly the Doctor asked: "Well, how do you like your pupil?"

From the beginning Rusk had been waiting for some such question, and answered at once: "I like him very much. He's so intelligent, and responsive."

"You've found him that—eh? Not by any chance a little too intelligent, a little too responsive?"

Rusk stooped mechanically to smell a clump of roses. "What makes you say that?" he asked.

The Doctor smiled. "Because I like him too, and I feel a certain responsibility."

Rusk straightened himself. The Doctor's words appeared to him to require elucidation. "What do you mean exactly?" he asked.

"Oh, just that. . . . I think it's quite possible, you know, to be too imaginative, too sensitive, too gentle, too affectionate. I'd rather there was more of the ordinary rough-and-tumble boy about him, more of the fighting animal."

"I see. No: he's certainly not that," Rusk admitted.

"Well, he ought to be."

Rusk was surprised. "But don't you think he's very much above the average—mentally, I mean? Or perhaps what I really mean is spiritually. . . . No doubt he's a little odd in some ways; but he has a fineness!"

"He has."

"And if he develops; if——" He suddenly paused and looked

straight at his companion. "Why are you anxious about him?"

Doctor Birch did not reply at once, and when he did it was in his turn to ask a question. "Who said I was anxious about him?" Yet, as if in support of Rusk's suspicion, he almost immediately added: "As you say, he's odd, and—and spiritually above the average. . . . So was Shelley. . . . The point is that with a mind of that type there is just a possibility of its losing in some measure its hold upon reality."

Rusk's thoughts instantly leapt back to the scene in the wood, and the vague apprehension he had then felt. "You mean there's a danger that—that——"

"I mean that I don't want you to jump to exaggerated conclusions," Doctor Birch took him up rather sharply. Then, having studied his companion's face, he went on in a different tone: "I'm going to be perfectly frank with you—plainly and unconventionally frank."

"I'd much rather you were," Rusk replied.

"Well then; I suppose you know that I was largely responsible for bringing you over here? Not that that matters. What does matter is that I thought, I hoped, we might perhaps work together."

"Work together?" Rusk repeated, not quite following him. "In what way work together?"

Doctor Birch took him by the arm. "Herford told me about you," he said, "and from his description I was so sure you were the very man I had been looking for that I dare say I left him a little in the dark as to one or two points I might have made clearer. To put the matter in a nutshell, I felt you could do a great deal for the boy. At the same time I wished you to form your first impression of him for yourself, didn't want to bias your judgment in one way or another, which is really why I avoided calling on you. As you know, there were several tutors before you came—his father's selection" (Rusk thought of the sound commercial education), "and it was that which exasperated me into interference." He stood still for a moment, his hand resting familiarly on the younger man's shoulder. "Well, does it strike you that all this is dreadfully tortuous?"

Rusk hesitated, hardly knowing what to think. "But isn't there a very great likelihood that he will outgrow his—his——"

"There is. That's why I'm delighted to hear you get on so well together." The Doctor's penetrating, rather cold eyes held his companion's for an appreciable space, during which the latter became conscious of a will much stronger than his own. "You, my dear fellow," he then went on genially, "are really more the physician he is in need of than I am. Of course it's hard in such matters to be absolutely sure, but I don't think he has lost any ground of late, and probably has gained a little. . . . Tell me, are you by any chance excitable or nervous? You don't look it, I must say, but I should like to have your own word for it."

Rusk wondered whither all this was leading. It was so unexpected that he half believed the Doctor had sprung it on him on purpose to give him no time to prepare his replies, and subconsciously he began to throw up small defensive ramparts, from behind which he could review his position before committing himself. "I don't know that I'm particularly nervous," he made answer.

"That's all right then. If you were, it would be no good."

But poor Rusk felt more and more that the Doctor was hardly being so frank as he had promised. "You seem to want to make me so," he retorted.

"I, my dear fellow! Why in the world should you imagine that?"

"At any rate you seem bent on putting me into a very responsible position: or rather to assume that I'm in one already."

"So you are, of course," Doctor Birch rejoined blandly. "But never mind that. I don't think you'll regret it. And after all, I'm asking you to do no more than keep an eye on our young friend, to influence him, make him more like himself—and occasionally give me a report as to how things are progressing, or anything else that may strike you."

Put thus, the Doctor's request seemed natural enough, and Rusk might there and then have embarked on an account of that afternoon's adventure in the wood, had he not remembered that this would necessitate a betrayal of Denis's confidence. He wished he could see his duty more plainly; but as it was he saw only that he could do nothing behind his pupil's back.

"Of course sending him to a boarding-school was the stupidest thing in the world," Doctor Birch went on; "but I was not consulted, and at that time I had not even come a great deal in contact with him."

His voice had now taken a very friendly and persuasive tone, in spite of which Rusk had a vague sense that he was being "managed". "I think, you know, that I ought to have been given a clearer idea of all this before I came," he protested. "I was told nothing except that the boy was delicate."

"I know; I know," Doctor Birch agreed. "You must see, however, that it would have been difficult to enter into details beforehand. Unwise too; since it might have prejudiced you—even made you refuse to give the thing a fair trial."

"Perhaps; but I should have been allowed to choose."

Doctor Birch agreed again. "At least you know everything now," he said; "and it isn't very much, is it? I'm afraid that unintentionally I've given you an exaggerated impression. Denis is just as you've found him: everything I have said would apply almost equally well to any other exceptionally sensitive and imaginative boy. The real trouble is that you're the only person coming in contact with him who has the faintest grain of common sense. Use it, use your own judgment, irrespective of what his people may tell you. And remember I'll always be there to back you up."

Rusk remained silent, while he dug holes in the grass border with the point of his stick. Then he said: "I'll do what I can. . . . I promise no more."

The Doctor, however, seemed perfectly content with this; and his very friendly smile for some reason brought a deeper colour into the younger man's cheeks. "You think we've treated you badly—eh?" he said good-humouredly. "If you do, blame *me*: his family aren't in this, and I dare say would be extremely annoyed with me for speaking as I have done." He paused. "Well, I don't know that there's anything more at present. I think we understand each other now and can work together, which is the great thing."

They had by this time completed their tour of the garden; and in fact very considerably prolonged it, and were again close to the spot where they had left the two ladies, who meanwhile had been joined by Denis. Rusk sat down for another twenty minutes, and then rose to take his leave.

"You must come back very soon," Miss Anna told him, and he promised to do so. He added that, though only a novice, he was fond of sketching in water-colours, and would like to make a drawing of their garden. Miss Anna thought this a delightful plan: so did Miss Harriet. And both sisters gave Denis strict injunctions to see that it was carried out should Mr. Rusk himself prove lazy or forgetful.

9

They returned home by the back way, and as they passed the lodge a small bent old woman curtsied to them from the door. From a yellow face, wrinkled like a withered russet apple, gleamed two bright black eyes. The nearly toothless mouth was twisted into a smile, and the whole countenance expressed a mingled obsequiousness and cunning. Rusk nodded briefly: he had taken a strong dislike to this person from the first moment he had seen her. A parrot screamed from his cage as they went by, and the old woman stood looking after them.

"How long has Rebecca been with you?" Rusk asked when they were out of earshot.

"Oh, she's always been there," answered Denis indifferently.

"I don't much care for her."

"Mamma doesn't like her either. She once tried to get her sent away."

Rusk reflected that this possibly accounted for her continued presence, but did not say so. "She's the mother of one of the gardeners, isn't she?" he said.

"Yes. She's got five or six sons, and all with different surnames—at least, so Johnson told me."

Johnson was the head gardener, and it should be added, for reasons of his own was not on good terms with the lady of the back lodge.

Rusk stared. "She's been married five or six times?" he marvelled.

"Oh no, I don't think he meant that; but very likely it isn't true."

Rusk made no comment, and they were nearing home when

the boy said with a sidelong glance at him: "I wonder how papa enjoyed Switzerland! He was to be back this morning, you know. . . . Do you like it better when he's away?"

"I don't intend to answer questions of that sort," Rusk returned half angrily. "And you ought to know better than to ask them."

"Sorry. Of course it can't make any difference to you whether he's there or not."

On reaching home, however, they were not long left in doubt concerning Mr. Bracknel's arrival. May was going upstairs, but she stopped at the top of the first flight when she heard them enter the hall. "Papa's here," she whispered, pursing up her mouth and looking at her brother. "Don't make a noise."

"Make a noise!" Denis echoed. "We're not going to cheer, if that's what you mean."

"S'sh! Dinner will be in in a minute. Hurry up."

At dinner, therefore, Rusk was prepared to encounter Mr. Bracknel: what he was not prepared for was the presence of Alfred. He had guessed, to be sure, that it had not been primarily for his pleasure that the father had undertaken a journey abroad, nevertheless the so speedy return of the prodigal took him by surprise, and he wondered what on earth could have happened. No light was thrown on this mystery by either of the travellers. Mr. Bracknel sat in moody and abstracted silence, so that all sorts of telegraphic communications took place across the table without attracting his attention: Alfred looked only sulky and bored. Forgetful of the proverb that it is well to let sleeping dogs lie, Rusk was foolish enough to ask the latter how he liked Switzerland, though the instant he had done so he realized his mistake. For the mere word "Switzerland" appeared to pierce through all Mr. Bracknel's gloomy reveries, and without waiting for his son to reply he pronounced curtly that Alfred was not returning there, while Alfred himself, taking no notice of his father's interruption, remarked indifferently that he was very glad to be home again.

Mr. Bracknel looked at him, and it was not a pleasant look. Fortunately the situation was saved by Denis, who quite unconscious of the storm hanging in the air had been pursuing his own thoughts and now gave utterance to them. "I took Mr. Rusk to the

Birches' this afternoon," he told his mother. "We had tea in the garden, and they sent their love to you."

"Did you, dear?" Mrs. Bracknel murmured. "That was very nice."

"He must have enjoyed it!" Alfred sneered. "But perhaps he's fond of cats."

"Oh, Harriet's not so bad," Amy chimed in. "It's only Anna who tries to be sarcastic."

"I liked them both extremely," Rusk declared, with an emphasis which drew a smile and a raising of her eyebrows from Amy.

"Did Harriet show you her embroidery, and did Anna read aloud to you?"

Mrs. Bracknel looked distressed. "You might be a little more respectful, Amy, if for no other reason than because you know they're very old friends of mine!"

"I'm afraid I'm not sufficiently sentimental," Amy laughed. "At all events they're no friends of mine." And she proceeded to give an imitation of Miss Anna reading aloud and of Miss Harriet listening and asking questions. For some reason this performance appeared to tickle her father even through the reveries inspired by his elder son, but Rusk was annoyed, and wished Denis had not mentioned their visit.

. . . . . .

An hour or so later, leaving his pupil at work in the study, he went out by himself to take a meditative stroll. He lit his pipe and sauntered across the lawn, thinking of all Doctor Birch had said to him. He hardly knew what to make of it, nor exactly how all the rather guarded hints he had received were to be of much assistance to him. On the contrary, they increased his anxiety by awakening fresh misgivings. Yet they were not to be ignored, for it was clear that the Doctor wished to do everything in his power to help the boy. Besides, Rusk himself had noticed most of the characteristics he had mentioned. He, too, had told himself that Denis was too imaginative, too gentle, too responsive, too sensitive. It was of his very essence to be these things; only it had not occurred to him before his talk with the Doctor that the very qualities which had struck him as lovable and rare might become, if slightly accentuated, perilous. . . . In the midst of his meditations he heard a sound of rapid footsteps behind him, and glanced round to see Amy, flushed and out of breath. "I've come to apologize," she cried, pouting a little. "I called to you to wait, but you wouldn't."

"Apologize?" Rusk echoed absently, his mind still busy with the problem of his pupil.

"I could see you were still thinking of what I said at dinner—you've no idea how cross you can look! What I said about Harriet and Anna Birch, I mean; though it was only in fun. Anyhow, I'll promise never to do it again."

Rusk shrugged his shoulders. He was on the point of telling her he had forgotten all about what she had said at dinner, but remarked instead: "I've an idea you think me a most thorough-going prig."

"I don't," Amy laughed. "At least only now and then—when you're particularly English. Are you going for a walk? May I come with you, or do you want to be alone?"

"Not at all," Rusk answered civilly, though to be alone was very much what he did want.

"You say that as if you were being led to the stake. I know, of course, you don't approve of me, but I'd like to know why. Please tell me."

"My dear Miss Amy, you get hold of the most extraordinary ideas!"

"Oh, that's just a way of getting out of it. You'd rather talk to May, wouldn't you? You've more in common with her. You're both intellectual, and can discuss intellectual things, while I *loathe* intellectual things."

"You seem to loathe a good many things," Rusk said, half laughing. "If you tell me what it is you like we can keep to that."

For a moment he thought she was going to say "I like you," but she didn't. "I like life," she answered, "and feeling and knowing I'm alive. And pleasure. I don't mean ethereal and poetic pleasure—mooning over sunsets and all that—but real pleasure—riding and motoring and playing golf and dancing and theatres and—oh, hundreds of things."

"You ought to be very happy, then," Rusk returned phlegmatically.

"So I am—when I get what I want. I'd do a good deal, you know, to get what I want."

She spoke as usual with an air of careless frankness, and there was as usual something about her which vaguely disquieted him. He was for ever telling himself that he did not particularly like her, yet it was impossible not to feel the abundance and strength of her vitality. There was something in her nature which had a kind of sweeping force, like the pull of a strong current. There was in fact a strong strain of her father in her, though superficially they might seem to have little in common.

"Were you surprised to see Alfred back again?" she went on. "You guessed, I dare say, that it was on his account papa went to Switzerland?"

"Not exactly. Indeed, I didn't guess at all: I supposed he had gone on business." It was a perpetual source of wonder to Rusk, the amazing way in which the various members of the Bracknel family took him into their confidence, and retailed, with the fullest particulars, matters one might have thought to be more or less private. "I saw I had put my foot in it at dinner," he added. "But it was quite unintentional."

"Yes, I know. It didn't matter. Anyhow *that* was papa's business. He got a wire from the house over there, saying they hadn't seen or heard anything of Alfred for a week, and wanting to know what they were to do about it. Papa posted over immediately, and discovered Alfred away up somewhere in the mountains with goodness knows who. So he brought him home, and naturally he's furious about it. What really irritates papa is the way Alfred would allow everything in the business to go to smash. He told him on the way back that he was only going to give him one more chance, and I know he'll keep his word. I've just been doing my best to get Alfred to turn over a new leaf."

Rusk was silent, while he puffed at his pipe. He had no desire to discuss these family affairs, but Amy apparently had, for she kept on, undiscouraged: "It's not all his fault either. I mean Alfred's. Papa keeps him far too close. I don't know what his salary is, but

I'm pretty sure he's up to his eyes in debt. Papa isn't generous in things of that kind: he's just the opposite. Alfred says there's not a man in the place who gets decently paid. In fact the office is filled with girls and apprentices simply because they come cheaper; and papa won't allow anyone to have the least authority. Alfred says that last year the firm must have cleared about twenty thousand pounds. Of course it was an exceptionally good year, and Alfred very likely is exaggerating; but still it does seem a lot of money, and it makes him mad when he thinks of what *he* gets. He ought to pay you more, Mr. Rusk, too."

Rusk winced. "I don't think we need——" he began hastily.

"Oh, I'm not going to say anything. You needn't be so frightfully sensitive. Only you do a lot for Denis: you're very different from the other tutors he's had. Besides, you're a gentleman, and they weren't. Poor papa, of course, doesn't know what a gentleman is; but we do—even Alfred has some idea."

They strolled on through the mild summer evening, Amy, in spite of Rusk's unresponsiveness, chattering freely, while the long twilight slowly darkened into night. Overhead the sky was clear, but a heavy dew was falling, and the cawing of the homing rooks had died away. Rusk thought of the well by the hawthorn, and had Amy not been with him probably he would have gone to look at it again. He thought of Denis and his lonely sacrifices to the moon; and somehow, at this moment, it was these things that were real; the girl beside him, so full of life and the passion for life, who was unreal.

"Rebecca was in the kitchen when I left the house," Amy went on. "She says she saw you this evening, but that you hardly noticed her: she says you never *do* notice her."

"I don't like her," Rusk answered shortly, and Amy made a little grimace.

"You're so hard to please! Yet you talk about me!"

"I'm certainly not pleased by Rebecca, and I don't know that I want to be."

"Well—you might at least say good-evening to the poor old soul. Besides, she's very interesting really—knows all sorts of queer things."

Rusk shrugged his shoulders. "If she knows anything worth knowing I'd be surprised. I don't think I ever saw a more villainous-looking old hag in my life."

"She says she was once the belle of the whole countryside, but that was a long time ago: she'll talk to you for hours about her dead-and-gone lovers. She can give you cures and charms, too, for whatever's the matter with you. She showed me a bit of a sheet that was once wrapped round a corpse, and told me that if I could get mamma to tie a corner of it round her head like a nightcap it would put away her headaches."

"It was excellent advice, then."

"Oh, don't be so sarcastic. I'm sure if I got the frightful headaches mamma gets I'd try it. What harm could it do? But apart from all that, she can tell you things to do on May Eve and Hallow Eve. Last May Eve I tried an experiment she told me about. I sprinkled ashes just outside the hall-door after everybody had gone to bed, and very early in the morning I went down to see if there was a footprint on them. If there is, and if it's turned towards the house, it means a marriage; but if it's turned the other way it means a death. I got a fright, I can tell you, because there *was* a footprint, and naturally I hadn't expected one. It was turned away from the house too. One of the maids had got up still earlier, to gather dew to put on her face. If you gather dew on May morning, you know, and put it on your face, it gives you a lovely complexion. And it was her foot-mark I saw. Only, of course I didn't find that out till afterwards, and at the time I got an awful shock."

More and more bored, Rusk had practically ceased to listen, when Amy suddenly came to a pause, as if expecting a reply. "So those are Rebecca's accomplishments!" was the only one he could find.

"Oh, you're perfectly horrid! I won't tell you anything more. I never met anyone so superior in my life!"

They had turned on their homeward way, and presently the house came once more into sight. He was not sorry. There was that in the girl's manner which warned him to be very careful. She had shown him pretty clearly that she liked him, and perhaps something more. He never knew, either, just how far she would go—that was the worst of it—though he was most careful to avoid all topics that so far as he could judge might develop sentimentally. Still, she was quite capable of choosing her own topics, or of doing anything else that might happen to suit her purpose. Latterly she had begun to seek opportunities to be alone with him, and it was difficult to frustrate these designs without being more or less rude. He had no desire to be rude, but he had a suspicion that this would be necessary sooner or later, unless he were prepared to play the role she appeared to wish him to adopt. In the end the situation might even become impossible, and then how was he to keep his promise to Doctor Birch?

When he entered the library Denis was sitting at the table, working. He looked up in the soft lamplight and smiled. Rusk went over and sat down beside him.

10

Sunday morning was always with the Bracknels a period of disturbance and confusion. Breakfast was fixed for a particular time—ten o'clock it happened to be—at which hour everyone was expected to be seated at the table. Mrs. Bracknel came down first; then her husband. Rusk also took care not to be late; but the others straggled down anyhow and in varying order, the gong sounding repeatedly, sometimes being rung by Mr. Bracknel in person. After breakfast there was the further rush and scramble of getting ready for church, while the master of the house fumed and fretted in the hall, calling up every now and then to his wife and the girls that they would be late. On the Sunday following Alfred's return, however, it seemed to Rusk that the atmosphere had been more peaceful, or at any rate more subdued, than usual—that is to say, until nearly the last moment, when suddenly it was discovered that Denis was missing. Nobody had seen him since breakfast; nobody knew where he was; and in the end they were obliged to set off without him.

Inside the church it was stuffy; the service dragged; the sermon was longer than usual, and the congregation apathetic. Amy had secretly planned to walk home with Rusk, but she was detained for a moment or two in the porch, and when she hurried out, found he had already joined her sister, who was saying: "Oh Mr. Rusk, you never told us you went in for sketching. I discovered it by the merest chance from Miss Birch. I'm going to make you help *me*, so there!"

Rusk's own words Amy failed to catch, but she heard him laugh as he and May dropped behind the others. As for his artistic accomplishments—these only interested her because she was sure May would work them for all they were worth. She had not opened her paint-box for months, nevertheless Amy was quite certain it would be in full evidence to-morrow. They would criticize each other's drawings; May would pretend to make fun of him, and at the same time show how much she was really impressed by what he said; and probably it would end in their arranging an expedition together, when they could take with them Denis, who would not be in the way.

So Amy worked it out while she accompanied her father and mother; but the moment they reached the house she went straight to her own room, where, after taking off her hat, she sat down at an open window to look out for the artists. And presently she saw them, sauntering slowly across the lawn, deep in conversation, now coming to a standstill, and again moving on. A few minutes later she heard May coming upstairs, and with that she rose and walked down the passage to her sister's room.

"What's the matter?" May asked, none too agreeably, for she had been interrupted in the midst of very pleasant thoughts and there was something particularly irritating in the way Amy simply stood in the doorway gazing at her, without uttering a word. "What are you staring at me like that for? You'd think I'd seven heads!"

Amy's laugh was unconvincing. "I hope you had a nice talk and arranged to go sketching together."

May shrugged her shoulders. "Are you mad?" she dropped contemptuously, turning her back and beginning to tidy her hair before the glass. "I don't even know what you're talking about."

"Don't you?"

"No; though I suppose it has something to do with Mr. Rusk as usual."

Amy took a step towards her. "That's a lie," she breathed in a low voice. "I never mention his name to you."

May gave another shrug. "Perhaps not, but your whole behaviour is sufficient without words."

For all answer Amy sat down on the side of the bed. There followed a silence, and then she asked again: "Are you going sketching with him?" but May did not reply.

"Are you going sketching with him?" Amy repeated for the third time; and this time May spoke.

"It's no concern of yours what I'm going to do; and since I don't intend to discuss the matter you needn't wait."

Still, for a minute or two Amy made no movement; but at last she got up. Her face was sombre, her eyes sullen, yet she appeared to be quite unashamed of having laid bare her feelings and of the manner in which she had done so. She went back to her own room and began to pace up and down, her mind filled with the tumult of unreasoning jealousy. There was a strange simplicity about this girl—something elemental, as if the primitive woman in her had been left almost untouched by the conventions of her class and education. She posed herself now before the mirror and looked long and intently at her own image reflected there. It seemed to her that in every way she was superior to her sister, and she continued to move before the mirror, taking fresh attitudes, as if she were a slave exhibiting herself to a hesitating and critical purchaser. Possibly the result was reassuring: at any rate it was with a less clouded countenance that she descended the stairs when the deep note of the gong rose from below.

II

Denis had awakened early that morning. He knew it was Sunday and that there was no hurry about getting up, so he lay in a half dream, listening to the sighing of the trees till gradually his drowsiness slipped from him and he sprang out of bed. He was the first to sit down to breakfast, and as soon as he could he escaped out into the garden, where for a few minutes he wandered among the flower-beds, shaking the dew from heavy crimson roses and burying his face among cool green leaves. It was a perfect summer morning, and remembering that if he lingered near the house he presently would be marched off to church, he decided to take a holiday, though it would certainly mean getting into trouble afterwards. However, that couldn't be helped. The sunlight lay on the grass all around him; birds were singing; clearly church was out of the question.

His heart was strangely uplifted as he ran across the lawn and down a wooded slope, till he was hidden from the house and in safety. Beside a stream he sat down in the fresh green grass, hugging his chin against his knees, and watching the water ripple past, dancing and sparkling in the sunshine. Above his head the branches of a willow dropped to the stream, the tips of the slender leaves almost touching the water as it passed. Denis rolled over and over like a dog, the earth smell in his nostrils, the earth murmur in his ears. From time to time a faint rustle passed through the tree-tops like the whisper of a spirit, from time to time a pale-winged butterfly flitted across the stream and on into the dimmer heart of the wood. . . .

He gazed up through the quivering heat at the sky, so soft, so pure, never so far off as to-day; and he wondered just where in all that immensity—untroubled by mortal joys and sorrows—lay the country of the gods. His brown thin hands rested on either side of him, motionless upon the green grass; and the sunlight grew stronger and stronger, till at last it beat down through the sheltering boughs above him, like a stream of liquid gold.

He shut his eyes tightly and crushed the grass in his hands, then he sprang to his feet and crossed the brook by a couple of stepping-stones. He was now in the thickest part of the wood; the trees were very close together, and their branches made a roof above him, while the ground was covered with a dense brown mould of withered leaves which had lain undisturbed for a long time. The light here was dimmed, like the light in a church: he knew where he was, and yet it all seemed strange and mysterious.

His progress was momentarily arrested by a thick clump of bushes and undergrowth through which he forced his way, reckless of his clothes. He tore his trousers and scratched his hands and wrists; and then, coming out on the other side, he found himself in the open glade where the great hawthorn grew beside the pool. The pool lay there now, surrounded by green level banks: it lay there in the sunlight, and the spring which fed it bubbled over on the grassy brink. The water was a shower of precious stones when he splashed it up against the blue. After the dusk and gloom of the wood the glade seemed to him wonderful and unearthly, and for a long time he lay looking down into the water, watching the sky in it, the passing clouds, the flight of a bird, his own face, very brown, half unknown. . . .

Then he turned on his back and shut his eyes. He lay there for so long that by and by he dropped asleep, and when he awoke had the feeling that he must have slept for a considerable time. He knew he ought to go home, but he did not: there would be trouble in any case, and it would make little difference *when* he got back. This place was his own; this pool was haunted; and he had come into its power long ago. But the spirit that guarded it was friendly to him. There had been times when sitting in the drawing-room at home, or in a crowded classroom at school, everything had faded away before him, and through the chatter of human voices he had heard a soft rustle like the sound of leaves, and had found himself back here—back where he was now, beside the pool and the old hawthorn and the half-buried altar, with its faint and faded stain of blood. He stood up and shouted aloud. A kind of ecstasy seized him and drew him up into the sun. He was lost in the spirit of the universe; he seemed to live through endless ages in the opening and closing of his eyes. . . .

Suddenly he heard the noise of someone approaching—someone who did not know the way and who was blundering through the bushes and undergrowth, yet always getting nearer. A quick thought of flight came into his mind. Who could it be? No one had ever come here before: no one even knew of his hiding-place. And then he remembered his tutor. It annoyed him that Rusk should break in upon his privacy—especially just now—and he slipped away between the bushes as quietly as a shadow, and in a thicket close by lay still to watch.

Very soon Rusk came blundering out into the open, looking flushed and hot. He gazed about him, and the boy could see he was disappointed at finding nobody. Then he began to call aloud while he parted the surrounding bushes with his hands, peering between them: "Denis—Denis—are you there?"

A half-mocking smile flitted across the face of the hidden boy, but he made no sign, and presently Rusk went away again. He could hear him crushing twigs and brambles and broken branches under his feet as he went. When the noise of his progress at last ceased Denis crept out once more into the sunlight, and crouched down again by his pool. But the magic was gone; the spell was broken; he was back in an everyday world, and very soon hunger reminded him that it must be hours since breakfast.

Hours indeed!—the shadows had perceptibly lengthened when he drew near the house, where the others were sitting out on the lawn. He was dirty, torn, dishevelled, but he sauntered across the grass with his hands in his pockets and an assumed air of unconcern. He smiled with a little friendly nod, which seemed to say, "Oh, here you are! I must say you all look very comfortable."

Nevertheless, there was a general outcry at his appearance.

"Where have you been, Sir?" Mr. Bracknel asked sternly. "Are you aware what day it is and of the condition you're in? Do you think I buy you clothes to have you go out and roll in the mud in them like a savage? If your mother is content to pass over such practices I'm not. Don't you know you've been missing ever since early morning? Where have you been? Don't stand there grinning like an ape! but answer my question."

Denis still smiled faintly; he still kept his hands in his pockets, and his head was slightly drooped. "I was out for a little," he said almost in a whisper. "I didn't mean to stay so long."

"Come with me, Sir," Mr. Bracknel replied grimly, getting up. "We'll talk about this inside."

His wife laid a timid hand on his arm. "Let him get something to eat, first, James: he must be starving!"

"I *am* rather hungry," Denis confessed. "Won't it do a little later, papa?—to talk, I mean."

There was something absolutely inoffensive in his manner and in his voice, nevertheless Mr. Bracknel's face, which had been hot and shining before, now grew purple. "Come with me," he repeated ominously.

Denis gave a slight shrug, and father and son went together towards the house.

The rest of the party watched them as if spell-bound, till at last May broke the silence by saying, "It's fortunate papa's bark is worse than his bite." She caught Rusk's eye as she spoke, and the latter broke into an irrepressible laugh, which drew from Mrs. Bracknel a glance of reproach.

"I can't help it," Rusk apologized, trying to recover his gravity. "He's got the cheek of the mischief! Only why on earth couldn't he have slipped in quietly by the back?"

"It wasn't cheek," May answered. "You don't understand him. It was just a kind of un-selfconsciousness. He never thinks of how he looks till somebody reminds him. Then he becomes extremely sensitive till he forgets again. . . . And he was really very nervous, though he talked in that way. Papa gets so violent! He never even tries to understand or make allowances. As if it mattered about his clothes!"

"Still, there was a triangular tear in his trousers about the size of my hand," Rusk chuckled.

"Even if there was! It's so stupid to get into a rage. For one thing, it doesn't do any good."

The advent of Denis had had the effect of breaking up the party on the lawn, and May and Rusk were now strolling together away from the others. "But I think I do understand him a little," the latter demurred in self-defence. "After all, you must admit that he *looked* uncommonly cool."

May let the matter drop there: but suddenly and most unexpectedly she said: "Mr. Rusk, I'm afraid I won't be able to go out sketching to-morrow."

"Oh well, the day after will do—or any day that suits you. I only suggested to-morrow because I thought it was going to be fine and

I didn't see any particular point in waiting."

May said nothing for a moment: then she added: "I don't know that I shall really take it up again at all."

"At all?" There was something in her tone which made him look at her.

The girl smiled. "I haven't done anything for so long that I shouldn't know how to begin."

"If that's all, you'll very soon get into it. Everybody needs practice."

"I don't think I can come, all the same."

A vague suspicion entered Rusk's mind. "Why?" he asked. "You seemed quite keen on it this morning."

"I know I was—but——"

Rusk was disappointed: also he was pretty sure there was something she had not mentioned at the back of her refusal. "You've surely changed your mind very quickly," he grumbled in a rather injured tone. "Of course if it will only bore you——"

May coloured. "I haven't changed my mind. . . . I mean I shouldn't like you to think me changeable. I hate changeable people."

"I don't know what you call it, then," Rusk replied.

She smiled again. "I'm still interested in *your* sketches," she told him. "I intend to see that you do a dozen a week. Why don't you get Denis to try? But in any case he *will* try, if he sees you at it. He can use my brushes and paints."

They had drawn close to the others once more, and Rusk was obliged to accept for the time being this most unsatisfactory decision.

12

On Sundays, if the Bracknels got up late, they went to bed early. By eleven o'clock only the light in Rusk's room was still burning; the rest of the house was wrapped in darkness, though not wholly in slumber. May was awake, and Denis too was awake—awake and dreaming—the day, in fact, was ending much as it had begun.

There was a difference in one respect. In the morning he had been happy, eager; now a profound lassitude had fallen upon him, and the sunlight of the morning was as far away as though it had never been. He felt depressed and lonely; his mouth was drooped and tired; and as he sat up in bed, hugging his knees and gazing out through the dim window, he seemed to be watching against the silent darkness the story of his life slowly weaving itself out in changing scenes and pictures. A complete reaction from the excitement of the past few hours had set in; he felt at present only a weariness of all things good or bad. He could have hidden his face on the pillow and cried himself to sleep; he could have welcomed the end of life as coming with the ending of the day. He was unhappy: he had never been very happy it now seemed to him, though sometimes he was able to forget everything but the moment actually passing. He had no illusions about himself, about what he had been, about what he was now, about what was still to come. He had no illusions about the people who formed his world, about life itself as far as he knew it, about anything. He knew he was unsound physically; that mentally also he was different from others—from healthy, normal people like Rusk, for instance—probably unsound there too!—that even in appearance he was peculiar. He had read love tales which had fired his imagination for an hour, but he was sure no one would ever love *him* in that way: it had not required his brief experience of school life to teach him he was unwanted. Doubtless he would be well-off some day, for his father was a rich man, but he did not see that this could make much difference. After all, he had everything he wanted now—everything of that kind—and what did it mean to him? Other boys, or many of them, had aims, tastes, ambitions; but there was nothing *he* wanted to do, nothing *he* wanted to be. He was only tired, tired to death. . . .

His hands caught at the crumpled sheets and he shut his eyes, his whole face and attitude expressive of an infinite dejection. At length he could bear his loneliness no longer; he felt he *must* speak to someone; and he got out of bed and softly opened his door. There was only one person to whom he *could* speak at this hour. It might be no good; might even lead to a rebuff; but the longing to unburden himself was stronger than any fear of rebuffs. He went along the passage and knocked at the door of the next room—knocked very softly—but he heard Rusk moving inside, and next moment the handle turned.

His tutor stood there in the lamplight, holding a book, his finger still keeping the place, while he looked in some surprise at the figure before him—barefooted and clad in pyjamas—with his coarse black hair straggling over his forehead and his narrow eyes unnaturally bright.

"I wanted to speak to you," Denis said. "I'm glad you haven't gone to bed: I thought you mightn't have; I thought you might be reading. Do you mind? I'll go away if you don't want me."

"But why aren't you asleep? Of course I don't mind. Only you'd better go back to your room and not stand there catching cold."

"I want to talk to you."

"I know, and I'm coming with you." Rusk laid down his book, and pushing Denis before him, followed him to the other room. There, when he had seen his pupil once more safely under the bedclothes, he sat down beside him. "What is it?" he asked. "You led us all a nice dance to-day, and I suppose I ought to begin by scolding you."

"I want to tell you I was there when you came to look for me," said Denis, suddenly reminded of this incident, and seizing on it as an excuse. "I was angry at your coming; I had always kept it a secret place. I was hiding in the bushes, watching you, when you called me."

"Oh, you were hiding, were you?" Rusk said good-humouredly. "I had a strong suspicion that you weren't very far away. And you were angry with me for going to your den? But, my dear boy, I didn't go till well on in the afternoon, when everyone was wondering what on earth had happened to you. Such considerations don't trouble you, I suppose?—your people imagining you've fallen into the river, or broken your leg, or been run over, or perhaps all three?"

"I didn't think about them. At any rate it wasn't the first time it had happened, and so far as I could see nobody looked particularly anxious when I came back."

"And what were you up to? Why didn't you get hungry?"

"I did. That's what brought me home. Anyhow, I wasn't doing any harm. What's the use of bothering about it?"

"Why can't you go to sleep now?"

"I don't know; but it's not because I have a bad conscience. . . . I feel rotten—that's all."

"What about?"

"About everything."

"I expect you're tired: it was a tiring kind of day: you'll be all right in the morning."

"I knew you would say that. . . . Well, it doesn't matter."

Rusk was puzzled. He knew he was not being very helpful, and yet he wanted to help if he could only think how. It seemed best, at any rate, not to take the matter too seriously. "Shall I read to you?" he asked.

Denis shook his head. "I don't feel like reading. Tell me about what you did when you were a boy. . . . Do you think if I had known you then we'd have been friends?"

Rusk very much doubted it, but he only said, "Why not?"

"We're good friends now at all events: that's one comfort," Denis replied. After which he lay quiet for so long a time that Rusk, thinking he had fallen asleep, went back on tip-toe to his own room.

But Denis was not asleep. He had realized that what he needed was beyond his companion's power to give—that was all. Rusk had always been sympathetic and kind, but the boy felt instinctively that he would never really understand. They were too different: his tutor's spirit seemed in many ways younger than his own: probably there was nobody on earth who could give him what he longed for.

He wondered if he should see anything of Rusk later on—when they had ceased to be master and pupil? He doubted it. Rusk would have his profession to follow. Yet his tutor was the only friend he had ever found.

The moon had risen above the trees and a silvery light lay across the floor. He watched it, and gradually he grew drowsy, and at last he fell asleep. It seemed to him that he was awakened by a slight sound. He opened his eyes and half sat up in bed. The room was almost as light now as it was by day. The white radiance of the moon was pouring in, and while he looked at it, it gradually grew denser and turned to something pale and cloudy—and then—and then to something else. . . . There was a figure bending over him, a pale, dim form that leaned down and took him in its arms. He felt a coldness pass into his body with a strange shivering joy; he felt a kiss upon his cheek and then a longer kiss upon his mouth: he lay in a half-conscious swoon. . . .

When he opened his eyes it was broad daylight and he had an idea that it was late. He felt languid and loath to get up, and he turned in his bed and then lay still. He began to remember things. What was it that had taken place last night? Had it been a dream? He felt an odd reluctance to inquire into it too closely. . . .

Outside on the roof, just above his window, a bird was chirping. He lay listening to it, not trying to think very clearly, and gradually he slipped back again into sleep.

13

May kept her word, and Rusk was obliged to go out sketching alone; or rather, accompanied only by Denis, who on such occasions brought a book with him and read, sometimes to himself, but more frequently aloud to his companion. A good many hours they passed in this way—hours that brought Rusk a greater, though by no means perfect insight into the peculiar character of his pupil's mind. Among other things, he learned that ordinary life, ordinary adventures, seemed to have little attraction for Denis, who would forsake *The Three Musketeers* or *Treasure Island* for any (to Rusk absurd and fantastic) tale or poem or treatise that dabbled in the unseen. The boy had some mysterious standard, too, by which he judged such things. He examined them all impartially, but the vast majority he threw aside as worthless. "The man doesn't know," was his formula on such occasions—the man of course being the author; though what it was exactly that he didn't know to Rusk never became very clear. For to himself, while varying in plausibility, the works in question all appeared to be of about equal value in relation to reality. He thought one or two of them clever; and one or two poetic, as he would have said; but the greater number struck him as merely silly; and all alike as singularly profitless. He was not successful, nevertheless, when he tried to wean Denis from a taste which was evidently inseparable from the very nature of his mind. Rusk, with disapproval, saw nothing in these productions but a stimulus to an imagination already far too little under control. He found it difficult to reconcile the boy's apparent credulity in such matters with his eager alert intelligence in other directions. There seemed to be a perpetual dream-life going on in his pupil's mind, the reflections from which now and then flared out with so dazzling a brightness as actually to obscure that of his sensual perception. And his imagination had a curiously Eastern tinge Rusk found it hard to follow. Beneath the wild fantasy of the *Arabian Nights*, for instance, he appeared to find hidden and obscure realities. He must know they were fictions, and yet he had bewildering moods in which he seemed to take them seriously. Or was it that he only *wanted* life to be like that? Rusk was not sure, and in all other ways he found Denis amenable enough. He had never known anyone with so sweet a temper, so affectionate, so pleasant. Of course he knew by this time that Denis was extremely fond of him; there had been moments indeed when he had almost wished that the boy's affection were a little *less* genuine—it seemed so to deepen his responsibility. And he found himself growing alarmingly serious under the weight of this sense of responsibility; not that it affected his manner so much as the whole way he had come to regard life. He had never particularly regarded life at all during his four extremely happy years at Cambridge: now he seemed to be plunged in it up to his eyes, as in some deep, possibly dangerous, river, and without the least notion as to how well he could swim. His conversations with Doctor Birch—for there had been more than the one recorded—doubtless had something to do with all this; but he found himself endeavouring to gaze on into the future, and it was Denis's future more often than his own which figured in the foreground of this temporal perspective. It was very fortunate indeed, he thought, that the boy was, or would be, in a secure position financially; otherwise he didn't quite see what would have become of him. Even as it was, he had somehow a feeling of discouragement, as if he foresaw the waste of a fine intelligence and an exquisite sensibility lost through a slight want of balance in one particular direction.

Denis sometimes had long fits of silence and abstraction which Rusk could not understand. He would be sitting reading, say, when he would drop off into a kind of dream from which it would be hardly possible to rouse him. Naturally the tutor got accustomed to it, but at first it had made him a little anxious, for more than once he had noticed that after he had been awakened the boy's mind would still seem to be filled with reflections and images from his dream; as if, indeed, he were hardly capable of distinguishing between it and reality. And now and then he appeared not even to know that he *had* been dreaming. Rusk was perplexed; yet he felt the problem to be so delicate a one that he hesitated to touch it lest his touch should prove too coarse. Besides, he did not care to question Denis, fearing that by doing so he might perhaps turn his thoughts into morbid and weakening channels. He could not forget their visit to the altar in the wood. The place obviously held some mysterious fascination for the boy, and any such influence, it seemed to Rusk, must be malign. He had a horror of mental aberrations. They struck him as far more dreadful than a twisted, misshapen body. His pupil, of course, was perfectly sane; but was there not an enemy somewhere, watching and waiting in the shadow?—crouching, ready to spring? Denis impressed him as having been in the past left absolutely to himself. Certainly, in things that mattered most of all, he had been allowed to struggle on alone as best he might. It was as if he had been left in the dark to find his way through a treacherous country where quicksands lay all about his feet. Possibly if a boy were born with a certain temperament this inevitably happened, and disaster was bound to follow. Nevertheless Rusk did not believe it, and intended to prove the contrary. He was filled indeed with a dogged determination to do so, highly characteristic. No doubt if he had not been fond of Denis his zeal would have been very much less, but it is probable that it would still have kept him at his post. He had ideas about duty (they coincided perfectly with those Doctor Birch had imputed to him), convictions that there are certain things worth doing and that those were the things he wanted to do. His present occupation, it seemed to him, dropped naturally into this category.

. . . . .

Towards the end of August, in order to be present at the wedding of his eldest sister, Rusk returned home for a week—a week which, by contrast, threw into extraordinary vividness the peculiarities of the Bracknel ménage. He had had half a mind to suggest bringing his pupil with him, but on his arrival was glad he had left him behind. His young brother was home for the holidays: he had left school and would be going up to the university next term. His young brother was rather a swell at games, and he had staying with him a congenial spirit whom Rusk had not hitherto met. He could not in truth quite see Denis getting on with either of these youths. They would have regarded him with a more or less contemptuous tolerance, and at best would have said he was mad. It gave Rusk something of the measure of the change that had been wrought in his own ideas, when he found himself impatient of a point of view he would doubtless not so long ago have shared—found himself, too, on a good many occasions bored by the society of these typical specimens of budding manhood, and mentally contrasting them, not very favourably, with the young boy of whom he had lately seen so much. He had a certain simple tenderness for Denis which was quite different from any feeling he had hitherto experienced. Rusk, it may be added, was not of a temperament to be easily carried away, and if he had formed no romantic friendship at school, he was certainly unlikely to do so later on. He was eminently sensible and practical: his imagination, if it could indulge in a respectable flutter now and again, was not given to sustained or lofty flights; his feet were planted firmly and sturdily on this earth, and above all he disliked "gush". Of course, he would have denied that there was anything in the least romantic in his affection for Denis, but the denial would not, in spite of its sincerity, have represented quite the whole truth. For undoubtedly he had come, by many little steps, to regard himself as in a way the boy's protector; while the very fact of his pupil's dependence upon him had strengthened this feeling, had given it just that quality of delicacy, of tenderness, which differentiated it from anything else he had felt in the past; while at the same time it deepened his whole sense of life.

Naturally his mother and sisters were eager to hear all about how he was getting on, all about his pupil, all about the other Bracknels; and for some reason appeared to have expected a less prosaic story than the rather bald account of his adventures proved to be, though what it was they had pictured was never revealed.

"He's a queer little chap," Rusk said, in reply to a question concerning Denis, "but he's as clever as they're made. I half thought of bringing him over with me. He'd have come like a shot, too; he'd have liked to come, and I'd have liked you to see him."

But he guessed that it was really in the other members of the Bracknel household they were interested. He told them that he liked Mrs. Bracknel and May, that May was a thoroughly decent sort, and that he didn't care so much for Amy. Yet in regard to this last statement he apparently could not, when questioned, give any particulars. A curious and possibly absurd idea had in truth taken possession of him—that he must say nothing derogatory concerning any member of the family. He did not tell them, for instance, of what had taken place on the evening of his arrival; he did not tell them about Mr. Bracknel and Alfred. His powers of description were not remarkable at the best, and to the feminine mind they seemed at present singularly inadequate. To supplement them he produced a photograph—a group Denis had taken—and his sisters discovered that Amy was very good-looking, but that May was rather plain. When he showed them a portrait of Denis himself, they thought he looked most peculiar.

His week at home passed quickly and pleasantly; nevertheless, at the expiration of it, he was not altogether sorry to return to his duties. On the day of his arrival he and Denis spent a good deal of their time in a canoe on the river. Denis had nearly as many questions to ask as Rusk's own family had had, for he was tremendously interested in everything relating to his tutor. He wanted to know how the wedding had gone off, what his brother was like, what they had done, if they had played much tennis, what his brother's friend was like. This last question reminded Rusk of something he had now and then thought of before—namely, that Denis himself appeared to have few or no acquaintances of his own age. He had never heard him so much as allude to any companion he might even have had in the past. Once he had asked him if he knew any boys whom they could get to make up a four at tennis, and on that occasion his pupil had said there was no one. Mrs. Bracknel thereupon had mentioned two or three names—Denis could write and ask them if Mr. Rusk liked—but the matter, viewed in this light, had seemed so formal that he had not pushed it further. Of course he could see in a way how his pupil would have little in common with his contemporaries; but he thought it a pity that he had been so isolated, so much thrown on the society of persons older than himself. It must have helped to accentuate, even to create, some of his peculiarities; and if it had not made him unbearably priggish, that really was rather surprising.

The day after Rusk's arrival they returned to work. Perhaps an hour had passed, and the tutor was looking over a Latin prose the boy had done for him, when the door opened and Amy came in. Rusk had known before he looked round that it was she; for no one else ever interrupted them, and just before his visit home she had come in on one pretext or another for two or three mornings in succession. It must be confessed that this was partly his own fault, since he had not yet screwed up his courage to the point of objecting overtly to such interruptions; but he determined to do so now.

She had brought him a letter which had come by the midday post. "How cosy you are in here," she said, seating herself in her customary armchair. "I always liked this room. . . . I can never read properly with mamma and May chattering and moving about. I simply can't read when people are talking, and it's so delightfully quiet here."

"I'm afraid we have to do a good *deal* of talking," Rusk rejoined. "We couldn't very well work without."

"Oh, but that isn't the same thing. What I mean is when people every now and then ask you a question, or begin to tell you something they expect you to listen to. I could read perfectly here."

"I don't think it would be good for Denis's work," Rusk answered quietly.

Amy's voice took a sharper key. "Oh, Denis's work! I'm sure he does a lot!" Then, dropping to her softest note: "I wish you would tell me what I ought to read, Mr. Rusk—really good books—I'm sure you know everything of that kind."

"I'm afraid I don't," Rusk replied, "and at present we really must go on with what we're doing."

He returned to his prose, and Amy sat silent for a minute or two. Then, happening to encounter her brother's eyes, she gave him a glare. Nevertheless she got up. "I'm sorry for having disturbed you," she said stiffly to Rusk as she stalked to the door.

"Oh, it's all right," Rusk returned; but he decided that now was the time to settle the matter definitely. "I think, all the same, if you'll forgive my saying so, that it would be better, when you want to speak to me, to choose some other time than the morning."

He had made this remark in perfect good faith, yet Amy appeared to discover a sarcastic meaning in it, and her cheeks flamed. "Want to speak to you!" she cried. "I brought you a letter, and that's all the thanks I get."

Rusk, who had risen, stood in silence, his eyes fixed on the opposite wall, at a point somewhere above Amy's head.

"Oh, you needn't look at me if you don't want to," she continued, her voice trembling. "I know you think I'm beneath your notice. It's a nice example to set Denis, that's all."

Rusk returned to the table and sat down, leaving her to find her own way out of the room. The boy had walked to the window while this scene was in progress, and he still remained there, with his back turned and his hands in his pockets, looking out. There was a minute or two of silence, while Rusk scored a phrase through with his pen. "Where did you get this from?" he asked nervously. "Why won't you use your dictionary? I don't see what objection you have to it."

Denis came back and looked over his tutor's shoulder. Then he sat down in his place again. Rusk could not see his face, but he could guess from his attitude, from the way he sat, a good deal of what was passing in his mind. Denis was ashamed, and Rusk felt that it was partly *his* fault. A few minutes ago he had been quite determined to be perfectly explicit. If Amy did not care to take what he said in good part it was her own look-out, and perhaps it would be better if she *were* annoyed. Yet now he suddenly felt he had been tactless. He should have chosen a more opportune moment to remonstrate with her; he should not have spoken before Denis; and if the girl had felt humiliated, so, naturally, in another and possibly deeper way, had her brother.

14

That evening a remark Denis let fall suggested that he had been turning the matter over in his mind, instead of forgetting all about it, which was what Rusk had hoped he would do. They were sitting together—Rusk and the boy—in the study. It was about nine o'clock; the curtains were drawn; and the lamp was lit. Rusk was in the armchair Amy had occupied, glancing over *Punch*; Denis was at the table, his books around him, busy over his work for the next day. Rusk, whose attention was not very closely riveted to his paper, had been watching him for some time, when the boy looked up and their eyes met. Denis pushed away his books with a half-impatient gesture.

"Well, have you finished?" the tutor asked.

"Yes, for the time being. . . . I've been thinking——"

"Have you? What about?"

"About you," said the boy unexpectedly; "about myself; about all of us. Don't you think we're very strange—taking the family as a whole?"

Rusk's glance dropped again to *Punch*, and he turned a page. "I'm principally concerned with one member of the family," he answered. "Of course I think *him* rather odd."

"Ah, but seriously."

"Well?"

"Will you answer me a question if I ask one?"

He leaned his elbows on the table as he spoke, and with his chin supported between his hands gazed across it at Rusk. The latter, half amused, returned his scrutiny. The boy's sallow, intelligent face was vividly revealed in the lamplight, and, as often before, Rusk was struck by its Oriental quality. Denis's lips were parted; his hair was ruffled where he had pushed it back from his forehead; his wide-set, elongated eyes were fixed upon him intently. "It depends entirely on the question," he answered cautiously.

"You're afraid, then?"

Rusk laughed. "Not much wonder—when you look at me like that."

The boy flung himself back in his chair. "No—but I'm in earnest. . . . Supposing you had known what we were like—everything you know now—would you have come to teach me?"

Rusk was still smiling. "Yes," he said.

"Ah, you're a humbug," Denis grumbled, giving him up. "We *are* queer, all the same," he went on after a moment, "and I know you think so, even if you won't admit it."

Rusk laid down his paper, still open, on a chair beside him. "Why do you want me to admit it?" he asked.

"I don't, if you'd rather not." Yet his next words contradicted this. "Has it never occurred to you that Alfred, for instance, is unusual? I suppose there must be other people like him, but——"

"But what?"

"Oh I don't know." He got up and walked over to the hearthrug, where he stood leaning back against the mantelpiece, in his father's favourite attitude. "What are you laughing at?"

"Nothing—nothing," Rusk murmured. "What were you going to say?"

"I was going to say I had seen him with his friends, and they don't like him. Of course they play cards with him and all that, but they don't really like him. I wonder——"

"Well? Now you've begun you may as well finish."

"I wonder what becomes of such people when they begin to get old?"

Rusk was puzzled. "I don't quite grasp what you're trying to get at," he said. "I should have thought your brother Alfred was about as 'usual' as anyone could be. Also, if I may ask, when did you ever see him with his friends?"

"I've seen them up here at the house. He has them up sometimes when papa is away. They talk about horses and prizefighters and women. The last is their special subject. They keep hovering about it—leaving it for a minute or two, but always coming back, like bluebottles buzzing over a cake of dirt. It suggests stories to them, you can see their faces lighting up, it's only Alfred who can make it dull."

Rusk—somewhat staggered—hardly knew how to receive this speech. "And were you often present when these discussions took place?" he asked. For he knew Alfred's type and could imagine the rest.

"Not often, but once or twice—when they forgot about me. You see, they usually began the moment the coast was clear after dinner, and it was rather interesting to watch them. You can discover a good deal by watching people's faces—what they're really keen about, what amuses them, even what they think rather deep. . . . Then there's papa——"

But at this point Rusk abruptly intervened. "My dear boy, I'm not going to sit here while you discuss your entire family. Doesn't it strike you that it's hardly the thing to do?"

"I'll not do it if you don't want me to. But why mayn't I talk to you? You're the only person I *have* to talk to."

"You may talk as much as you like—about other things. After all, you're scarcely in a position to criticize your people. They're all a good deal older than you are, you know—particularly your father."

"And I'm to say nothing about what happened this morning?"

"Not the least little word: it's none of your business."

"It *is* my business," cried Denis in sudden indignation. "It's my business if I have to put up with it. I hate it. It's not fair to you."

Rusk blushed crimson. "Oh I can look after myself," he said hastily.

The boy turned his back and stood with one foot on the fender. "I'm sorry," he muttered.

"Would you like a game of chess?" Rusk asked, to change the subject. "Or would you care to come for a stroll before bedtime?"

Denis, still gazing into the black dead grate, shook his head. "No: I don't want to disturb you: you're reading. I've said all I've got to say. I know you know what I mean."

He went back to the table and opened a book, but his tutor, giving him a sidelong glance from time to time, guessed that he was not very deeply absorbed. . . . So he had wanted to apologize! For of course what he had said really went back to Amy. Rusk was sorry that he should take this matter of her silliness so much to heart. After all, though a nuisance, apart from that it was of little importance. Certainly he himself didn't intend to give it more consideration than it was worth. A rather childish outburst of rudeness and ill-temper, having its origin in a very easily wounded vanity—this was about what it amounted to. Amy seemed completely devoid of self-control, but was there anything new about that? The only thing which really mattered was that Denis should have been there to witness it, which certainly was unfortunate. And half in self-ridicule, Rusk recalled an episode of his knickerbocker days, when he had been publicly kissed at a party by an affectionate little girl. He had not responded to that particular demonstration, which had indeed only been rendered possible by some foolish game they were playing, nor had he felt in the least flattered by it. And it was much the same now. His personal vanity was slight, and did not lead him to picture Amy's interest in him as very profound, though it might easily make him look absurd.

"Come," he said to Denis; "you're not really working: we may as well go out for half an hour." He walked over to the window and pulled aside the curtain. "It's a beautiful night. Shall we go?"

The boy pushed back his chair. "If you like."

He followed his tutor from the room, and they went out into the garden. They walked slowly and in silence over the lawn down towards the gate. The night was warm, a little close even. From time to time a flash of distant summer lightning threw for a moment into vivid distinctness every leaf and twig hanging motionless in the still air. Then, while they sauntered on, like a lamp of gold swinging under a deep vaulted roof, the orange moon floated out from behind a cloud. In its ghostly light the grass was dim and faded as some old tapestry, and the garden behind them was a well of deepening shadow. A bat flew past, the noise of his leathery wings distinctly audible in the stillness. The quiet trees were dark against the paler sky, and a falling grace of weariness had drawn the whole world closer to a dream.

Rusk drew his pupil's arm beneath his own. "What is the matter?" he asked kindly. "Why do you bother about things of no importance?"

"I suppose it's my nature," Denis said. "You're so decent, so nice, that I hate anyone to be rude to you."

There was something in his voice that touched Rusk deeply, that made him suddenly more serious. "It's you who are nice," he answered unaffectedly. "You've always been so—from the first day I came."

He felt his pupil's hand tighten ever so little on his arm.

"If I have," Denis said shyly, "it's because I like you—more than you know perhaps—more than I have ever liked anybody else—much more."

Rusk answered nothing. There was no particularly appropriate remark to make, so he kept silent.

"You don't mind?" asked Denis presently.

"Mind!" Rusk repeated in surprise.

"My having said that."

"It gave me great pleasure," answered Rusk simply.

The boy looked up at him and smiled. "I wanted to tell you before—a good many times—but I didn't like to. I wanted you to know, awfully, but somehow it was hard to say."

"I think I did know," Rusk replied.

"Well, it's better like that, isn't it?"

"Much better."

They had reached the gate, and now they passed out on to the road. They walked a short distance and then turned back. They walked in silence, and the silence all round them was broken only by the noise of their own footsteps as they moved on through the lonely, listening night. A strange sense of dreaming had crept over Rusk. He seemed to have drifted back into some forgotten past that had been washed up to him again from the deep mysterious sea of time. Presently the lighted windows of the house came once more into view. They slackened their pace a little, but still continued on their way.

Denis was very happy, though, as always, there was a melancholy mingled with his happiness. Never before had he felt himself so close to his friend, yet oddly enough, what hovered in the background was a sense of loneliness, of the impossibility of knowing, even in such a moment as this, anything save the few sad or happy impressions that passed through his mind. He seemed to be moving to a dark shadowy garden from which there was no discoverable way out, a place all dim secluded glades, and dimmer walks, shut in by high interlacing hedges, so that he could see only the solitary path he himself followed, and now and then, as tonight, catch a faint sound or a swift gleam, showing that he was not quite alone there—that something or someone was moving in the distance and at times approaching, but always in the end to pass out of sight.

He did not know why, but he felt that this was his life. Perhaps with others it was different—yet he hardly saw how it could be. . . . Only, they didn't seem to mind, while he—he. . . .

In the sudden light of the hall Rusk, glancing at him, thought he looked pale and tired, and packed him off to bed then and there.

15

A few days later, at lunch, May announced that she had met Miss Anna Birch. "She asked when Mr. Rusk was coming over to paint a picture of their garden. She says he promised ages ago to do one, and they're beginning to think he must be trying to draw out of it. . . . She wants us all to go over this afternoon—you mamma, and Mr. Rusk, and Denis, and Amy."

"As an afterthought evidently," Amy interjected. "I hope you'll enjoy yourselves."

"I'll go," said Denis. "Mamma and I'll go and talk, while Mr. Rusk and May do their drawings."

His mother looked at him uncertainly. "But you always shut

yourself up in the library, dear, and you'd be so much better in the open air on a lovely day like this."

Denis patted her hand. "Oh, I get plenty of the open air. Besides, one must be polite!"

All through the meal Amy sat in enigmatic silence; but as they were leaving the table she rang the bell and ordered the car to be round in half an hour—she was going into town.

"What do you want to do in town?" her mother asked, lingering by the door. "And are you sure your father doesn't want the car? I think you'd much better come with us."

"To sit all afternoon with Harriet and Anna Birch?—thank you for nothing."

No further attempt was made to induce her to change her mind, and when Rusk and May started off they left her on the doorstep talking to Dixon, the chauffeur. Denis was waiting for his mother, who was not quite ready, but the artists wished to take full advantage of the fine afternoon. There was a golden quality in the sunlight, in the colouring of everything—a quality which seemed to combine the richness of summer with the first change of approaching autumn. Rusk and May walked over the smooth close turf in the green shadow of the trees, Rusk carrying their painting materials, May swinging a parasol. Out on the road, they had only gone a short distance when Amy passed them in the car. She did not turn her head, but gave a brief wave of the hand, and in another minute was out of sight.

May gazed straight before her at the settling cloud of dust. "I know papa wants the car this afternoon," she said, with inscrutable face. "Isn't it like Amy to take it!"

"But Dixon will tell her."

"I'm sure he's already told her. That probably was what they were talking about—but you don't know Amy if you think it will make the least difference. She's like papa himself: when she once takes a thing into her head nothing can budge it, even though she realizes perfectly what the consequences will be."

Rusk could not help thinking that if one or two other members of the family also stood up now and then to Mr. Bracknel it would do no harm: in this respect, at any rate, he was entirely in sympathy with Amy. "She's taken something into her head concerning me," he remarked. "I mean I've offended her in some way. She's hardly spoken to me for the last week."

"You asked her not to interrupt Denis at his lessons, didn't you?"

"Did she tell you that? I don't think it was my fault. I had to do something about it."

"You were perfectly right," May declared. "But Amy is always like that. The best thing is simply to take no notice. Of course you couldn't have her poking round when you were working with Denis. The thing was ridiculous, and she'd have seen that for herself if she'd had the slightest tact. We none of us have much, perhaps—except mamma and Denis—but Amy has least of all. You saw how she wouldn't come with us to-day; and it was just because she's taken a violent dislike to Miss Anna Birch on account of something she once said. They had a nephew staying with them—Jimmy Temple—— However, I needn't go into that, and there's a quite different side to her which you've never seen. She's very generous, and if she likes you will do a good deal for you: she's got Alfred out of ever so many scrapes. Alfred's her favourite. She likes you too, Mr. Rusk, only she thinks you don't like *her*."

As she gave utterance to these words May looked at him with an air of candour which Rusk found it not so easy to meet. "I'm sure I don't know why she should think anything so—so——" he mumbled lamely.

"Isn't it true, then?" May asked innocently. "I thought it was, myself."

"But why?"

"Oh, I dare say it was only from your manner. You sometimes seemed rather reserved. Anyhow, I'm glad I was wrong."

Rusk was in a difficulty, since he could hardly explain that his reserve had been due to discretion. "I hope I haven't been rude," was his somewhat feeble reply.

May smiled up at him. "I can't imagine your being rude," she said.

"You're very kind."

"No, it isn't kindness, *or* flattery: it's just that I don't think it's in your nature to be rude—any more than it is in Denis's. I'd say the same thing about him."

They had entered the garden now, and after a preliminary lookround decided to make their sketches from a spot near the library window. Here Mrs. Bracknel and the Miss Birches presently joined them, seating themselves within easy conversing distance, while Denis, as usual, went indoors to prowl among the books. Mrs. Bracknel, Rusk decided, looked more at her ease, more in her natural element, than he had yet seen her. And the effect of this somehow had been a kind of rejuvenescence, so that he could even find traces of the lovely girl of Miss Anna's portrait.

The roses were still blooming in a rich glory of crimson and yellow and pink, but Rusk was principally occupied with a bed of Shirley poppies, which stretched away from the porch and figured in the foreground of his sketch. As he worked he occasionally glanced sidelong to see how May was getting on. He liked May: he imagined she was nearly always happy, and that in itself went a long way towards making her a pleasant companion. It was a pity, he thought, that they should by-and-by have to return to the other house—to Alfred, and Amy, and Mr. Bracknel—where things were so different.

From time to time his pupil would lean out over the windowsill to encourage the artists, and at last he came out altogether, to make a closer inspection of their efforts. Mrs. Bracknel thought it would be very nice if Denis, too, were to learn to draw, and Rusk himself had a theory that it was "rather a good thing to sketch a bit"—if nothing else, it helped you really to see places, and fixed them in your mind. They were all agreed that it was a most desirable accomplishment, and Miss Birch recollected a time when she also had adorned various domestic articles, such as terracotta plates and vases, with groups of chrysanthemums and sweet-peas—it had been before she had taken to embroidery. She had never got so far as drawing from nature, however—at least, unless you counted flowers as nature.

Denis moved about with his hands in his pockets. In his grey eyes a light gleamed and danced just as the sunlight gleamed and danced among the leaves. He declared that to his mind what was most worth sketching at present was his mother, sitting there among the roses. He was charming himself as he said it, and Rusk saw a faint flush of pleasure come into Mrs. Bracknel's cheeks. There were a good many not very brilliant jokes in the air, and they dropped softly into a general atmosphere of intimacy and friendliness, which rounded them off and made them fulfil their easy purpose.

After tea, when the drawings were finished, and the painters had been congratulated, and Denis had borrowed an armful of books, the visitors rose to go. The Miss Birches accompanied them part of the way. It was getting late; the evening sun was already dipping to the trees; and birds were flying home in the softly-coloured light.

. . . . .

All the peaceful charm of the afternoon, however, was broken rudely enough half an hour later at dinner. Mr. Bracknel had been kept late for an appointment. The car had not called for him, though he had given Dixon full instructions in the morning. It had not even called to bring him home; and now, though the car was in the garage, he could find no trace of Dixon anywhere; nobody appeared to know where he was or what had happened to him. Such a thing had never occurred before: there must be a reason for it; though, whatever the reason, Dixon would have to be dismissed. Even if something had gone wrong with the car at the last moment he could at least have telephoned.

"You needn't bother dismissing him: he's gone already," Amy interrupted brusquely. "I had a row with him in town this afternoon. He refused to do what I told him, and left on the spot, so that I had to drive the car home myself."

Mr. Bracknel stared at her, his soup dropping from the ends of his moustache. He could hardly believe his ears, and he sat back further in his chair, while a look of amazement overspread his face. "So it was *you*, miss, who prevented him from coming for me! It was *you* who countermanded my orders!" The very enormity of the offence overpowered him.

"I didn't countermand anybody's orders," Amy replied impatiently. "I told him to drive me home, and he said he hadn't time; which was nonsense; he had plenty of time. If he'd hurried he wouldn't have been more than ten minutes late in calling for you."

"Ten minutes late!" Mr. Bracknel repeated weakly.

"He wouldn't do what I told him; and when I insisted he got insolent."

"Insolent!"

"Yes, papa; you needn't keep on repeating everything I say."

"What right had you to tell him anything, miss?" her father exploded. "Who gave you permission to take the car at all? You know I've forbidden you to use it when I want it. Do you hear me? Don't look at me like that!"

Amy raised her eyebrows. "Really, papa, to listen to you one would think I was a child! How could I prevent the man from going away? It wasn't very pleasant for me to have a dispute in the middle of Donegall Place. You don't appear to realize that."

Mr. Bracknel choked. To all seeming he had realized quite enough. But Amy went on calmly with her dinner, and the servants moved noiselessly about the room, handing dishes, with fixed inscrutable faces. There was a kind of painful absurdity in Mr. Bracknel's position which made Rusk, for once, sympathize with him. He had hitherto regarded him as at any rate a man of very strong character, but he now began to doubt the accuracy of this judgement, and to wonder if what he had taken for strength were not merely the violence of a bully exploiting other people's weakness. These frequent puerile outbursts of anger in the bosom of his family, for instance—though the present one he admitted to be justifiable—were more neurotic than anything else. At all events, there could be no denying that Amy had come off victorious. There was in fact a kind of insolence in her triumph which must have been particularly galling to her father. To Rusk the man's whole existence seemed a pretty miserable affair. He glanced round the table with a new curiosity, looking from one to another of those seated there. Was there not a lack of restraint about all of them—a want of balance—a something, which if it had been carried to a slightly higher power, would have amounted almost to hysteria? What other people could have been so insensible to the indecency of squabbling like this in public? He could imagine the scene which must have taken place in town between Amy and the chauffeur! Probably there had been a little crowd gathered to witness it! For himself, he was now more or less accustomed to such happenings, but what must other people think? Surely they must be very much talked about, must have an extraordinary reputation! Of course it was horribly unfair to lump them all together like this. Denis he had always considered apart; but Mrs. Bracknel and May also were different from the others—from Amy and Alfred and the father. Only, was there not something wrong there too?—might there not be even more than he was aware of? He began to feel doubtful. Denis, though so sweet-tempered and lovable, was certainly not normal. And May—May whom only that afternoon he had decided was so pleasant and sympathetic—would one, after having lived as he had done in close intimacy with the family, want to marry her? But next moment he was ashamed of so ungenerous and unreasonable a judgement. He raised his eyes and encountered those of Mrs. Bracknel fixed upon him—large, dark, and gentle—with something in their expression which he felt almost as an appeal.

16

The book-keeper tapped at the door, and without waiting for an answer entered Mr. Bracknel's private office. "There's a woman here, sir, wishes to speak to you."

Mr. Bracknel looked up. His face assumed an expression of irritation, and he waited for a moment before he spoke.

"What does she want? Begging, I suppose? Surely you can interview such people yourself without bringing them to me!"

"I did speak to her, sir, but she wouldn't tell me what her business was. She said she must see you herself."

"Well, she can't see me. God bless my soul, you'd think I was made of money and had nothing to do but throw it about. Tell her I'm busy and can't talk to her now: tell her I'm always busy."

"Yes sir."

The man turned to leave the room, but on the threshold a woman pushed firmly by him. Mr. Bracknel looked up angrily, recognized her, frowned, but gave no other sign of recognition till the book-keeper had discreetly withdrawn. Then he said briefly: "Well?"

Mary Brooke took the precaution of seeing that the door was quite shut before speaking or sitting down in the chair he had motioned her to. He himself stood up, leaning his back against the chimney-piece. His face had relaxed into a partial smile, which was not genial and very quickly vanished.

Mrs. Brooke did not smile. "I came to tell you something I only learned an hour ago," she said. "I had it from Rhoda herself. She was married to Mr. Alfred last Monday."

The words dropped with the abruptness and finality of an explosive bomb, leaving Mr. Bracknel to stare hard at the speaker—so hard that his eyes seemed to glaze and bulge in their sockets. Then he took a turn across the room, his hands behind his back. "Married to Alfred!" he repeated aloud, and before she could reply broke into a disagreeable laugh. It was the crowning-point! Nothing so complete as this had happened before. "Well, I wish her joy of him," he sneered.

Mary Brooke coloured faintly. "At any rate he's been honourable with her, so far as that goes."

Mr. Bracknel gave her a strange look. Perhaps he detected a comparison, a reproach, in her words, for a sort of sardonic humour, which had at the root of it a smouldering fury and contempt, took possession of him. "Yes—so far as that goes," he agreed. "Unfortunately it *doesn't* go very far." He laughed again. "Well, as I say, I hope she'll be happy with him; and I'm glad to see you approve of the match."

A spark showed itself in Mrs. Brooke's eyes. "I only want to know what you're going to do?" she returned with some spirit.

"Do! Do! Don't you think enough has been done already? What do you expect me to do? It's rather late in the day now to interfere. Perhaps you expect me to be overwhelmed with joy!"

"No, I don't."

"You're quite sure there's no mistake about it?"

"Quite sure. What mistake could there be? They were married, and in church."

"Ah, that's a comfort anyhow!" He repeated the words with a venomous sarcasm. "Married, and in church!"

Mrs. Brooke's mouth grew hard, and the lines of her face were drawn into an expression of rigid obstinacy. "I dare say we can leave that for the present," she said.

"Married, and in church!" The perfectly harmless phrase appeared to irritate Mr. Bracknel extraordinarily.

"In the meantime, what are you going to do about it?" As she repeated her question the woman's face darkened with a slowly-gathering wrath, which he met with an answering anger of his own.

"I'm going to do nothing about it," he snapped. "Did you hope I'd take Alfred into partnership, and present your niece with a motor-car and—and—a tee-ara?"

Again Mrs. Brooke coloured. "My niece is as good as your son is, and perhaps better," she retorted.

"I don't doubt it; I don't doubt it. God help her if she isn't. My son's not good enough for me, however; and I don't think any more of him because he happens to have made a fool of himself in this as in every other way."

"I don't know what you mean," said Mrs. Brooke, rising slowly to her feet. "You speak very strangely. Do you think I had anything to do with it? Perhaps you do: perhaps you think he was trapped into it?"

Mr. Bracknel regarded her unpleasantly with half-closed eyes. "I haven't got as far as that yet," he said. "Give me time."

"I'm not any better pleased than you are, maybe.... And anyhow I've had enough of this sort of talk. You didn't want your son to marry Rhoda. I can understand that——"

"Oh, you can understand that, can you?"

"Yes; and without your going on in that way." Her voice rose with her increasing indignation. "I want to know what it is you're going to do now he *has* married her: and if you don't mind you'll please give me a civil answer."

Mr. Bracknel had been walking up and down at intervals, but

now he came to a definite standstill. "My good woman, be reasonable, and don't lose your temper." He spoke himself with a studied calm, as if to set her an example. "Believe me you'll gain nothing by doing so. To begin with, she's no real relation of yours; and secondly, what *can* I do? Come, Mary, you used to have plenty of sense: try to have some now."

"There's a good many things you can do," she returned sullenly.

Mr. Bracknel shrugged his shoulders. A kind of freakish humour again flickered in his dark eyes. "Are there?" he answered, and appeared to meditate. "Let me see! I'm not going to raise Alfred's salary, if that happens to be one of them. And I'm not going to take your niece to live in my house, if that's another. Upon my word I don't see any further way I *could* come in, even if I wanted to—which I don't, you know; I confess I don't. Really, when you come to think of it, so far as I'm concerned there seems nothing even to be said. They're not children. They're both of age. Their marriage is their own affair; and as they didn't see fit to consult me—or apparently you—beforehand, I don't see that we've any duties or responsibilities in the matter now. If Alfred neglects or illtreats his wife—as I've no doubt he will—she can take an action against him. But there will be plenty of time to consider that later."

Mary Brooke took a step towards the door. Her back was turned to him, and she did not look round as she said in a dry constrained voice, which nevertheless trembled slightly: "Well, I won't keep you any longer. I may have to speak to you again after I've seen Mr. Alfred: I don't know. I'm going to look after Rhoda, I may warn you. And in the meantime I've told her she can't come back here."

"That is obvious; but I don't suppose she wants to. I'm sorry she made this mistake, though I suppose she must have known what she was doing: people can't be married against their will."

There might have been a covert irony in his words, but Mrs. Brooke took no notice of it. She opened the door, and he watched her go out. He was on the point of sending for Alfred, when he remembered that Alfred had taken the day off. "Fool—stupid fool!" he muttered as he went back to his desk. In his eyes it was indeed the ultimate folly, and he saw his son's future, never very promising, sunk at last to the depth of abject futility. An irregular connection he could have understood; but this! At the same time the remark about Alfred's honourableness rankled in his mind. Well, they could live on Alfred's honour and see where it landed them. He strode over to the door and called out sharply to his shorthand clerk.

17

Up at the house nobody learned anything of the interesting news, for Mr. Bracknel did not telephone to his wife, nor did he go home to announce it to her. Rusk, coming out on to the lawn after lunch, found Denis playing a game of croquet with his sisters. As both May and Amy were much more brilliant players than their brother, when the tutor proposed that he should join in, the match promised to become a more even one. May, who had been playing against the other two, naturally took him for her partner, but when she declared that they must start all over again Amy demurred. She evidently was not enchanted with the prospect of having Denis for a whole game, and suspected that Rusk had waited to make sure that it was May who was playing single-handed before offering to join them. She could make no overt objection, however, because at present she had adopted a policy of treating Rusk with cold politeness; nevertheless the game began inauspiciously. Presently Amy made a break of half a dozen hoops, but unfortunately Rusk and May had become so absorbed in conversation that they did not notice when it reached its conclusion and she stepped off the court. Amy would not have interrupted them for the world, and in sombre silence sat down on a bench.

Actually a minute or two elapsed before May glanced up. "Oh, you've finished!" she cried, looking round to see what her sister had done. "We're red and yellow, aren't we? You play, Mr. Rusk. Have a shot at blue."

Rusk had a shot, and even a successful one, thanks to a happy cannon off the post. "Oh, good!" May applauded. "Now we must be very careful. What hoop are you for, Amy?"

"You can see the clips, can't you?" was the courteous response.

Now croquet is a pastime in which a vast amount of advice may be requested and given (especially when one of the partners is a novice), and as Rusk and May discussed each of the former's shots for several minutes before he attempted it, and then, on its failure, became promptly oblivious to the game, Amy, with some justification, began to feel more and more exasperated. She grew sulky, and no longer either tried herself or helped Denis. Several times the boy was obliged to shout to their opponents from the other side of the green that it was their turn; Amy would have waited in smouldering rage for a quarter of an hour rather than do so. At last, when May had played the wrong ball twice in succession, her patience gave way, and without a word she stalked off to the house. Rusk and May did not even notice her departure till they saw Denis alone, and apparently wrapped in slumber, in one of the deck chairs.

May glanced round quickly. "Where's Amy?" she called out.

"Gone," Denis murmured without unclosing his eyes.

"Gone! Where has she gone to? Has she stopped playing?"

"I expect so."

"But why? What's the matter?"

Denis perfectly understood what was the matter, and thought that both May and Rusk ought to have understood too. He also thought that their behaviour had been distinctly stupid; but all he said was: "Oh, I don't know. She's in a wax with me, I suppose."

"With you! Why, what have you done?"

"Nothing—except boss the same hoop three times. She thinks I spoil the game." He glanced at Rusk. "Somebody usually gets like that over croquet anyway. It's the most interesting thing about it—trying to pick out who it will be."

May sat down in the chair beside him. "What shall we do?" she said, tapping the toe of her shoe with her mallet and looking vexed.

"I'll play against you and Mr. Rusk, if you like," her brother volunteered. "But you'll have to give me heaps of bisques: we'll say twenty to begin with."

The game now proceeded less strenuously, but much more pleasantly, till by and by Mrs. Bracknel made her appearance.

"Where is Amy?" she in turn asked, before settling herself in a chair. "Run and tell her tea is ready, dear," she added to Denis. "They're bringing it out now. I thought it would be nicer to have it in the garden."

Denis went off, but returned without his sister. "She's going to have tea in the house," he said. "She's got a headache."

"Is it bad?" his mother questioned anxiously. "I thought I saw her out here only a few minutes ago. It's the hot sun, I expect. I'm sure it would be better to wait till the evening to play your games. . . . Denis dear, do take your hands out of your pockets. It makes you look so—so I don't know what. And give Mr. Rusk his tea. You never see *him* lounging about like that. Where are your manners?"

Denis did as he was told. "Manners make the man," he agreed. "Mr. Rusk, kindly accept this cup of tea and select some grub." Then he sat down on the grass at his mother's feet.

"I wonder what's the matter with her?" Mrs. Bracknel went on, her thoughts reverting to Amy. "I don't think she's well, and I wish she would see a doctor. Don't you think she's looking very white?"

The question was addressed to May, who replied indifferently: "Amy never had much colour."

"She had more colour than she has now. I've noticed it for some time past: she isn't looking at all well."

"She ought to go away for a bit," Denis suggested.

"Yes, if she only would! It's what I've been trying to persuade her to do. I know her Aunt Lizzie would be delighted to have her. But she says she hates going away and that she's much better here; and she's so headstrong there's no getting her to do anything she doesn't want to. . . . You too, Denis, would be much better with a hat. I know you don't like wearing one, but the sun is so strong it may give you a sunstroke."

"Do you say you've spoken to her *already?*" May asked.

"About Aunt Lizzie? Yes, I spoke to her this morning. But it only seemed to irritate her."

"I shouldn't advise you to say anything more, then. If you do, she'll think we want to get rid of her. You know what she's like."

Mrs. Bracknel's mild gaze expressed astonishment. "Such nonsense!" she exclaimed. "As if she could possibly think such a thing!"

"It's exactly the sort of thing she *would* think—or say, at any rate."

"But why should we want to get rid of her?"

"Oh, we don't, of course," May returned half impatiently, though she laughed. "I'm only telling you what she'll think. You know yourself the extraordinary notions she gets hold of, without rhyme or reason."

"We might all go away, for that matter," her mother murmured; "only your father doesn't like the idea. It seems to him to be a waste of the garden."

"I quite agree with him," Rusk interposed. "The garden couldn't be nicer than it is at present."

"Oh, for my part, I'm perfectly content to be here," Mrs. Bracknel replied hastily. "It's only that a change might do the children good."

"But Amy and I were away in the spring," said May, "and you know perfectly well you'd never leave papa and Alfred to look after themselves."

"Well, I'm sure I don't wish to make any of you do what you don't want to," Mrs. Bracknel sighed; "but I never know what will please you."

"Don't you think we'd better finish the game in the meantime?" Denis interposed. "It's Mr. Rusk's shot."

Rusk took up his mallet, and crossed the court to where his ball lay. May, the moment his back was turned, bent down and kissed her brother. Neither Rusk nor Mrs. Bracknel saw her, and Denis made no sign.

"I knew you'd do that," he cried gaily, as Rusk, failing to go through his hoop, left everything in beautiful position for the next player. "It was rather nice of you, all the same," he added. "As papa says, it's so hard to trust anybody nowadays."

The tutor returned to his seat, and Mrs. Bracknel smiled upon him. "You're so good to Denis, Mr. Rusk!" she said. "He looks a different boy ever since you came!"

"I'm afraid we all impose upon Mr. Rusk's good nature," May put in. She got up as she spoke, and walked towards a corner of the ground where Denis had knocked her ball, while Mrs. Bracknel went on:

"Don't you think yourself he's really much better? Last spring I was beginning to be a little anxious about him, but he looks quite different now. I wonder if it is only that he is happier with you. I know he *is* happier, very much happier, of course; but don't you think there may be something more than that? Don't you think he is better physically, I mean?"

"I'm sure he is," said Rusk hopefully. "I gathered from what Doctor Birch told me that he thinks so too."

Mrs. Bracknel's dark eyes rested upon him in confidence. "I'm very fond of Denis, Mr. Rusk," she said softly.

Rusk was oddly touched, though he smiled. He remembered how she had used those same words on the night of his arrival. "I know you are," he answered. Then, after a slight pause: "As a matter of fact, I am too."

Mrs. Bracknel was silent a moment. "I can't tell you how grateful I feel to you for all your kindness to him."

"Oh, the kindness is just as much on his side as on mine," Rusk laughed. "I mean, for not exposing me. He's about ten times cleverer than I am, you know."

Mrs. Bracknel looked at him in surprise, as if doubtful whether to take this as a confession or a joke. In the end she decided to see it in a humorous light, and smiled.

It always embarrassed Rusk to be thanked for anything. He would much have preferred, so far as he himself was concerned, that people should take things—especially things of a certain sort —for granted. Next moment, however, Denis came up, and saved him from any further expressions of gratitude. The boy sat down beside them. He lifted the book his mother had brought out with her, and began to turn the pages.

"Miss Anna Birch lent me that," Mrs. Bracknel said, speaking to Rusk. "I can't say I find it very interesting. It's by Henry James, and I remember reading some of his other books when I was a girl, but this seems quite different. The others were historical—like Scott, you know. This isn't: but perhaps you've read it, Mr. Rusk?"

"What's it called?" asked Rusk, whose thoughts had been wandering.

"It's called—oh, I never can remember names." She took the

volume from her son and consulted the title-page. "It's called *The Princess Casamassima*."

"No; I don't think I've read it."

"There's such a strange person in it—a Madame something or other——" Mrs. Bracknel again had recourse to the volume. "Madame Grandoni. . . . A most peculiar character, and I can't think at all natural. She says she's a hundred-and-twenty, yet she appears to be quite active and have all her faculties—going about to theatres and parties and all the rest of it, like anybody else."

"A hundred-and-twenty," Rusk repeated in astonishment.

"Yes. Here is the place. And she says it again somewhere else."

Rusk took the book and read a few lines. "Ah. . . . yes. . . . I fancy she's speaking figuratively, don't you think?" he ventured.

"I suppose she must be," Mrs. Bracknel answered doubtfully. "But isn't it strange to make anybody talk like that. I mean, so few people—even elderly people—want to make themselves out older than they really are."

"Very few indeed," Rusk agreed. Then, seeing that Mrs. Bracknel had half unconsciously begun to read, he decided that it was an excellent opportunity to take a stroll with May. For the game of croquet appeared to have been mutually abandoned, and she had wandered off among the flower-beds, where she was gathering a bunch of roses.

18

Alfred returned home that night. He had been at a race-meeting, but the day, so far as he was concerned, had proved a failure. This wasn't so much because his luck had been foul, as because everything had been overshadowed by the worries he saw looming ahead. Perhaps he had been foolish, perhaps he had acted too precipitately, for what after all was the good of being married if it entailed most of the difficulties and discomforts attendant on illicit loves! True, this was only temporary; he had every intention of making his position known on the first suitable opportunity; but he might, all the same, have done better to have waited. . . .

When he reached the house it did not tend to put him in an easier frame of mind to find that his father was still up, though all the rest of the family seemed to have gone to bed. Coming in from the obscurity outside, the strong light in the dining-room dazzled Alfred, and he was conscious that he did not show to advantage. This increased his annoyance, for he was not nearly so drunk as probably he appeared to be.

"Ah, you've got back," Mr. Bracknel remarked genially. "I hope you've had a pleasant day."

"Very," answered Alfred, making a sudden plunging movement to get out of the room. He distrusted the cordiality of his father's manner, though as yet no suspicion of Rhoda's betrayal had crossed his mind.

"I'm glad to hear that; but you'd better wait a moment; I've something to say to you. . . . I've been hearing news about you—quite unexpected news—bright and festive news one might almost call it."

Alfred, who had already reached the door, paused there, with a sudden premonition of disaster. The shock sobered him. "What have you been hearing?" he asked, turning round.

"About your increased responsibilities," Mr. Bracknel replied, in the same tone of sinister jocularity.

A dark flush overspread Alfred's heavy face, and a vicious spark showed itself in his small eyes: but he knew he must be propitiating, that it was his only chance. "What responsibilities?" he asked, coming back into the room, and trying to throw into his voice a conciliatory note, which was far from expressing his real feelings.

"I mean the responsibilities usually incurred by matrimony."

Mr. Bracknel spoke now in a soft, almost purring fashion, and the playfulness of his manner, taken with the prolonged sarcasm of his words, exasperated his son as nothing else could have. Nevertheless, with an effort, he controlled himself. "Who told you I was married?" he asked.

"Your wife's aunt," replied Mr. Bracknel with great relish. "Your wife's aunt." He repeated the words, rolling them on his tongue as if he took a particular pleasure in their sound. "You might at least have given us a chance of attending the ceremony, which I understand was conducted in church, with every regularity. Well, well; of course you're of an age to know your own affairs best."

Alfred said nothing, and there was a silence till his father broke it once more. "How, if I may ask, do you propose to live? What are your plans?" He rubbed his hands softly together and smiled. "What do you propose to do?—but possibly such questions are indiscreet?"

"We haven't settled yet. We were going to keep it quiet for the present," Alfred mumbled. It may seem strange, but he actually *had* hoped that his father, once he got used to the idea of the marriage, would put him in a position to support his wife in comfort. For this reason he had intended first to get his mother on his side; but now he saw these hopes rapidly dwindling. "I suppose she wormed it out of her," he added gloomily, alluding to Mrs. Brooke and Rhoda.

"I don't know—I don't know," Mr. Bracknel rejoined. "By the way, your salary is two hundred, isn't it?"

"It is—at present."

"At present?" His father, after a moment's hesitation, seemed suddenly to grasp everything in a new light. "Ah, I see—I see. You have something better in view: you're thinking of leaving us—thinking of taking up another job . . . ?" Then, as Alfred remained silent; "No . . . ? *Not* thinking of leaving? Ah well, of course it isn't impossible to live on two hundred. Lots of people do it, and your wife, I dare say, hasn't been accustomed to luxury. . . . Only *you* may find it difficult just at first. These little excursions—such as the one you've returned from to-night, for instance—though I'm sure quite harmless and delightful in themselves, might be imprudent for a man in your altered position and with your new ties. . . . You'll have to allow for so many things—food and clothing as well as household expenses—unless you propose to live with your aunt."

"I don't propose doing so," Alfred muttered. The flush on his face had deepened, spreading over his neck and ears and up to the roots of his hair.

"I see. . . . You'll rent a little house, then? One of those houses with four rooms, including the bathroom. I shouldn't advise you to spend too much on it. A small house in a street where your wife will be near her aunt and her former friends might be best. I'm sorry your abilities and the very intermittent attention which is all you are able to give to business don't permit me to offer you a better position."

The fingers of Alfred's hands opened and closed; he stood for a moment watching his father; then, with his mouth twisted into an ugly sneer, he gave vent to his real feelings: "No, I should think you'd want to keep anything of that sort for your bastard."

He had said it; and a silence followed—a silence during which the ticking of the clock became audible, a creak from the stairs, then nothing but the ticking of the clock. Father and son still faced each other, but all Mr. Bracknel's mock geniality had vanished. When he spoke again there was an icy note in his voice: "Well, I needn't detain you longer. Good-night."

Alfred did not move. He was conscious that he had burned his boats with a vengeance; he had even, for a moment, been slightly shocked by the sound of his own words, though now that they *were* spoken he would have liked to see them have more effect. For they appeared to have had little or none; his father had not so much as changed colour. Could there be any mistake, Alfred wondered uneasily? But no: he had received his information from Rhoda in the intimacy of a long discussion of their mutual affairs. It had been startling, but almost at once he had accepted it as true. Rhoda, it seemed, had worked it all out long ago, and she supplied Alfred with the various clues that had first put her on the track. *He* had been aware of nothing beyond an undue favouritism. Even a certain physical resemblance, though undoubtedly there, had not struck him until she had mentioned it. As all this flashed through his mind it seemed to touch a spring, releasing a jealousy which till now had been bottled up within him—a sense of injury, a sense of wrong. "You've treated me badly from the beginning," he spluttered, resentment goading him to an unaccustomed eloquence: "you've treated me meanly and you've favoured John Brooke. I've never had a chance. I've been kept down and he has been pushed forward. You've never given me any authority in the place. I'm nothing more than a clerk; yet you accuse me of not taking an interest in the business. What have I to take an interest in? I'm not allowed to do anything on my own initiative. But that's what you like. You like everybody to go down on their knees and lick your boots." His flood of words suddenly subsided; he could get no further, though his father politely waited for him to go on.

Mr. Bracknel, indeed, had listened with a perfectly impassive face, and he now answered calmly: "If you have no authority it is because you've never shown yourself fit to have any. As for John Brooke, he isn't drawing as much pay as you are."

His tone of half contemptuous indifference renewed Alfred's fury. "I don't care what he's drawing. I'm quite sure you give him as little as you can. He has a position, all the same, and I haven't. He does things on his own responsibility: he isn't a mere machine. I've heard you asking him his opinion when I was standing by, but of course not worth consulting. Others have heard it too; and do you think it has no effect on them? doesn't make them look on me as of no importance?"

"Why *should* I ask your opinion?" Mr. Bracknel put it to him with a kind of brutal deliberateness. "What value do you imagine it has? You must surely know that if you weren't my son I wouldn't keep you in the place an hour longer than I could help! All you've ever done has been to set an example of idleness and dissipation. Where have you been to-day? What did you do when I sent you out to Switzerland? It's been the same story from the beginning:—cards, betting, drinking, and I don't know what less mentionable pursuits. Do you seriously expect me to entrust my business to a man of your stamp?"

"Oh, damn you and your business," said Alfred violently. "I hope you'll take it to hell with you." And turning on his heel he pulled open the door with a vicious jerk. But on the threshold he came face to face with his mother, who was standing there, pale and frightened, clad in a long, dark dressing-gown.

"Oh Alfred!" she exclaimed, horrified. "How could you speak so to your father!"

But Alfred only muttered something incoherent, as he pushed past her, and on upstairs.

Mrs. Bracknel entered the dining-room. In her dark, flowing

gown she looked strangely wraith-like. Her husband regarded her in sombre silence, but since he did not actually repulse her, which she had half expected him to do, she ventured to draw nearer.

"What has happened, James?" she asked, in a low tremulous voice. "What is it? What is the trouble?"

For a moment Mr. Bracknel found it a relief to have somebody to whom he could unburden himself. "The trouble?" he answered bitterly. "The trouble is that he's done for himself."

"Done for himself?" A vague vision of some dire deed floated before the mother's mind, though without taking precise form.

"He's married," said Mr. Bracknel laconically—"married a typist out of the office, that's all." He uttered the words with a kind of gloomy contempt, and his wife gave a sigh of relief, having imagined something infinitely worse.

"But when was it? To-day?" she asked.

"Oh, a few days ago. What does it matter when it was!"

"And you didn't know anything? You didn't——"

He looked at her angrily. "Of course I didn't know. Do you think I'm a fool? They took precious good care that I shouldn't know. A silly little doll of a thing, with a pretty face and the brains of a hen."

"But is she—is she a nice girl?—is she a good girl?"

"Oh, damn her," said Mr. Bracknel simply. "I don't know how nice she is. Nice enough for him, I dare say."

But his wife—in spite of her shrinking attitude—persevered. "Is Alfred fond of her?—what does he say about it all?"

"Fond of her! What do you mean by 'fond of her'? You don't think he married her for her position, do you? Whether he's fond of her or not he'll be sick of her at the end of a month—and God help her then!" He looked straight before him with unmitigated pessimism.

"Oh, don't say such dreadful things!" Mrs. Bracknel quavered. "Why should he be like that?"

"Because he's a brute and she's a fool." He spoke thickly, which was a sure sign that he was much agitated, but quietly, and even with a sort of gloomy fatalism. "What's the use of sentimentalizing about it?" he went on less violently. "You ought to know him well enough by this time, though he *is* your son! At any rate, if you don't, I do." And he began to pace up and down the room.

His wife watched him for some moments in a kind of fascinated silence. Then she asked timidly: "What are they going to do?"

Mr. Bracknel gave a short harsh laugh. "They're going to be sorry they ever saw each other," he replied. "They're going to live in some squalid little house in a back street till they hate the very sight of each other. God knows what they're going to do! Alfred can't afford to keep her at any rate—with his tastes, and on his salary."

Mrs. Bracknel's gentle countenance was filled with woe. She sank into a chair. "Where is she now?" she asked helplessly.

"She's at her aunt's, I suppose. She lives with an aunt; and she'll have to go on living there unless he takes a house."

"She has no father or mother, then?"

"It appears not: it's the one redeeming thing about her."

Mrs. Bracknel sighed. She tried to see some ray of light in all these gloomy pictures, but she had not yet had time to take in the full significance of what had happened. "Perhaps she's a nice girl," she murmured, with a weak return to her former position. "After all, we don't know her, do we?"

Mr. Bracknel glowered. "If she was a nice girl she wouldn't have married Alfred," he said. "It was to get him away from her that I sent him out to Switzerland!"

"Then you *did* know——?"

"I didn't. I only took precautions—because I got a hint that he was running after her."

"But we don't know her," the mother repeated. She was beginning to resent these attacks upon her son. Surely he had committed only an indiscretion, not a crime.

"*I* know her—as well as I'll ever know her. She'll never cross this door: you may put any idea of that sort out of your head."

"Do you think she entrapped Alfred, then? Do you think——"

"Oh, how do I know what she did! She hasn't drawn a prize at all events, though I suppose she thought it worth the risk. I can't live for ever, and I suppose they calculated that then it would be all right. The intention was to keep it a secret."

"Still, we must do something for them, mustn't we?" Mrs. Bracknel pleaded.

"Must we? I'm pretty sure we won't. Fortunately you've no money of your own to waste on them."

"But why are you so bitter? Is there—is there anything against her character?"

If he had wanted to, he could have told her why he was so bitter; he could have repeated to her the remark her son had let fall, have repeated those few words, for he remembered them perfectly, they still rang in his mind, in spite of the fact that he had been able outwardly to ignore them. Those words had sounded like a menace, but a menace he would never yield to. "I tell you I know the type," was all he said. "If he had married some simple country girl it would have been different. But a girl like this—no, it won't do."

"Still, now that it *has* happened," Mrs. Bracknel persisted, "mustn't we make the best of it? You can't cast Alfred off. If you allowed——"

"I won't allow him a penny more than his present salary. He's overpaid as it is." Suddenly he sat down in a chair. The colour drained from his face, and he began to breathe queerly. His wife flew to his assistance, but in a minute or two he was better and able to get on his feet again. "I'm not going to lose my night's sleep over it either, whoever else may," he added, with a poor attempt to carry off his strange collapse. But his face was still colourless, and little drops of sweat had broken out on his forehead. Rejecting his wife's aid, he moved a little uncertainly across the room and up the stairs, leaning heavily on the banisters. Mrs. Bracknel followed him closely.

19

The moon-worshipper sat on his narrow white bed, hugging his knees. The posture was a favourite one with him when he was in deep thought or dreaming. He had only partially undressed, for though he had been lying down on the bed he was going out again presently; he was merely waiting till he thought it would be quite safe to do so, and it seemed to him that he had been waiting a long time. By leaning out of the window he could see that Rusk's light was still burning. He had heard Alfred coming upstairs half an hour ago: later, his father's step as he too came up, the sound of the shutting of a door. It was past one o'clock; Rusk must be going to bed soon; and even as he looked the light went out. At last the coast was clear, yet the boy lingered on for another five minutes. Then he got out on to the window-sill and, with a surprising agility, the result of much practice, let himself down by a rope. He stood upon the grass below the window and looked up. The house, so far as he could see, showed a blank and sleeping face to the night. A radiant moonlight flooded the lawn, and he ran on, looking neither to right nor left. On the border of the shrubbery was a weeping ash whose branches swept the ground. He paused here and gazed down the low hill which separated him from the dim strange secrets of the wood and the stream. The grass was faded and wan in the moonlight, and there were dark mysterious shadows that were like crouching beasts. The boy was very lightly clad, but the night air was warm and there was no wind. A wonderful moon floated high and clear in the sky.

As he stood motionless a momentary fear suddenly crossed his mind—a fear of something that was there and yet not there. He watched the shadows and they seemed to become alive. One of them was like a huge sprawling sphinx, lying waiting for its prey, with curved cruel claws dug into the ground, and half-raised head, expectant, listening. Then his fear vanished, gave place to a wild excitement which made the blood drum in his ears, as he ran lightly down the slope to the stream. He was quite close now to the wood, yet still he lingered, conscious that he was approaching the innermost shrine, the secret temple. He crossed the shallow brook, and in doing so seemed to pass from one world to another. He stood for a moment upon the bank—and the water went murmuring away into the darkness.

. . . . .

He had been very quiet, he thought, but for all that not quiet enough. Rusk, from his own room, at any rate, had heard him, though the sound was but slight and he hardly knew why he should connect it with Denis, since he had not even been thinking of him. Nevertheless he did so connect it, and lay still, listening for a minute or two longer; but the sound was not repeated. Still uncertain, he got out of bed and went to the window. He was only just in time—in time to see what he believed to be his pupil gaining the shadow of the trees. A few seconds more and he would have missed him. He hesitated, but not really for long. Obviously it would be better that he should learn once and for all what actually took place on these nocturnal expeditions—it would set his mind more at rest, no matter how the adventure should turn out: besides, there was always the chance of discovering that the whole thing was merely a kind of boyish prank.

If he *was* to follow, however, there was no time to lose. He hastily put on a few articles of clothing, and going straight to Denis's room discovered the rope just as the latter had left it. Rusk had expected something of the kind, and he decided that it would be better to make use of it than to risk waking anyone by going downstairs and letting himself out in the ordinary way. In another minute he was on the grass and moving rapidly in the direction where he had seen his pupil disappear. His idea was to get to the moon-temple before Denis, for he thought it quite possible that the boy would loiter by the way. When he reached the shrubbery he proceeded more cautiously, but almost at once he caught sight of the fugitive, a slight dark figure standing motionless on the top of the hill. Here was his opportunity, and Rusk made a rapid detour, approaching the boy's hiding-place from a point lower down. Fortune favoured him again, and in a much shorter time than he could have expected he reached his destination, coming upon it simply by chance, and actually before he had begun his search.

His next proceeding was to hide himself carefully in the brushwood, and after that he had only to wait. Until now it had all been plain sailing, but just here he became conscious of a check, an unforeseen embarrassment, which presented itself in the shape of conscientious misgivings—moral scruples as to the honourableness of what he was about to do. It occurred to him that it was rather shabby—was in fact as clear a case of espionage as one could well imagine, and such a thought was most unpleasant to him. Of course there were plenty of reasons why he should act in this secret way—though the really convincing one, perhaps, was that no other was possible. The essential gravity of the case, the impossibility of learning indirectly what really took place on these occasions, the heavy responsibility which Doctor Birch, which everyone for that matter, had thrown upon him—all these things surely formed sufficient excuse, to say nothing of the full confession he intended to make to Denis afterwards. There was no doubt in the world that here, if anywhere, was an instance where the end justified the means, though so jesuitical a policy might not appeal to him. As the minutes passed, indeed, it appealed to him less and less, till in the end he was on the point of getting out of his hiding-place and going home. But a rustle close at hand sent him crouching back into the brushwood, gazing in amazement at Denis, who had emerged into the moonlight, moving through the dim, delicate beauty of the darkened wood, like a figure in a dream.

For the boy was naked, and this simple fact, so unexpected and astonishing, had in some inexplicable way the effect of banishing from Rusk's mind all hope that the whole thing might merely be an elaborate game. He lay still and watched, the strangeness of the performance holding him more and more, as by the force of some hypnotic spell, which drew his mind from its accustomed sphere. Denis advanced into the middle of the grove, and there was something in his movements, a kind of rhythmic precision and alacrity that was yet not haste, which gave Rusk a momentary impression that he might be walking in his sleep. The possibility brought him a sudden hope, but of this hope he was doomed to swift disappointment, when he watched the boy uncover the altar and place a moon-shaped object upon it. This object, Rusk saw, was decked with white tapers—tapers Denis was now lighting. When all were ablaze he bowed low before them as to some unseen presence, and then proceeded to go through the most amazing ceremony

Rusk was ever likely to behold. He must surely have invented it, and yet it suggested an actual survival from a half-forgotten pagan ritual. The boy poured out a libation. He burned incense as he moved about, waving it up to the pale divinity that hung in the deep sky above him. The thin aromatic smoke rose up in slender spirals, while the young priest, like a white sylvan creature of a primeval world, performed his simple rites. Half an hour ago Rusk had asked himself how far it was all real, how far a mere exploit of boyish romance; but somehow as he watched it now, alone, at this hour and in this place, with the dimness of night and the stillness of motionless trees all around him, stretching away into what might have been the very womb of the past, he found it difficult to see it in the light of anything childish or trivial. On the contrary, there was something in it which imposed itself upon his imagination, as if a fantastic lunar influence were working upon him also. It was real—only too real. What, then, was the relation of this naked pagan boy, with body bared to the whiteness of the moon, to the young Presbyterian who sat Sunday by Sunday in his father's pew? The thing was perplexing, inexplicable, and innumerable disquieting suggestions passed through Rusk's mind, making him more and more uneasy. Suddenly, as Denis drew closer to him, he had a clear view of his face, and his heart sank. That strange, rapt expression was not the expression of a boy playing a game. If he were to reveal himself now, would Denis even recognize him? A sudden chill came over him as he realized the import of this question. But he could not watch the thing any longer; he had seen enough; he must break the charm; he had already suffered it to go on too long; and he rose to his feet, coming out into the open, while at sight of him the boy gave a low cry. Denis made no attempt to hide himself, but stood perfectly still, trembling a little.

"It's only me," said Rusk, gently. "Won't you come back to the house?"

Denis looked at him without speaking. Then a sudden consciousness of the situation seemed to awaken in him, and with it a burst of anger against the intruder. It was the first and last time that Rusk was ever to see him in a passion. He himself felt horribly in the wrong, though his reasons for doing what he had done were surely good enough. At all events the spell was broken, very effectually broken, and he knew he need have no further fear to leave Denis to himself. He knew that the boy would follow him back to the house: he thought it better not to wait, better to leave him alone—for the present at all events. Such explanations as he had to offer would do well enough in the morning, and he was conscious that they would sound particularly feeble. It was not the first time he had played the part of intruder, and though before it had been more or less accidental, he certainly could not make that excuse for to-night's action. He was afraid, indeed, that it might alter their whole relation to each other. He was afraid it could hardly fail to do so, hardly fail to make Denis distrustful of him, even if it did not awaken actual dislike. Certainly the boy would have every reason to be distrustful. No matter with what excellent intentions, it could not be denied that Rusk had taken advantage of his confidence to spy upon him. The more he considered the matter the more he feared he had made a serious blunder—a mistake which might cost him all the ground that up till to-night he had gained. But it was too late now to draw back: what was done could not be undone.

Therefore it was an intense relief to find next morning that things seemed to be all right. Denis came down late, looking pale and tired, with heavy black lines under his eyes, but otherwise much as usual. He smiled somewhat listlessly at his tutor, but apparently bore him no ill-will. He behaved, indeed, as if he had forgotten the whole affair, though Rusk could not believe this to be really the case. Over his work he was languid and indifferent—so obviously so, that at the end of an hour the tutor proposed taking the rest of the day as a holiday. Denis instantly rose from the table with a sigh of relief, and without a word curled himself up in an armchair, where he seemed to drop asleep over a book.

Outside it was raining heavily. The branches of the trees, soaked and dark, stretched above the sodden grass, and from all around there rose a continuous drip—drip—drip. But to Rusk, for some reason, the melancholy sound was soothing, and the soft rush of the rain down the windows, the patter of rain on leaves.

Now that Denis had taken the matter so quietly he was even

glad that he had obeyed the impulse to follow and watch him; it was so much better that he should know all. He began to write a letter home—a rather overdue letter, for he was a poor correspondent—and from time to time he glanced at his charge, still with a certain anxiety, having an idea that he ought to speak to him, that in fact he *must* speak to him sooner or later, of last night's adventure. It would be easier, no doubt, to imitate Denis's attitude of apparent forgetfulness, especially as he hated the idea of perpetually forcing the boy to deliver an account of his doings. But there was his promise to Doctor Birch; there were also Doctor Birch's warnings, the memory of which kept cropping up constantly in his thoughts. He felt he should like to consult Doctor Birch, that if they were really to work together he certainly *ought* to consult him; though on the other hand he was afraid Denis would regard this as a betrayal. He could not make up his mind what his next step should be. So between the sentences of his letter he looked at the sleepy boy, and tried to decide where his duty lay.

It is possible that Denis was not wholly unaware of the psychological problem he had given rise to, and this occurred to Rusk while he watched him. He looked very young—almost a child—as he half sat, half lay, in the big chair, with that big old book in his brown, slender hands. Rusk felt there were few things he would not do to help him, even if there were no more than a bare chance. . . .

The volume Denis had taken from the shelves was the second of the complete works of that exquisite and fanciful divine, Jeremy Taylor: and in *The Life of Jesus* he had come upon a passage describing the flight into Egypt:

"'Then he arose and took the young Child and his mother, by night, and departed into Egypt.' And they made their first abode in Hermopolis, in the country of Thebais; whither, when they first arrived, the child Jesus, being by design or providence carried into a temple, all the statues of the idol-gods fell down, like Dagon at the presence of the ark, and suffered their timely and just dissolution and dishonour, according to the prophecy of Isaiah: 'Behold the Lord shall come into Egypt, and the idols of Egypt shall be moved at his presence.'"

Characteristically, this passage stirred the boy's imagination, which plumed its wings and spread them for a very distant Egypt, where he became busy with a scene that curiously blended the quaint picture of the learned bishop with a wilder wonder borrowed from *The Arabian Nights*. He read no more except in his own fantasy, and the heavy calf-bound book slipped unheeded to the floor. To Rusk, still watching him, his face just now had a purely spiritual quality, and it sent a sharp pang of regret through him to think that this spirit should ever be troubled, as surely it had been troubled only a few hours since. A sudden tenderness swept over him—a tenderness which almost from the beginning had been there, but which now was crystallized into a definite sense of regret at what might be the waste of a beautiful intelligence—an intelligence so fine, so rare, that it appeared to be capable of the very highest things. Rusk was quite firmly convinced that his pupil was made of a finer clay than anyone else whom he had hitherto encountered. He was different—it was of his essence to be different —but the difference lay not so much in any superficial peculiarities as in a greater delicacy, a rarer quality of mind, a more perfect sensibility, a higher, a subtler power of imagination. And what was there, perhaps, in the most striking degree of all, though hitherto it had not occurred to him to take note of it, was a complete absence of anything gross, of anything that could, even with the passage of years, associate itself for an instant with vulgarity or sensuality.

20

On the afternoon of the last day of October Rusk was strolling along the river bank by himself. He had left Denis fishing in a stream hard by, where he had once caught an extremely small trout, and had haunted assiduously ever since. Rusk had left him with the intention of returning later on, but at the present moment he had forgotten all about him, and was completely absorbed in his own thoughts. The path he followed was heavy, and covered with a clinging brown mud. The ground sloped up on either side from the dark river, down whose nearly black surface a few brown and scattered leaves drifted slowly. Rusk came to a pause and leaned against a broken stile. On the opposite bank the curve upward was broad and low and sweeping—a smooth meadow of a yellow-green hue, washed across with waves of darker green, and crowned towards the top of the incline by trees of every shade of brown and red and gold and green. In the mildness of the season, though the ground was drifted over by a carpet of dead leaves, most of the trees were still well covered, the blacker, stouter limbs alone being visible through the thinning foliage. Two horses and a donkey moved slowly over the grass, nibbling lazily. Grey clouds floated overhead. The reflections of tall grasses and reeds, of hawthorn bushes and stooping trees, of tangled shrubs and naked prostrate logs, were motionless in the still water; all the colour of the upper world was imaged there, hardly dimmed in this deep dark mirror. The lower clouds in the west were tinged with a faint cold sunlight, looking almost silvery behind the deeper red-bronze of the trees; while in the east a heavier cloud-bank was black and threatening, gradually approaching though hardly seeming to move.

A barge came drifting along, pulled by a white horse with mud-splashed legs. It passed so smoothly, low in the dark oily water, that it seemed the sleepiest thing in the world. When it was gone the silence closed in once more, broken now only by the occasional note of a bird and the distant sound of the weir. And the quiet of the passing afternoon had a melancholy that brought with it a curious consolation. Rusk acquiesced in its dreamy stillness; his mood became sympathetic with it and with the somewhat austere beauty of his surroundings; but he was thinking of things which might have seemed far enough removed from the scene before him, things which were altogether practical. . . .

After a while he climbed over the broken, rickety stile and ascended the incline till he reached a road leading in a homeward direction. He had been walking for some time, still lost in thought, when he saw someone approaching, whom he took to be Miss Anna Birch. It was indeed Miss Anna—Miss Anna coming from the village, and she had recognized Rusk at the same moment as he had recognized her. He quickened his pace, and when they met turned aside with her, both entering a narrow high-banked lane, a short-cut to the Birches' house.

The country everywhere was clothed in brown and yellow autumn tints, with richer notes of gold and crimson. The yellow leaves had fallen from the chestnut-trees; the beeches were a deep red-brown; the willows still a delicate silver-grey; but the last lingering traces of summer were gone, and there was a rustle of dead leaves in the air.

It was a country of mingled wood and pasture-land, stretching between the river and the hills, and lying now under a white drifting light of mid-afternoon. The sunless landscape had already a somewhat wintry charm; the cold wan light was slowly fading; from all around rose whispering voices—the thin low trembling notes of withered grasses, the fuller, sweeping murmur of the trees.

They skirted the garden wall, built of crumbling red brick stained with patches of dark green moss and crowned with tufts of wallflower, till they reached a small green wooden gate, where they came to a pause. Here Rusk was about to take leave of his companion, but Miss Anna would not allow him to go.

"Now you've come so far you must come in and have tea," she said; and the young man yielded without much persuasion.

He had a weakness for drinking tea with the Miss Birches. The society of these ladies he always found to have a homely unexacting pleasantness which was most agreeable. Miss Anna perhaps was not perceptibly old-fashioned: she liked to talk about Wagner's operas, for instance, and Rusk had once discovered her reading a novel by Gabriele D'Annunzio. This work, it is true, she subsequently confessed to have taken up more for the sake of her Italian than for any great pleasure it afforded her; but she read Henry James, and Anatole France, and was indeed much more familiar with the works of these authors than was Rusk.

They had tea indoors—the garden days had been over for some time—and the tutor, looking out at the denuded flower-beds, the faded leaf-strewn grass, felt a vague sense of regret. He found a sadness, delicate and half-fanciful, in the passing of summer; and never before had he been so conscious of its personal significance, its suggestion of the passing of other things one cared for—hours, some of them, one would gladly recall. These sentimental reveries were prosaically interrupted by Miss Birch discovering that he had a slight cold. She insisted on preparing some special kind of tea for him, in which tea itself appeared to be the least important ingredient; and Rusk allowed himself to be doctored and made much of, with a half-amused sense of slipping back into a not very remote boyhood. Miss Anna found that he was becoming far too serious. She declared that when she had met him he had frowned at her as if he carried a thousand cares on his shoulders.

"They were only selfish cares," said Rusk, smiling. "I was wondering what I should do when I leave here—leave the Bracknels, that is. I had intended to go in for teaching, you know; but I've almost decided not to. I don't think I should like it—I mean in a school; and of course one can't go on being a tutor all one's life—once is enough for me at any rate."

"But you're getting on all right, aren't you?" Miss Birch ventured. "You're not thinking of leaving just yet?"

Rusk laughed. "Oh no. It's not so immediate as that. I'll stay as long as they want me—for another year or two, that is. But then will come the difficulty. I somehow don't see myself taking on another pupil."

Miss Anna found something in his manner or his words, or perhaps both, which prompted a question. "Did you ever suggest that you and Denis might go abroad for a few months? It would do him a world of good and would be rather nice for both of you."

"It would indeed," said Rusk regretfully. "The only thing is that it might be considered a little *too* nice. Mr. Bracknel would call it an unnecessary extravagance, and he doesn't like unnecessary extravagances."

"Don't you think he perhaps might in this case—if you put it to him very artfully—as being ever so much to Denis's advantage and all that?"

"Unfortunately he has his own ideas as to what is to Denis's advantage," Rusk said dubiously. "And then—well, he's not exactly the kind of man you can suggest things to. You never know whether he'll insult you or not. Quite without intending to, of course; but he's got a most peculiar mind. He might think I only wanted to travel at his expense; and if he did he'd probably say so; and—oh well, it would be very unpleasant all round."

"But still——"

"All this fuss about Alfred, too, seems to have made him more suspicious than ever."

"He'll get over the Alfred affair now Alfred is settled in a house of his own," Miss Birch said.

Rusk was not convinced, but he did not argue the point, and soon afterwards rose to go. While he walked back he turned Miss Anna's suggestion over in his mind. It had an undeniable fascination, but unfortunately all the turning over and all the fascination in the world could not make it appear very practicable. He was so sure that Mr. Bracknel would take it as he had said that he did not even think it would be worth while going through the highly distasteful task of approaching him on the subject. At present their relations were perfectly amicable, and it was most important to keep them so.

Rusk did not take a direct route back to the house, but feeling in the mood for a lonely ramble, wandered on down a series of lanes and field-paths till presently he perceived a solitary figure coming towards him through the twilight. The figure, as it drew closer, proved to be that of Denis, carrying a fishing-rod over his shoulder, though apparently this was the only trophy he was bringing back from his afternoon's sport. Lack of success, however, had not put him out of humour, for he was whistling, and as soon as he caught sight of Rusk called out gaily: "Where are *you* off to?"

"Just taking a stroll," Rusk replied. "I've been over at the Birches'."

"You never told me you were going or I might have come with you. Do you know that this is the last day of October—Hallowe'en —and that you certainly shouldn't be wandering about alone on 'this night of all nights of the year'?"

"I don't suppose the risk is very serious," Rusk returned inattentively.

Denis caught him by the arm. "Don't be too sure. On just this one night the dead can leave their graves and dance in the moonlight on the grass: the more light-hearted ones at any rate. Do you imagine they're going to miss such a chance for you?"

Rusk glanced round into the damp foggy evening. "I don't see any graves—or moonlight either," he murmured, still thinking of the continental tour.

Denis prattled on undiscouraged. "It's a new moon," he said, his fresh young voice sounding with a very infectious charm, though having begun to break it was subject to sudden and surprising alterations of pitch. Rusk turned to where he pointed, and saw in the western sky a faint, almost imperceptible crescent.

"The old Irish feast to the moon was held on this night," the boy continued to chatter. "Amy and May will be trying all kinds of things after dinner. At least they used to, other years—to find out who they're going to marry and all that."

"Well, you and I aren't in a hurry to know," Rusk supposed. "Are we?"

"*Aren't* we, you mean," Denis corrected him. But after a brief pause he went on in a different tone: "I saw Alfred yesterday. Mamma —though you mustn't breathe a word about it—went to visit Mrs. Alfred; and I went with her, though I didn't go in. She didn't want me to; but she told me to call back for her in half an hour, and I did. It was then I saw Alfred—in the distance. It's rather stupid, don't you think—all the fuss that has been made? To listen to it you'd think we were of the most exalted lineage and mixed exclusively with the aristocracy. Mrs. Alfred must hate us like poison, and that's about the only effect it can have. Personally I have a theory that she's rather nice."

"I dare say it's as good as any other," Rusk said, with a shrug.

"Are you bored?" Denis asked, smiling at him, and leaning on his arm.

"Bored?"

"With my attempts at conversation."

"You're a wonderful humbug," Rusk replied. "But I suppose you're fishing for a compliment."

"Yes," Denis sighed, "and I don't seem to be any luckier than I was down at the river. You'd better tell me what you talked about to the Miss Birches."

"As a matter of fact we talked largely about *you*. At any rate Miss Anna did. Later, if anything comes of it, which is most improbable, I'll perhaps tell you what she said."

"You're very mysterious. Why won't you tell me now?"

"Come along," said Rusk; "it's getting late."

They quickened their pace. It was very dark, and now and then they stumbled over some unevenness in their path, and occasionally had to scramble across a ditch or over a gate, for they still kept to the fields.

"If we'd gone by the road it would have been easier," Denis grumbled.

"But longer, and unless I'm greatly mistaken we're in for a downpour."

21

Rain, in fact, had already begun to fall by the time they reached home, and the wind was rising. The son of a neighbour, a boy who was supposed to have looked after Denis—or who at any rate had been requested to do so—during the latter's brief period at school, was present at dinner. He had ridden over on his bicycle, the bearer of a message, and had been invited to stay.

Mrs. Bracknel introduced him to Rusk as a friend of her son's, and Rusk could guess just how far the friendship went. But he had a chat with this youth—later in the evening, when Denis was out of the room and while the girls and their mother were discussing some bazaar at which they had promised to help. The two young men talked for a little about cricket, and then by a question Rusk brought the conversation round to his pupil. One of the first things he learned was that Denis was a "freak" and should never have been sent to school at all. "He did the maddest things, and was always getting into rows—silly kinds of rows that no one else ever got into. There was no harm in what he did, of course: it was just mad. And for some reason the masters couldn't stand him. They had an idea half the time that he was 'ragging' them, but could never be quite sure. You see, he's a facetious little beast in his own way."

"But how did he get on with the other boys?" Rusk asked. "Did they like him?"

"Oh, I dare say they liked him all right—in a sort of way. There's nothing much to *dis*like, is there? The only thing was that most of the chaps couldn't get the hang of him. And then, as well as being rotten at games, he took absolutely no interest in them, which naturally didn't help. He seemed, all the same, to be getting along not too badly; but of course you never can tell; and after he got ill it came out that everything had been wrong from the beginning— one or two beasts had been giving him as bad a time as they knew how. If I'd guessed, I'd have done something, or at any rate tried to do something, about it, but naturally I didn't see a great deal of him: I mean, when a chap's two or three years younger than you are, you can't very well, can you? What it really amounts to is that a boy like Denis oughtn't to be sent to a public school. He's bound to have a rotten time, and the chances are he'll get into bad ways and go to the mischief."

"I don't think there was much danger of that at all events," Rusk replied.

"No, I suppose not, but—— I like him, you know; he's quite decent, if only he wasn't so queer. I must tell you one thing he did. It sounds like a fairy tale, and it was before he took ill, before all the row——"

Rusk, however, was never to hear the remainder of the story, for at that moment Denis himself entered the room. He held a slim narrow green volume in his hand, and as Rusk and the young guest came over to join the little group by the fire, he opened it and began to read aloud slowly, with a slight upward wrinkle of his eyebrows:

"'What is your favourite musical instrument?'

"'The harp.'

"'What do you consider to be the most beautiful thing in nature?'

"'Ruins by moonlight.'"

But at this point May made a sudden grab at the book, which in the struggle that ensued fell to the ground, where she pounced upon it. Once it was safely in her possession, she began to laugh. "It's a Confession Album," she told the mystified Rusk. "I don't suppose you've ever heard of such a thing, but in Aunt Lizzie's young days they were all the rage. This one belonged to her, and she passed it on to me when I was about fourteen, because at that time I was dying to write in it. Where Denis discovered it I don't know. I haven't seen it for years."

"I discovered it in the bookcase," Denis replied, "and if we're not to have confessions I propose we go down to the kitchen. They're burning nuts and doing all kinds of things. Cook was trying a most mysterious experiment with a red herring when I was there. I couldn't make out what it was exactly, but I'm going down again now. I'm going to burn myself with Cook. She's really very fond of me, mamma, though she lets 'concealment, like a worm i' the bud——'"

. . . . .

In the ebb and flow of his present existence Rusk had for some time been conscious of what appeared to be a favourable current, but never had it so strongly revealed itself as on this particular evening. Amy was in a normal mood again, and her relation with himself and with May seemed perfectly natural and friendly. In fact when he retired that night to his bedroom it was with a reassuring sense that things after all had worked out satisfactorily—an idea which gave a pleasant encouragement to his innate conviction that in the long run, if you only let them, they usually do. To-night, in his own room, while the wind was rocking the trees outside, and coming in gusty blasts against his window with a sweep and rattle of driving rain, he had been indulging in these optimistic thoughts, and at last had taken up a novel by Le Fanu which promised to be full of mystery and suspense. It was a little past midnight, and he was beginning to abandon himself to the spell of his book, when suddenly above the bluster and moaning of the wind, coming like an echo of the passage he was reading, he thought he heard a cry. True, it was very faint and distant, yet at this hour, when he believed everyone but himself to be in bed and asleep, it was sufficient to make him stop reading. He listened intently for a minute or two; then, though hearing nothing further, got up and opened his door, going even some little way along the passage, still listening.

Evidently he had not been mistaken, for at that moment Denis too came out. They stood together, uncertain as to the direction the sound had proceeded from, and were still standing there when the door of May's room at the end of the passage opened, and Amy appeared. Rusk took a step forward, but the look he received brought him up abruptly and he advanced no further.

"What do you want?" she asked in a clear cold voice that rang out with a metallic distinctness in the silence of the house. "And what is Denis doing there, prowling about at this hour?"

Rusk, feeling rather foolish, began to explain. "We thought we heard someone calling," he said awkwardly.

"I suppose you heard May calling to *me*. I'm sorry if it alarmed you."

Rusk coloured and muttered an apology, but already Amy had disappeared, going back again into May's room, the door of which she closed in their faces.

"I told you they'd be trying things," Denis whispered, but Rusk, who resented Amy's words, and still more her manner, returned to his own room, extremely annoyed.

There, moreover, while his indignation cooled, his earlier sense of dissatisfaction revived. He had been very easily put off, for in spite of Amy's lofty attitude he was now persuaded that the cry he had heard had been a cry of fear. On the other hand, very likely Denis was right, and in that case it was none of his business. So having placed his reading-lamp on the small table beside his pillow, he undressed, got into bed, and resumed his novel.

He read a chapter or two, after which, though still not feeling in the least drowsy, he was on the point of extinguishing the light and trying to go to sleep, when there came a tap at his door.

"Come in," he called, and Denis entered.

Rusk looked at him. "What's the matter?" he asked, for the boy's face had an odd expression, and his eyes were unnaturally bright.

Denis slowly approached the side of the bed. "Will you let me sleep with you?" he faltered.

The tutor hesitated; then in silence made room for him; and in silence they lay side by side for several minutes, Rusk not wishing to ask questions which might be embarrassing to answer. But Denis spoke at last of his own accord: "It was something I heard. I heard it last night too: but to-night somehow—— I didn't want to disturb you—— I—— Do you mind?"

"Of course I don't mind," Rusk answered. "I'm very glad, if it makes you feel more comfortable. . . . What was it?" he went on, for he could tell that the boy's nerves were for some reason very much over-strung. "It wasn't just what we heard before, was it?"

"No: it was a kind of ticking: but it wouldn't stop. It came from somewhere at the head of the bed. . . ."

A sudden light dawned on Rusk. "I know what you mean now," he said. "But it's only a small insect that gets into the woodwork. Surely you know that yourself."

"There isn't any woodwork," Denis answered.

"Well, into the wall then. We'll have a hunt for him in the morning."

Denis said nothing further, though Rusk, mentally anathematizing the inventor of death-watches and all similar bugaboos, suspected that he was still nervous, and instinct told him that a little sympathy would be of much more use than any amount of reasoning. He put out his arm, and Denis lay with his head against his shoulder. It now occurred to him—and he wondered he had not thought of it before—that possibly it was not uncommon for his pupil to be nervous at night. He remembered certain things he had been told by Miss Anna Birch about his childhood—things Miss Anna herself had learned from Mrs. Bracknel—and it looked as if he had not altogether outgrown those old fears.

"Do you often have bad dreams?" he asked—immediately adding, so that the boy should not feel ashamed to tell him the truth, "I know *I* did when I was a youngster; but fortunately one outgrows them; I haven't had what you might call a really first-class nightmare for years."

"Sometimes," Denis replied. "Not so often as I used to. I used to hate going to bed: I used to dread it for an hour before the time—and sometimes it was horrible; I could still see things after I woke up. There was one figure in particular. It used to stand at the foot of the bed—very tall, and with a long, white, smiling face. It was its smile that was the worst—its teeth. I used to be frightened of meeting it after dark—on the stairs—anywhere—for it seemed to belong here...."

Abruptly Rusk made up his mind. "Tell me," he said; "would you like to have your bed brought in here? The room is quite large enough for both of us, and there's no reason on earth why we shouldn't share it. It wouldn't disturb me in the least.... That is absolutely true. It won't make the smallest difference so far as I'm concerned, and if you would like it you might just as well be here as not. I mean this, Denis: I mean it literally; I'm not trying to be kind or anything like that; so you need have no hesitations or scruples about telling me the truth."

Denis waited, but not for very long. Then he said simply: "I would like it."

"I wonder I didn't think of it sooner," Rusk muttered. "It was stupid of me, but I never understand anything till it's more or less pushed down my throat."

"You do understand," cried Denis indignantly. "There's nobody understands so well. Only you didn't think I was such a baby. How could you?"

"My dear boy, it's merely a matter of temperament, of imagination: there's nothing babyish about it."

Denis made no reply, and presently Rusk thought he must have fallen asleep, when suddenly he said: "Don't mention it before papa, will you? He wouldn't allow it." After which he was silent again for a minute or two till he added: "I'm afraid it won't do. The others would be bound to get to know, and they'd think me a coward, and perhaps talk about it. They're not like you."

"Will you *leave* it to me?" Rusk asked.

"But what will you do about it?"

"I don't call that leaving it! I'll speak to nobody but your mother, though I fancy if I spoke to Doctor Birch as well, he could make it all right at once. Anyhow remember, if nothing else you can always come in as you've done to-night, without anybody knowing. But I'm perfectly certain it can be arranged, so don't worry."

A little later he could tell from his low regular breathing that Denis had dropped asleep. It showed him that he had taken the right course—the course which evidently had brought consolation. Rusk himself lay awake for some time longer. He was again busy with the idea of taking the boy away, and curiously enough the difficulties to be surmounted did not now strike him as nearly so formidable as they had appeared before. He determined at all events to do his utmost in the matter, and not to give in till he had exhausted every means in his power.

22

It was about half an hour before lunch. From the study window Rusk had seen Mrs. Bracknel leaving the house, and thinking this to be probably his best chance of getting her alone had sallied forth in pursuit. She was only going as far as the front lodge, he discovered, but his offer to accompany her thither was accepted, and they paced slowly down the drive together, Rusk asking after May, who had not appeared at breakfast, and whose absence he had guessed to be in some way connected with the mysterious alarm of the previous night. He had said nothing about this, thinking it better to avoid the subject in Amy's presence, and Amy on her side had also kept silence—an unusual discretion, not tending in any way to remove the young man's suspicions. And now Mrs. Bracknel's rejoinder to his inquiry seemed amply to justify them.

"I don't understand what is wrong with May," she told him. "You saw she didn't come down to breakfast, and she says she fainted last night. They *will* try those senseless tricks! Just think, Mr. Rusk; at midnight she shut herself up in her room in the dark and began to comb out her hair before the mirror. It's an old Hallowe'en custom, and after a time you're supposed to see the reflection of a face in the glass—the face of your future husband. But I'm sure it must be wrong to try such things. If one *did* see anything, how could it be anything good? May says she only tried it because she knew it was all nonsense. As the clock was striking twelve she began to comb her hair before the glass, while she stood gazing and waiting. The room was nearly pitch dark, but she says that after a minute or two she distinctly saw a dim white face staring at her. That is all she remembers, and when she came to, Amy was with her. This morning she seems convinced that the whole thing was due to Amy, who knew beforehand what she was going to do, and had hidden herself in the room on purpose to give her a fright. You see there's a clothes-press built into the wall, and of course it *would* be quite possible for anyone to hide there and creep out."

"But——" Rusk began, and then paused.

Mrs. Bracknel turned to him, waiting a moment before she continued: "Amy's story is that she heard a cry, and guessing something had happened ran to May's room, where she found her lying on the floor in a faint. She says you and Denis heard it too, and that all the rest is May's imagination."

Rusk reflected. Amy must have been remarkably quick if what she said were true, but he had a strong suspicion that it *wasn't* true. Nobody could prove this however, and he thought it better to keep his doubts to himself.

Mrs. Bracknel's gaze rested on him in uncertainty. "They're so strange!" she murmured plaintively. "I never know what to do or what to think. I'm sure it's Rebecca—that horrid old woman at the back lodge—who puts these ideas into their heads—or rather into Amy's, for I don't think May ever goes near her. I've tried to get Mr. Bracknel to send her away, but he won't listen to me."

It occurred to Rusk that all this was not exactly leading up to what he himself desired to discuss, but he sympathized as best he could, and acquiesced in the view that Rebecca was an undesirable person. As he did so he reflected on the curious fact that it was almost impossible to agree with any one member of the Bracknel family without tacitly criticizing some other. He had grown accustomed to the position, however, and latterly had begun to disregard it, saying on every occasion what he actually thought. Meanwhile they had reached the lodge, and he waited for Mrs. Bracknel while she spoke with the gardener's wife.

"I wanted to talk to you about Denis," he began, as soon as she reappeared and they had turned back towards the house. He told her of his idea of having his pupil's bed brought into his own room; and then, carrying his plan still further: "Don't you think it would be good for him to get away for a bit, to have a—a complete change of scene—to travel for six months or a year—two years perhaps?"

"To travel!" Mrs. Bracknel almost gasped, gazing at him as if he had said something most extraordinary—which indeed he felt he had.

Nothing daunted nevertheless, he continued to enlarge on his idea: "Yes. I should be very happy to look after him. Of course I only mention it because I suppose the matter of expense would be of no importance to Mr. Bracknel."

"Matters of expense are always of importance to my husband," Mrs. Bracknel rejoined naïvely.

Rusk laughed. "You see, I'm quite convinced it would be the very best thing for Denis," he went on. "It's really just what he needs. It would set him on his feet: the good it would do him would never be lost."

"What makes you say so? What is the matter with him?" Mrs. Bracknel questioned anxiously.

"Well—this nervousness is the main thing. He needs to be taken out of himself; needs something to—to interest him and amuse him."

"To amuse him!" Mrs. Bracknel's eyes expressed a surprise not unmixed with alarm.

"I mean something that will give him a new interest in life—in places, in people. I know it would be good for him. If you trust him to me for a year or two now, you will never regret it later."

The note of conviction in his voice would have been more than sufficient to overcome any objections that might have existed in the mother's mind, but she knew she had not herself principally to take into account, since her acquiescence would mean nothing in the face of her husband's refusal. "Mr. Bracknel would never agree to such a thing," she exclaimed, as if a little frightened at Rusk's audacity in even suggesting it. She herself had perfect confidence in the young Englishman; she had in fact come to regard him almost as Denis's elder brother; but she also knew that this would count for very little in any decision her husband eventually might make.

"I'll speak to him," said Rusk. "Or rather, I'll get Doctor Birch to speak to him; that will be better." He had a sudden assurance of success, and continued enthusiastically: "We'll all speak to him. Surely everyone must see it's a good plan." Then, in case he might be displaying rather too much jubilation at the prospect of taking Denis away from home, he moderated his tone, though he continued to press the point.

Mrs. Bracknel remained more than dubious. "He won't see it at all," she sighed, referring to her husband. "He'll say that when he was Denis's age he was earning his own living, not being taken on pleasure tours through Europe. He might possibly agree to his going away for a month. Do you think a month——"

"A month's not the slightest use," Rusk returned impatiently, his last night's impression of his pupil still fresh in his mind.

Mrs. Bracknel laid her hand gently on his arm, and the instinctive gesture told him that she was at least grateful, even if she could do little to help him. "Don't count on Mr. Bracknel's consent, Mr. Rusk," she said. "I think you are almost certain to be disappointed. And in the meantime it would be much wiser not to mention the matter to Denis."

"To Denis! Of course not. But if everybody knows it is the right thing, I don't see——"

"He can't go without his father's consent," Mrs. Bracknel reminded him, "and until he has that we can do nothing."

23

It was comparatively early on the following evening when Rusk returned from dining with the Birches, and he went straight to the study, expecting to find his pupil at work. But though the table showed numerous traces of him, Denis was not there. Doubtless he would be back soon, however, for he had left the lamp burning, and Rusk sat down to consider the most recent development of his scheme.

During dinner it had come in for a good deal of discussion—in fact they had talked of very little else—and in the end the Doctor had decided to walk over with his guest and put the matter before

Mr. Bracknel entirely as his own idea. He had laid particular stress upon this, having found out that, so far as Rusk was aware, Mrs. Bracknel had as yet said nothing to her husband. And Rusk himself could see the advantage of the Doctor's plan. The proposition would come with much more weight from him: he was the family physician; he had been consulted about Denis on more than one occasion; and could argue the whole matter from a detached and scientific point of view.

After dinner, when they were alone together, Rusk and his host had returned to the subject, this time discussing it to the accompaniment of the Doctor's excellent cigars and the Doctor's excellent wine. Perhaps indeed, for one of them, they had lingered a little too long over the excellent wine: at all events now, seated before the glowing study fire, Rusk felt somewhat sleepy, and perfectly at peace with all the world. In this happy mood of optimism (for he had great confidence in the Doctor's powers of persuasion), he heard the door opening behind him and, without troubling to look round, concluded that his pupil had come in. But no further sound following, after a few seconds he turned to see why; and it was only then he discovered that his visitor was Amy, not her brother. She stood there, neither advancing nor retreating, still holding the door ajar, as if slightly disconcerted at finding him alone.

"Where is Denis?" she asked, suddenly smiling with a peculiar intensity, which covered him with a physical sense of light and even of warmth.

"I don't know. Isn't he downstairs?"

She shook her head. "It doesn't matter: it's nothing of any importance. . . . You look dreadfully lazy and dreadfully unsociable —I suppose I'd better go away again." The last words were uttered in a tone somewhat at variance with their literal meaning, and she made no attempt to put them into practice; seeing which, and partly also to show that it was only during teaching hours he was so grumpy, Rusk begged her to come in and sit down.

"I *am* rather lazy," he confessed. "It must be the demoralizing effect of a comfortable chair and a fire. Such things are fatal."

"Do you feel demoralized, then? I love to feel that way, but it's so difficult."

"I was enjoying it immensely." He looked at her with his frank smile. His fair hair was ruffled, as if he had been out in the wind without a hat; his face was rather flushed.

The sudden softness of her manner surprised him. The coldness and reserve with which she had treated him of late had entirely disappeared, and it was the very midsummer sun of favour that she turned upon him now. He had risen to his feet on her entrance, but he sat down again, since Amy, forgetful of her intention to leave him, had already found a chair. Moreover, she had given it a push that brought it in front of the fire and very close to his own; while she leaned a little forward as she sat, the warm, coloured light playing over her face and in her eyes, which rested upon him from time to time with an expression he had not seen in them for quite a long while. He had an idea that she must have come in purposely to make friends again, and that, when all was said, it was rather decent of her.

Amy drew her chair still closer. He felt that she was very near, and through the dreamy passivity of his mood the sense of her proximity grew gradually stronger. "You look very lonely," she sympathized, with a lingering sweetness in her voice. "I'm sure you must often feel lonely. I've thought so before."

"Oh, I'm all right," answered Rusk prosaically.

"But you must find it so different from what you've been accustomed to. You must have so many friends in England!"

"Well, of course I have a few friends," he admitted. "But sooner or later men are bound to get scattered, to lose sight of one another. It's inevitable."

"I suppose so. And girls don't make friends."

"Don't they?"

She shook her head. "Not really. Of all the girls I knew at school there isn't one I even write to now: and yet we used to sit for hours with our arms round each other and pretend to be ever so affectionate."

"Well, I can understand the not writing part of it," Rusk laughed.

"But I don't mean what you do: it isn't the trouble that prevents me: I haven't the least inclination to write. I suppose the truth is that I don't particularly like girls. I never did. They're well enough in some ways, of course, but they aren't made for friendships between themselves."

"Why not? My sisters don't seem to find much difficulty."

"Perhaps they're like you," Amy said softly.

"They're not—not a bit."

"Most girls are jealous of one another," she went on. "Besides, you can't trust them not to do mean things. You don't understand; you don't know. No man, I expect, ever really understands women. Sometimes they may tell him he does—when he flatters them or idealizes them—but he doesn't. They're both better and worse than he thinks: at all events they're different. The only women who are really popular with other women are the very plain ones, but it's not because they're plain, it's because they have—a better chance."

Rusk was interested: Amy as psychologist was something quite new. "A better chance in what way?" he asked.

"To be different; to live their own lives; to be genuine. I suppose it's more or less like the difference between children and grown-up people. There isn't the same spirit of competition, the same struggle to attract admiration and attention; you can watch them without feeling sick." She paused, but Rusk had no reply to make, and for a few minutes they sat in silence.

Then Amy began again: "Don't you feel it strange to have nobody who calls you by your Christian name? I've seen your name so often on your letters that I've got into the way of calling you by it in my thoughts, but I've never once heard anybody say it aloud. That's because I don't know any other Huberts."

"Oh, I expect a man doesn't notice these things much," Rusk returned vaguely. "You see, he's accustomed to being called by his surname, except by his own people and perhaps one or two others. It begins when he goes to school."

"I'd hate that," Amy declared. "I like everybody to call me Amy."

"They do, don't they?" Rusk asked innocently.

"You don't."

"Well, of course I couldn't," Rusk said, with a rather awkward laugh.

He felt her hand touch his. It rested there for a few seconds and then was withdrawn. He felt a sudden quickening of his blood, and made an effort to shake himself free from the fascination that was closing about him. He did not look at her, but he knew her gaze was fixed upon him. A silence followed, which seemed very long. To break it he moved uneasily, lifted the poker, and began to stir the fire.

"Doctor Birch is downstairs talking to papa," Amy murmured. "I think about your going abroad with Denis. . . . That would be very nice for both of you. . . . I know you're fond of travelling."

"I'm afraid I can hardly say *that*," Rusk replied. "I mean I haven't had much opportunity up to the present."

"Perhaps when you get married you will have more. If you were to marry somebody with plenty of money, then you would be able to please yourself and do exactly what you wanted to do."

"I'm not so sure of that," Rusk answered. "Things don't always work out quite so simply, I imagine."

"They would if your wife wanted chiefly to please you. If you met someone who—— But you're spoiling the fire: give me the poker." She knelt down on the hearthrug beside his chair. One of her hands rested on his knee as with the other she gave a few touches to the glowing coals. "See!"

He saw, but he did not move, and she raised her head. She was so close to him that her hair brushed his cheek. For perhaps three seconds her face was there before him, turned to his, smiling: then he had kissed her, while simultaneously there came the sound of the opening door.

Denis and May were both there, but the latter stopped short on the threshold, and with a quick exclamation of "Oh, mamma isn't here!" turned back, leaving her brother to enter alone.

Whether he had noticed anything or not, Denis gave no sign, but went straight to the table and began to gather up his books and papers, while Rusk rose to his feet and stood on the hearthrug, flushed and confused. He knew that to anybody coming into the room at the precise moment when May and Denis had entered, the picture presented by himself and Amy must have appeared one of remarkable intimacy, even if its full significance had not been grasped. Disgusted with himself, half inclined to believe he had been trapped, his eyes met Amy's with a resentful light in them; and she turned away without a word, leaving him alone with his pupil.

He felt horribly ill at ease, and Denis continued to keep a provoking silence. He looked at the boy, who kept his face averted, and presently sat down at the table. Rusk could learn absolutely nothing from watching him, so he opened a book, though he felt far too angry, humiliated, and suspicious to read. Suddenly he spoke: "Where were you?"

The question came with an abruptness and in a tone that rather startled even himself, and caused Denis to glance up for the first time. "I was out. Amy asked me to go a message for her."

Rusk's frown deepened. So that was it! She had known all along he was by himself! He filled his pipe and began to smoke in no very enviable frame of mind.

24

Meanwhile Amy, on coming away from the study, wondered if the inopportune entry of May and Denis had really been accidental. On the part of the latter of course it had been; but May? Denis might easily have told May that she, Amy, had asked him to post a letter for her, and May might have suspected she had had some ulterior motive for doing so. Yes, it must be that. Why otherwise should she have come to look for their mother in the study? When was their mother ever in the study? And now she would go and tell what she had seen; Rusk would be sent away; and everything would be at an end....

Filled with resentment, Amy went straight to the drawing-room, where she found her sister beside the piano, sorting some music—songs of Rusk's. Apparently she had not yet told, but this might only be because she hadn't had an opportunity. A wave of nervous exasperation swept over Amy, a mood of recklessness urging her to any act of folly which might suggest itself. She flung herself down in an armchair and took up an illustrated paper, over the pages of which she watched her sister in silence, waiting, longing for her to say something—no matter what—but May said nothing. She had now begun to practise an accompaniment, and the more difficult passages she repeated several times, humming the air while she did so. There was something in this innocent pastime, and in May's diligent pursuance of it, which Amy felt she would not be able to stand much longer. She was more certain than ever now that May intended to tell their mother, and suddenly she yielded to an insane impulse. May had reached the end of one song, and was on the point of beginning another, when abruptly, half defiantly, these startling words reached her: "I may as well tell you I'm engaged to Hubert Rusk."

The moment she had spoken the words Amy realized that they were worse than foolish, absolutely disastrous. But it was too late to recall them, and she waited, watching with a kind of jealous cruelty an expression she obviously was struggling not to show come into the elder girl's face.

"Engaged!" May at last repeated. "What do you mean exactly?"

"I mean what I say," Amy replied. "I suppose you've heard of such things before!" At the same time she told herself that she *was* engaged to Rusk. Even if there were nothing on his side, her own troth had been plighted, therefore she was speaking the truth.

May had risen to her feet, leaving her music open on the piano. "I don't understand you," she said, but apparently she did understand, for her gaze, at first incredulous, slowly faltered and fell. She turned away, and walked to the door, through which she passed without looking back.

Amy, left there alone, sat very still, her face filled now only with apprehension. And more and more, as the minutes passed, her courage failed her, so that it came almost as a relief when she heard the sound of footsteps, and next moment her mother hurriedly entered, looking extremely worried and perplexed.

"What is this May tells me," she asked at once, "about your being engaged to Mr. Rusk?"

Amy hesitated, though she could still smile faintly. "Did she tell you that? She's so stupid!"

Mrs. Bracknel stopped short in amazement. "But she said

she had just come from you—and that you had used those very words!"

"Did she? That's so like her! Of course I didn't intend her to take it seriously; but she ran out of the room before I could explain. She's so strange sometimes: you really don't know where you are with her."

Mrs. Bracknel for a few seconds did not reply. "It's you who are strange," she then said slowly. "Is what you told May not true? In that case why did you tell her? What has happened? What is there between you and Mr. Rusk?"

"Nothing. Nothing, I mean, that I can tell you—nothing definite." Her voice shook slightly, but she still kept up her smile.

"Nothing? Yet May says she saw you together in the study, and that. . . . What have you been doing? What have you been saying? Why are you looking at me like that now if there is nothing, and why should May have come to me?"

"I'm sure *I* don't know: you'd better ask her. There *is* nothing definite."

"What do you mean by 'nothing definite'? What——"

But her words were abruptly cut short by a pair of arms flung round her neck. "Mamma—mamma—I love him. . . . I can't tell you how much I love him. Surely you might have seen! Promise—promise you'll help me. I won't let you go till you promise. My life won't be worth living without him. I'll never care for anybody else. I can't help it. It's this that has been making me ill. You don't know what it means to me. Often I lie awake half the night, and sometimes I think—things that would frighten you if you only knew them."

Poor Mrs. Bracknel tried to draw back. Amy's words shocked her profoundly, but Amy's arms held her tightly clasped, so that she could not free herself. "I don't understand," she said helplessly. "I must speak to your father. You shouldn't say such things—it isn't right. What have you been doing?"

"You mustn't. . . . You mustn't speak to papa," cried Amy in desperation. "Tell me you won't. . . . Promise—promise. . . . You must. . . . Promise you won't speak to-night at any rate. He might come in at any moment. Promise you won't tell him."

Mrs. Bracknel yielded. Amy had always been an insoluble problem, but now she felt really frightened, and very much distressed. It was not in her, however, to resist such an appeal, and in her helplessness she said weakly, "I don't suppose it matters for a few hours; but I can't understand; I've never seen anything in Mr. Rusk's manner to suggest—— When did he first lead you to think he cared for you?"

"I don't know. . . . This evening. . . ." And suddenly releasing her mother, Amy burst into tears. Dropping back into her chair, she buried her face in the cushion, and the noise of her sobs became stifled. The paroxysm continued for only two or three minutes, however, and when she lifted her head she had regained control of herself; nevertheless, while it lasted, that brief abandon had been startling, and her mother accompanied her to her own room, where she left her only when she had promised to go to bed and try to sleep.

Mrs. Bracknel was now intensely anxious about her. The girl looked wretched, and she certainly must be far from well. She wondered if she ought to tell her husband that night—at once—in spite of her promise, and though she was still so uncertain as to what the situation really was. Only she hardly knew what she *could* tell him; it was all so very vague, and there might, she hoped, be so little in it. In the morning they would have to go into everything thoroughly; in the morning they must get to know clearly just how far things had gone, and decide what it would be best to do. They would have to settle about Mr. Rusk, too; Mr. Rusk, she feared, would have to be sent away. And any worry or excitement was so bad for her husband; one never knew what might happen. He had been much worse after the trouble about Alfred. Any excitement was dangerous to him, and he was so easily excited. . . .

In addition, there was Denis to be considered. Mr. Rusk had done so much for Denis. . . . As she thought of all this poor Mrs. Bracknel couldn't help feeling perhaps more angry with her daughter than compassionate. And then abruptly Rusk's plan of taking the boy away recurred to her. How could he have been so eager about that had there been anything between him and Amy? There could be nothing—nothing on his side at least. Suddenly, with a feeling of profound thankfulness and relief, she saw that the plan itself offered a perfectly natural solution to the problem. Amy would get over her infatuation were Rusk not there; and she had always heard that the more violent such emotions were, the more quickly they passed. At all events they would have to trust to this, since it was clear that some kind of action must be taken immediately.

25

"Do you think the lamp will keep you awake?" Rusk asked.

It was a reading-lamp and threw a bright light only in one direction, leaving the rest of the room in shadow.

Denis was already in bed. "No," he murmured drowsily.

"You're sure?"

"Quite sure, thanks." And he turned over on his pillow.

Rusk put on his dressing-gown and sat down. He would have given a good deal to know what had been, what was now, passing in Denis's mind; but how in the world was he to find out? The boy was inscrutable; it was really amazing how little Rusk could count on his betraying himself.

For an hour the tutor sat in an attitude of one too comfortable or too drowsy to go to bed, but actually he felt extremely *un*comfortable, extremely wakeful and depressed. He came to the conclusion that he had made a hopeless fool of himself, and that he might hear a good deal more of the matter before he was done with it. Why had he been such an idiot—he who up till that fatal moment had been so careful? There was something incredibly stupid about the whole episode, and it might have all kinds of consequences. It might mean that he would have to go, and he knew what this in its turn signified. Nothing could have been further from his desire than to sacrifice Denis to Amy, yet what else had he done? And he did not even like her! Moreover, the thought that Doctor Birch attached so great an importance to his remaining with his pupil awakened in him not only remorse and self-contempt, but all sorts of obscure anxieties as well. Doctor

Birch had never entered fully into particulars but his failure to do so left Rusk's imagination all the freer now to conjure up sombre forebodings, with the result that he felt an increasing resentment against the girl directly responsible.

Denis had dropped asleep long ago, and his low, regular breathing was the only sound audible in the room. Rusk, leaning his head back, gazed up at the ceiling without discovering much inspiration there. He was still gloomily pondering when the handle of the door turned noiselessly and the door itself opened. He started, for he had heard no footsteps in the passage outside, and with the movement he gave knocked a book off the edge of the table. It fell to the floor with what seemed a quite unnecessary bang—enough, he thought, to arouse the whole house. Furious, he saw that it was Amy again—Amy standing in the doorway, her long red hair floating about her shoulders. She advanced a step or two into the room, closing the door carefully behind her. "I came to see if you were still angry with me," she said in a low voice. "I thought you might be sitting up reading; I looked for a light under your door. If there'd been none I would have gone away again. I wouldn't have come at all, only there is something I absolutely *must* tell you before to-morrow—even if it makes you angrier still."

In the comparative obscurity of the room, and with her gaze fixed on Rusk, she had not as yet noticed the other bed. But now it gave a sharp creak, and glancing in that direction she saw her brother sitting up and staring at her, his eyes still dark and liquid with sleep. The sight was so unexpected that she could not quite check the little cry that rose in her throat. "What are you doing here?" she whispered, struggling to recover herself.

"He has come to keep me company," Rusk answered coldly. He had risen, and stood, erect and frowning, in an attitude that barred her further progress.

But Amy's eyes were fixed on her brother. "I suppose you were frightened to sleep by yourself!" she said. "Miserable little coward!"

Denis, still half asleep, blinked at her without replying. He turned instead to his tutor, whose face was scarlet. "What does she want?" he asked quaintly.

"Nothing. Lie down and go to sleep again."

Denis obeyed. At all events he lay down and shut his eyes, having first turned his back to the other occupants of the room. Rusk took a step towards him; then halted; and when he looked round again Amy had disappeared. He swore softly, though savagely, to himself, put out the light, and proceeded to undress in the darkness. Denis lay in absolute silence, but Rusk knew he must be wide awake and felt strongly inclined to question him, make him say plainly just what ideas had been forming themselves in his mind during the past few hours. He did not yield to this impulse, however, though it cost him an effort not to do so. "Damnation!" he muttered again, under his breath.

26

At breakfast next morning Rusk, horribly uncertain as to how things stood and what he ought to do, felt that Mrs. Bracknel's manner was slightly constrained, and at once jumped to the conclusion that she must know something, if not all. It was Sunday, yet neither May nor Amy had put in an appearance, and what was even more surprising, their father, who barely uttered a word throughout the meal, accepted their absence without comment. On its conclusion, not knowing what to think, Rusk went out into the garden, his mind still turning over the problems which had kept him awake half the night. He wondered if he had really got himself into a most lamentable mess, or if it could be that he was making a mountain out of a molehill. He paced up and down the lawn for what seemed a long time, inclining now to one view, now to another, and was half relieved when he saw May coming towards him from the house. Almost immediately, from the way she greeted him, he guessed that she had come out with the express purpose of speaking to him. "I don't know whether I ought to tell you or not," she began nervously, "but I think it's only fair to give you some idea, some warning——" With this, however, she ceased as abruptly as she had started, so that to Rusk, listening with the most painful anxiety, it immediately occurred that she must have heard Amy either going to or coming from his room last night.

Only, would she mention it if she had? He remained silent, waiting for her to continue, while he felt the blood burning in his cheeks.

When she spoke again it was rapidly and disconnectedly, though quite plainly enough for him to make out what was happening indoors at that very moment—to visualize the whole scene, indeed, as clearly as if it were actually taking place before him. For a single instant he looked blankly at her, and then gazed straight in front of him, while her voice continued to sound in his ears.

May's colour had been almost as bright as his own, but it faded before she reached the end of her tale, and both simultaneously came to a halt within a few yards of the house. Rusk even then did not look at her: all his worst fears were realized, more than realized.

"Is she with them now?" he asked.

"Yes, I think so. . . . I must go in. . . . They don't know I'm with you, and I don't want them to."

"Oh Lord!" he muttered. Then he thanked her for telling him, but when she entered the porch he turned abruptly on his heel and walked away down the drive.

He felt as indignant as he had ever felt in his life, though as the moments passed his anger became mingled with bewilderment. Amy must be mad! She might at that very moment be inventing all kinds of further lies! She seemed capable of anything! One point was clear; he would have to leave Mr. Bracknel's house as soon as possible. He had had enough of them: they might work out the problem of his relation to Amy among themselves and as was most pleasing to them or to her; *he* was going home at once; he would leave that night. He was so certain of this, so sure it was the only thing left for him to do no matter what conclusion they might reach, that he determined then and there to place the whole matter before Doctor Birch. He felt he must talk to somebody. He wanted advice; he wanted sympathy; above all he wanted to be understood; and nobody could advise him better than the Doctor.

Having made up his mind, Rusk hurried, and in a few minutes was at the gate of the other house. There he met Miss Birch coming down the garden path, but on mentioning what had brought him learned that the Doctor had gone out immediately after breakfast, and she had no idea when he would be back. Better go on to the house, she added, and wait for him there, unless, of course, he preferred accompanying her to church.

With this little joke she left him, and Rusk found Miss Anna in the parlour, seated by the fire, a small heap of papers and an open account-book on the table beside her. She seemed pleased, though also somewhat surprised, by so early a visit, but he explained how it had come about and that he had really called to speak to her brother. Possibly, in an effort to appear quite at ease he overdid it, for he saw at once from the way she looked at him that she guessed something to be wrong. Indeed, after the exchange of a few conventional remarks, he decided that it would be wiser to prepare her for what in any case she was bound to get to know soon. So, though confining himself to the bare announcement, he told her he was going home.

He certainly surprised her, but at the same time it was obvious that she did not in the least grasp the true significance of his words. "I hope you'll have a very pleasant journey," was all she said. "Are you going soon?"

"To-morrow," Rusk answered, and there followed a pause.

Miss Anna looked at him more doubtfully, and seemed to hesitate. "I hope you've had no bad news," she said.

"No." Then, realizing he was only puzzling her, and that he could not keep up this attitude of uncommunicativeness for ever, he abruptly took his plunge. "It's not that. I've had no news of any kind. It's simply that I'm leaving."

There could at least be no further doubt as to his meaning, and for a minute or two Miss Anna gazed at him in silent consternation. "But—isn't this rather sudden?"

Rusk coloured. "Yes," he said. He very much wished now that he had turned back when he had met Miss Birch. It would have been so easy merely to have left a message with her for the Doctor, saying he would call again later.

Miss Anna, however, quite unconscious of these belated regrets, could no longer repress her curiosity. "What in the world has happened?" she cried. "And what about taking Denis abroad? You can't rush off like this! Do they even *know* you're going?"

Rusk smiled faintly. "I'm afraid I'm not so indispensable as you think."

"Fiddlesticks! You needn't tell me it's *their* idea."

He avoided her eyes. "I'm sorry," he mumbled, "but I'd rather not go into it, and—and—they'll probably tell you themselves."

Miss Anna, more mystified than ever, regarded him irresolutely. "It hasn't by any chance to do with your plan of taking Denis abroad, has it?" she said. "If so, it's more my brother's fault than yours."

"No. There are several things."

"And you don't intend to come back?"

He shook his head. "I'm afraid not. I'm awfully sorry in many ways, I needn't tell you. For one thing I'll be very sorry to say good-bye to you and your sister. You've been so kind to me. . . . And there is Denis. I promised your brother to look after him. But—— If I could I'd take him with me, only I don't think they'd allow him to come. Besides—I'll have to look out for another job."

At this juncture, to his relief, he saw the Doctor's car turning in at the gate, and shortly afterwards the Doctor himself entered the room. Miss Anna appealed to him before he had even time to close the door. "Herbert!" she cried, "Mr. Rusk declares he has come to say good-bye—that he's going away—probably to-morrow night. And he says it's not just for a few days, but for good."

Whatever may have been his private reaction to this, the Doctor maintained his customary air of imperturbability. He merely turned inquiringly to the younger man. "You're not taking your pupil with you, I suppose?"

"I don't think so," Rusk stammered. "I'd be only too glad to if they'd let me."

"And you feel you have to go?"

"Yes."

Doctor Birch asked no further question, and there was a silence, during which Rusk stood with bowed head, apparently studying most carefully the pattern in the carpet. His face, however, was anxious and troubled. "I *must* go," he repeated. "I can't help it. You know I'd stay if I could."

"I must say——" Miss Anna was beginning irrepressibly, when her brother by a movement of his hand checked her. He continued to regard the young man before him, as if considering something, while under the perspicacity of his gaze Rusk's own eyes remained lowered, like those of a guilty schoolboy. Doctor Birch, however, laid a hand on his shoulder with a very kindly pressure, which at the same time had the effect of conducting him to the door. "I'll see you later," he told him quietly. "Don't say or do anything till I *have* seen you. I want to talk to you, but not just now."

27

As the long night had drifted slowly away, and a cold livid dawn grown brighter, for Amy the whole aspect of life had altered. The last flickering colour had faded from an impossible dream, and now, in the chill white light of this early Sunday morning, the dream itself seemed an empty pitiful thing, threadbare, curiously futile, like all dead things. She could not even understand how she had done what she had done; it appeared at present so senseless, so ugly. She had seen her action in its true light more or less from the moment she had left Rusk's room, from the moment of its last abject and irremediable failure; and she felt now that she would like to steal out of the house before anyone was awake, and disappear, never to return. But she had nowhere to go—and besides—it was impossible. . . . It had been then for this that she had quarrelled with May; that she had humiliated herself to Rusk:—for this! One task, indeed, still remained before her—she *must* speak to him, must tell him what she had said to May, what she had said to her mother; and leave the rest to his generosity. . . .

She heard the servants moving about downstairs, the opening of the hall-door, the rattle of milk-cans. Still another two hours passed before she got up and dressed herself, while even then she did not leave her room, where presently her mother came to her. "Amy, you must come downstairs: your father is waiting to speak to you. About Mr. Rusk. He thinks it best——"

Amy interrupted her. "You've told him, then?"

"Yes; he's in the drawing-room, waiting to see you. We've finished breakfast."

Amy lifted her gaze to the window. She did not look at her mother; her face expressed only a profound weariness and lassitude—in part, no doubt, due to loss of sleep. "What does he want to see me for? He knows everything: I've nothing more to tell."

Mrs. Bracknel regarded her uneasily. "You're quite sure, dear, that you're not keeping anything from us?" But the question broke off abruptly, for both women had heard the sound of heavy footsteps mounting the stairs, and next moment Mr. Bracknel's voice was raised as he called to his wife.

Mrs. Bracknel, after exchanging a rapid glance with her daughter, went to the door and opened it.

"Might I ask when you intend to come down?" her husband inquired from the threshold. "Do you know what time it is! Well—I don't suppose it matters; I daresay we can settle this business here as well as anywhere else."

He pushed past his wife, and Amy, who had sat down in a chair near the window, waited motionless and to all seeming utterly impassive for what he might say.

It came in the form of a question, and to his wife's surprise was spoken in a tone suggesting that he had decided not to take the matter over-seriously. "What is all this nonsense about you and Mr. Rusk?"

Amy made no reply, and as her silence continued, Mr. Bracknel presently went on almost lightly: "Your mother tells me you would like to marry this precious young man—whose only prospects, so far as I can gather, are matrimonial: that you want us to encourage him, in other words. Of course that is nonsense, but if he has done or said anything to try to—to—put such ideas into your head, I consider he has behaved most dishonourably; that he has taken advantage of the confidence we placed in him to—in short, to do whatever he *has* done."

"What has he done?" Amy asked.

"That's for you to tell us, miss. I suppose he must have made some kind of advances?"

"I don't know what mamma told you," Amy returned dully. "Mr. Rusk is not dishonourable, as you know very well."

Mr. Bracknel began to show signs of impatience. "If he has done or said nothing, why did you come off with all this story to your mother and sister? There must be something behind it."

"I said I cared for him. . . . And that——"

"Well—go on—and that what?"

The girl flushed faintly. "That is all."

"But it isn't all. Your mother says you asked her to help you to marry him. How could you ask such a thing unless he had given you some kind of hint that that was *his* wish also?"

"There was nothing definite," Amy faltered.

"What do you mean by 'nothing definite'? At one minute you say one thing, at another another. Answer plainly, can't you. In what way has he ever made you think that he wanted to marry you?"

"I love him," said Amy, in a low, dogged voice.

"And that is all? He has never told you that he loves *you*?"

She did not answer, and for a minute or two nobody spoke. Mr. Bracknel, in spite of his annoyance, secretly felt relieved. "What do you find in him that is so remarkable?" he pursued, in a tone that almost approached playfulness. "Why do you think him so wonderful?"

"I don't think him wonderful."

"You would like to marry him though; and live, I suppose, on the allowance I might make you." He blew out his thick lips and laughed not unkindly. "Pooh! You're only a child. Wait a few years and you'll find there are better men in the world than this—this schoolmaster."

Amy at last lifted her eyes and allowed them to rest on her father's face. She felt a sudden and irresistible desire to speak the naked truth. "I'm not a child," she said slowly. "If he asked me to go away with him I would go, whether I was married to him or not."

A pause followed this simple speech—a pause in which Mrs. Bracknel began to weep silently, while her husband turned a deep, purplish red. Amy looked from one to the other of her outraged parents, but without any visible alteration in her own countenance. "You might have spared me this, Amy," her mother reproached her.

"I'm only telling you the truth," Amy answered bitterly. "I thought you wanted to know. I don't see that my loving him now is any more disgraceful than it would be if he had asked me to be his wife; and I only told you because papa seems to find it impossible to believe me or to regard the matter as of any importance."

Mr. Bracknel took a step towards his daughter. "Be silent," he cried. "You needn't advertise your shamelessness further."

"If I'm shameless, it's not my fault. People can't be ashamed just because they want to be. You railed and stormed at Alfred because you said he had married beneath him. Well, Mr. Rusk isn't beneath me. And now you know everything."

Mr. Bracknel turned helplessly to his wife, who had already risen. She had even captured a certain air of quiet dignity, though her voice faltered a little when she spoke. "We had better leave you, Amy," she said. "I will come to you later." She opened the door, and taking her husband's arm drew him gently but firmly from the room.

Once outside, however, Mr. Bracknel began to recover himself. "Your children are certainly doing you credit!" he exclaimed, as if his own share in them were at most that of an uncle. "Well," he added impatiently, "I suppose Rusk will have to go, and the sooner the better,"—though the mere fact that Amy was compelling him to send the tutor away had already considerably enhanced that young man's value in his eyes.

"But—what are we to do about Amy?" Mrs. Bracknel urged unhappily. "You can see yourself how altered and ill she looks."

"You may thank heaven things are no worse," her husband returned grimly. "Fortunately there seems to be nothing in it except her own brazenness; and as she has been like that from childhood, I imagine nothing will alter her now. I don't expect Rusk ever even gave her a thought." Then, as if he felt a kind of belated compunction, he went on more kindly. "Come, come; we'll have to get rid of him; and that will be the end of it. It's a pity, for he was doing very well so far as Denis is concerned, and he's a decent young fellow. But what else can we do? He can't stay on here, unless you want to send Amy herself away, and I don't suppose you wish to do that."

28

Rusk was surprised on his return to the house to receive no intimation from either Mr. or Mrs. Bracknel that they wished to speak to him. He had taken it for granted that they would demand an immediate explanation, and he wondered what had actually occurred between them all. Lunch, or rather dinner—for on Sundays the Bracknels dined in the middle of the day—proved in this undecided state of affairs a distinctly embarrassing repast. As at breakfast, Amy was not present, but even without her a kind of forced naturalness was depressingly in evidence as the keynote of the gathering.

Nobody lingered longer over the meal than was necessary, and as soon as he could Rusk, too, escaped. He made his way to the study. Now was the time, he felt sure, when he would be summoned to give an account of himself; but an hour later, when he left the house with Denis, Mr. Bracknel had not yet given any sign of desiring an interview.

Their walk for the first mile or so was a singularly silent one. The boy saw that his companion's mind was occupied, and forbore to interrupt him. Rusk, on his part, was considering how he could best put to his pupil what he had to say. He found it difficult, for there was a good deal more in it than the mere announcement of his approaching departure, though this in itself was not easy. To begin with, he did not wish to leave Denis with a false impression, yet he did not see how, if he were to avoid, as assuredly he must, any reference to Amy, it would be possible to give him a true one. And if he could not tell him the real reason why he was going, on the other hand he did not want him to think that it was simply to better himself, or because he had grown tired of his present occupation. Their relation had been altogether too close to admit of any light parting now, with the probability of their rarely or never meeting again. After all, their homes were in different countries, and Rusk could not tell to what far abode Fate, in the shape of pecuniary necessity, might not lead him. Despite the disparity in their ages, his friendship with Denis was the most intimate he had ever formed, and it meant a great deal to him to have it broken off so sharply, and with so little prospect of their taking up again later on the snapped thread. His pupil had come to occupy a certain place in his life—a place which it would be difficult for anybody else to fill. What it would mean to the boy himself he could of course only guess, but he decided that in any event it would be better to tell him before they returned to the house, and presently an opening seemed to be offered when Denis suddenly asked, "Why are you so quiet?"

Had he heard no rumour, Rusk wondered? Had he not heard the others talking?

They had come down to the river and were following the brown deserted tow-path. The afternoon was grey and dull and cloudy. On one side lay a marsh of coarse grass and reeds, with here and there a twisted stunted ash-tree, delicate and fantastic, like a decoration in a Japanese print. On the other side the ground rose abruptly in a thickly-wooded slope. The damp sodden grass was bleached to a greenish yellow and drifted over with fallen leaves—brown, yellow, and dull red—rotting slowly into the soil. There were leaves floating on the dark oily water, and a shifting, waning light played over the whole landscape, filtering between livid clouds that hung, sullen and motionless, ready to drop down in rain.

Rusk had become conscious of these things while the boy's question still remained unanswered. They seemed to draw them closer to each other in a loneliness that might have been that of an unpeopled world, and he felt a profound depression which grew deeper and deeper as they wandered on through the fading, soundless afternoon.

"There is something I must tell you," he at length began; "something which cannot be very pleasant for either of us."

"You're going away," Denis answered softly and at once. He did not look at Rusk, but kept his eyes fixed on the sandy path before him. A quick flush passed across his face, fading as rapidly as it had come.

There was something in his voice, a kind of uncompromising fatalism, which it was against all Rusk's instincts to accept. "Oh come," he said, with a feeble attempt at cheerfulness, "we'll meet again before very long—and you'll come over to stay with me; we'll have to arrange all that before I leave."

He had a vision, as he spoke, of their first meeting (already it seemed long ago), of Denis being brought to speak to him, of the early summer evening, the interrupted game of tennis, the boy before him in his flannels, a little flushed, his hair tossed, his eyes bright and friendly. And then, even as he watched it, a veil dropped down, leaving them once more here with the dim winter twilight, the sadness of naked trees and faded fields, a dark sluggish river.

"You'll come to stay with me," he said again, but Denis met this suggestion with a head-shake of immovable conviction.

"Papa wouldn't allow me to," he answered. "He'll get someone else to teach me and that will be all."

"I hope he'll be nice," said Rusk weakly.

"I hope so."

A silence followed, and Rusk unconsciously slackened his pace, though they had been walking slowly enough before. The boy's acquiescence surprised him. He had expected to be questioned. Yet he was vaguely aware that Denis understood, that he was in a way letting him off, and that it would be better for him, too, to take it like this. "You must write and tell me all about him. Perhaps he will be somebody I know."

"Perhaps." Denis lifted his head and their eyes met for a moment. The boy's face seemed to be blown across by a strange white light. He smiled dimly and Rusk lowered his gaze.

The sound of falling water following them in the lonely place seemed to exercise an almost narcotic influence upon his mind. He was haunted by thoughts and images from the past, memories of hours he was loth to leave behind him, yet from which he knew the sharp change he was about to bring into his life would cut him off for ever.

"When are you going?" Denis asked.

"Very soon. To-morrow night."

The boy said nothing more.

It was rapidly getting dusk, yet still they wandered on, as if they felt that this walk might well be their last together. Presently they paused by a wooden gate, set across the path to keep cattle from straying. The sad lonely cry of a bird seemed to draw down the darkness about them, and in the gathering obscurity the shadowy trees and winding river grew faint and ghostly. They drew closer to each other. They were absolutely alone. All suggestion of human life had been blotted out from the scene: everywhere was struck the strictly impersonal note of nature—of earth and water and sky. A low sound from the weir, a soft murmur in the trees, and the increasing darkness of approaching night—all met and mingled.

At last, when they turned to retrace their steps, the path itself became uncertain, and Rusk allowed the boy to guide him, while more than once he stumbled over some unevenness in the way. The landscape in every direction was now black and impenetrable. Twice the stillness was broken by the noise of falling water, and the sound followed them for a long distance. All the way home they spoke but little, and among their few words was no further allusion to their approaching separation. A faint moon had floated out above the trees, diaphanous and pale, like a slender wisp of luminous cloud.

When they reached the house Rusk was informed that Mr. Bracknel desired to speak to him, and was awaiting him now for that purpose in the drawing-room.

29

On entering the room, however, he found only Mrs. Bracknel there with May. The elder lady was unoccupied, but May had her writing materials spread upon her lap and was evidently finishing a letter. Both looked up on his entrance and smiled.

"Did you have a pleasant walk?" Mrs. Bracknel asked gently.

"Yes.... A little damp under foot, and rather dark coming home—we went by the river—but Denis kept me from falling in." He was not at his ease, though he did his best to appear so.

"I don't like the river in winter," May said. "It's too cold and melancholy—especially when it's beginning to get dark. There are such queer shadows among the trees, and they seem to come down to the water like ghosts."

"Oh, I don't believe in ghosts," Rusk replied.

He had by this time the impression that something must have happened in his absence. Some subtle alteration in his relation to the others, or rather in theirs to him, had come about since he had last seen them. He could feel it in the general atmosphere, could hear it in the tones of their voices, from which all constraint had completely vanished; could see it in their manner, in their faces; and he wondered what had caused the change, wondered where exactly he now stood. He had a sense of being in the dark, or rather of being very much in the light, while the others moved in shadow, their eyes fixed on him as on the central figure occupying the stage in some dramatic piece as to the meaning of which he was not at all clear.

"We were talking about you, Mr. Rusk, when you were out," Mrs. Bracknel began, in her low sweet voice, "about you and Denis."

"Oh!"

The darkness seemed at last about to be illuminated, and he waited a trifle nervously for what he should find there.

"You don't look very pleased," May remarked. "If you'd only heard all the nice things that were said—especially by mamma; though Doctor Birch happened to drop in and he said some too."

"Mr. Bracknel has walked back with him," the elder lady murmured. "They only went a few minutes before you came in. I wonder you didn't meet them.... Do you remember, Mr. Rusk, talking to me a short time ago about Denis—about taking him abroad?"

Rusk looked up quickly. "Yes, I remember."

"That really was what we were discussing, and Mr. Bracknel was wondering if you would still be of the same mind—that is, if you would still be willing to take him."

A deep flush rose to Rusk's cheeks, and he felt an odd, choking sensation in his throat. He glanced at May, but her head was bent as she addressed and fastened an envelope. "I shall be extremely glad to," he stammered.

"Ah well, then," Mrs. Bracknel softly breathed, "it can all be arranged. We think that perhaps it would be better if you could start soon. In a day or two if that would be possible. Of course we don't want to hurry you, but as you know, once my husband takes an idea into his head he never rests till it is carried out. It's sometimes inconvenient, I'm afraid, but there it is. However, you must take your own time, and never mind him. We are leaving it altogether in your hands: Denis can be ready for whatever day you settle on."

"I could go to-morrow night, I should think," Rusk replied.

Mrs. Bracknel smiled. "Well, that perhaps would be pressing matters a little *too* much. After all, we must make some plans, we must talk over where you will go, and all that. Perhaps we had better fix on Wednesday or Thursday—just to give us breathing-time. Denis of course doesn't know anything about it yet."

"Of course not," Rusk said.

"There'll be no difficulty so far as Denis is concerned," May interposed. "He'll be nearly out of his mind with delight at the mere thought of it."

"It's awfully good of you," Rusk faltered, turning to Mrs. Bracknel, but she only smiled.

"It's you who are good," she told him. "There's no one else we would trust him to. It is you who make the scheme possible. Our idea is that he should be with you for about a year at any rate—after that we shall see. It was largely May's doing, I ought to tell you—May and Doctor Birch between them."

"Oh, *I* did very little," May said quickly; "Papa is really quite in favour of the idea. The only thing is that for the next day or two he'll worry Mr. Rusk to death with questions about every imaginable detail. You'll have to give a reason, Mr. Rusk, for everything you propose to do, and you'd better try to think of the kind of reasons papa will understand. Bring in the word 'advantage' pretty often: he understands all about 'advantages', and he'll be quite happy so long as he thinks you're both getting good value."

"It would be very foolish if they didn't," Mrs. Bracknel broke in hastily. "There's no use going away if one isn't going to make the most of one's opportunities."

"We've always made the most of ours," May pursued, with a rather strange smile. "You ought to have been with us in Paris, Mr. Rusk; it would have been a lesson for the rest of your life. Enjoyment was the last thing we thought of. If we sat down for a moment to breathe, papa used to tell us that if we only wanted to sit in chairs we could have done it much more comfortably and less expensively at home. I was never so thankful for anything in my life as for the sight of the train that was to bring us back."

Mrs. Bracknel seemed vexed. "I don't know why you should exaggerate so!" she said. "And surely it was natural that your father should want to see as much as possible, when he takes a holiday so rarely."

"He certainly didn't take one then," May replied. "The only things that might have amused him he left alone. His one idea was to see everything mentioned in Baedeker, and he used to get furious because the people didn't speak English."

Mrs. Bracknel changed the subject. "I should like very much to go to Italy myself," she confessed. "Ever since I was quite a young girl I've wanted to go. One hears so much of the scenery and the pictures and the beautiful buildings. But I've never been able to manage it."

"We've never been abroad except for our solitary visit to Paris," May persisted, with a strange obstinacy. "Mr. Rusk is filled with astonishment, knowing our 'advantages'!"

"Not at all—not at all," said Rusk. "I know any amount of people who prefer spending their holidays at home."

"Oh, but some of us don't prefer it," May rejoined. "We haven't any choice, which is even simpler." Fortunately she allowed the matter to drop there, and a few minutes later Rusk left the room in search of Denis.

May and her mother sat on by the fire in a somewhat constrained silence, till Mrs. Bracknel began again to talk of the proposed journey, making desultory and wandering conjectures concerning it, with occasional digressions on the subject of the new assistant minister, on the fact that Doctor Birch was very bald for so young a man, and on the advisability of giving the housemaid notice. She alluded once or twice to Amy, but they had already talked a great deal about Amy, and May was not sympathetic. With the departure of Rusk a kind of dullness seemed to have crept into the room, which to the girl suggested all the still duller hours that in the future were to be passed there. She saw them stretching on and on into interminable years—monotonous, trivial, wasted. . . .

It was only by an effort that she roused herself to listen to her mother, who was again talking of Italy, and how she had so much wanted to visit that country in the past; but there was something in her uncomplaining, unquestioning acceptance of the idea that this desire should have been considered of no importance which had the effect of alienating May's sympathy. "It's really too ridiculous when you come to think of it!" she at last burst out. "What on earth is the use of having money if you are to be cooped up in one little spot all your life, and never allowed to see or do anything! And money is all we *have* got. When you think of what some people would have made of even a hundredth part of our chance, while we aren't even properly educated! Look at the difference between me or Amy and Miss Anna Birch! Look at the difference between Alfred and Mr. Rusk! Denis is the only one of us who has anything, and he has it simply because he's ten times cleverer than an ordinary boy. *We* have nothing—not even passable manners. We do the wrong things and say the wrong things. We never meet anybody who is worth knowing. And so it goes on, day after day, year after year, and I suppose will continue to do so till it's too late, if it's not too late already."

Mrs. Bracknel regarded her in dismay. Was her elder daughter, too, who had never hitherto given her a moment's anxiety, going to fail her? "May dear," she expostulated uneasily, "what is the matter with you? I never saw you like this before."

The girl laughed. She sat there, still a little flushed, but the momentary bitterness had gone out of her face, and as her eyes rested upon her mother their expression grew softer still. "Dearest mamma, it's not your fault, I know. You have all the things we ought to have. I'm sorry. It was stupid of me to talk like that. I suppose I must be jealous of Denis and Mr. Rusk."

She came over and knelt beside her mother, throwing her arms about her and kissing her.

30

Rusk meanwhile had gone in search of Denis. He wanted to tell him of this unexpected alteration in their plans—he knew that it would make him very happy—but Denis was nowhere to be found.

As he approached the door of the library for the second time, Rusk fancied he caught a glimpse of a white face peering down from an upper landing, but it vanished too quickly for him to be quite sure that his imagination had not deceived him. He wondered what had happened to Amy, and what had been the result of the family conference? To send him away with Denis for one thing—that part of it at all events was highly satisfactory. So he sat down by the fire and betook himself to planning out an imaginary tour. He was so absorbed in this that he was unconscious of a figure standing near the door—a figure which had stolen into the room noiselessly as a ghost, and in the fitful light had even something ghostly in its appearance, in its attitude of watchful stillness, of a kind of sadness and remoteness, as of one gazing into a lost world. It was Amy, and she had been there for two or three minutes before he at last looked up and saw her. When he did so, he started and half rose to his feet, but she motioned to him to sit still.

"I wanted to see you before to-morrow. I'm going away to-morrow morning and you are going abroad with Denis—aren't you? I wanted to say good-bye."

There was a note in this sad voice which Rusk had never heard in it before. It seemed to him to have had all life crushed out of it; it was like something that had been living and full of colour, but was now white and dead. He made a vague sound of acquiescence. "I want you to forgive me before you go. I won't see you again."

Rusk did not meet the gaze that was bent upon him. "I'm sorry," he muttered. "I don't know what else to say; but I'm sorry."

They were both standing now, and he longed for her to go. The fire, blazing up, showed him for a few seconds the paleness of her face and its unhappiness. He felt desperately afraid lest somebody should come in, and tried to think how he could get rid of her without being brutal. But of her own accord she turned from him, and next moment had gone, closing the door softly behind her.

Now he had really seen the last of her Rusk could afford to be more charitable. Nevertheless he breathed a deep sigh of relief, for he knew he still did not like her. Very soon, however, his thoughts reverted to Denis and their prospective journey, and a few minutes later Denis himself entered the room and sat down quietly at the opposite side of the hearth.

Rusk could see his strange, expressive face as the flicker of the firelight passed across it. He watched him without at once beginning to tell his news. Then he remembered that his pupil believed this to be their last evening together, and told him.

Denis came over and sat on the arm of his chair. There was a deep happy light in his eyes, but Rusk could see that they had filled with tears. His tears did not fall, however, and his affection and gratitude—for he insisted on looking upon the whole thing as entirely due to his friend—shone out with a warmth and sincerity which made the tutor feel ashamed of the little he actually *had* done. In fact, what he had done most of all was very nearly to spoil everything, yet Denis was radiant, and Rusk learned that this long journey to be made with him was of all things what the boy had most desired. He had regarded it as too improbable, too delightful, ever to come true; he had never mentioned it on that account; but he had sometimes dreamed of it: this all came out now, in the gladness of realization. Then he seemed to notice his companion's silence.

"What's the matter?" he asked slowly. "Don't you want to go? You seem——" He paused, and Rusk answered quickly:

"Of course I want to go. There's nothing I want more."

But Denis was only partially reassured. "Why are you melancholy then?" he asked doubtfully.

"I'm not melancholy," Rusk said, smiling, and laying his hand on the boy's shoulder. "Aren't you sorry a little yourself . . . ? I mean —to say good-bye to everything here for so long? We've had some very happy times together, you know, and they'll never come back again."

"Of course they'll come back," cried Denis. But he was satisfied with his tutor's explanation, though Rusk himself knew it had not been quite genuine.

. . . . .

It was in another tone, however, that the boy said an hour or two later: "I'm glad we're going away." He was silent after this, but not with any intention of eliciting a reply from his friend, who had been unusually quiet all evening. Denis himself had been unable to sit still, had jumped up every now and again to wander restlessly about the room, dropping disconnected remarks in relation to their travels, and he was now standing at the window, his back turned, his forehead pressed against the glass, while he gazed out into the darkness. Presently he pursued his thoughts further: "There's something strange about this place. . . . I don't know what it is—but I've always felt it, it's always there, and I'm glad we're going to leave it behind. . . . There was a time when I liked it, I think—but I don't like it any more."

These mysterious words were uttered with a good many breaks between them, and they reached Rusk where he sat in an attitude of extreme laziness, his legs stretched out to their full extent and a pipe in his mouth. A faint sound of wind came and went in the trees with a musical sighing.

"I'd like to go somewhere where there is sunlight—plenty of sunlight," Denis went on. "It's too dark here. . . . There's something strange about this place," he repeated. "Other people have lived here—I don't know when—I don't know how long ago. But they've influenced it; they're still here; they have a kind of power."

"I haven't the faintest notion what you're talking about," Rusk answered, laughing, "nor where you pick up your ideas."

Denis was still gazing out of the window. "I pick them up here," he said. "They're floating in the air, and I want to get away from them."

Rusk returned no answer, not being in a mood for argument.

"They're there," the boy went on, pointing into the darkness. "They're there, coming and going; you can feel them like the cold touch of a fog. . . . However, I know you hate talking about such things."

"I don't particularly like it," Rusk admitted good-humouredly, "but since it seems to give you an unending pleasure I dare say it's all right."

"Does it?" And Denis began to draw with his finger on the glass.

"Well, aren't you for ever producing such fancies?"

"I don't know. I suppose I am, if you say so."

There was a longish pause, and then he came over and sat down on the hearthrug at his tutor's feet. "Why should I be like that?" he asked thoughtfully, looking into the red heart of the fire.

"I'm afraid I can't tell you," Rusk replied.

"I suppose I must always have been that way. I remember a thing I did more than once when I was a kid, and which I can't understand now at all. . . . Shall I tell you?"

"Fire away," said Rusk simply.

But Denis stared at the red, glowing coals for a long time in silence. Then, still with his eyes fixed on the fire, slowly, and as if describing what he saw pictured there, he began his tale. "There was an old, deserted, decaying house which I half pretended, half really believed to be haunted. You see, quite accidentally I had overheard some talk about it—that years ago its last owner had hanged himself in one of the bedrooms, which was why it had lain empty for so long. It stood in its own grounds; the gates were always wide open; and two or three times when I managed to get away from my governess—I had a governess then, a Miss McAlpine —I visited it by myself in the late afternoon. It was a big house, low and square, a sort of pale fungus-colour, with a flat roof railed all round by low stone pillars. Some of the pillars had been broken, and the doorstep was broken too, and partly covered with blackish moss. The plaster was mouldering away, and the knocker was thick with rust that came off on your hand. All the windows had tall narrow shutters, closely fastened, but worn and decayed, so that one of them on an upper floor had broken loose from its fastenings, and by climbing a tree you could get a glimpse of a bare, dismal-looking room inside. For some reason I imagined this was the room where the man had hanged himself. The kitchens and pantries were underground; an iron grating with a stone passage beneath it ran all round the house; and bushes of barberry grew close up to the side windows. The garden had grown wild; weeds and shrubs and flowers all grew together in a kind of jungle; while the paths between the spreading box borders had almost disappeared. Even in broad daylight the place had a gloomy and desolate appearance, as if a kind of shadow or blight rested upon it. I used to be as scared as anything when I came up the front avenue; the sound of a twig snapping under my foot would make my heart bump—and then suddenly, at a turn, the house would be there. The mere sight of it, so quiet and ghostly with its closed shutters, used to send a chill into my stomach. I imagined that it, or something inside it, was watching and waiting; that the hall-door might suddenly open; and I know that if by any chance it *had* opened I should have died. Every minute I was jerking my head round to see what was behind me; what I wanted to do was to run away as hard as I could; yet what I actually did do was just the opposite—and that is the queer part, for really it was as if something dragged me on against my will. I would climb the six stone steps up to the hall-door, stand there for perhaps a minute, and then give a tug at the bell. The wires, I think, must have got entangled in some way, for they made a hideous noise that echoed all over the house, and, even though I was expecting it, I would nearly collapse on the steps. And then—then somehow it was over and I could take to my heels without once looking back. But it was queer—queer—— Why should anybody do such things?"

Rusk sat puffing at his pipe. "I never did them," he answered stolidly.

"I know I was an awful wee fool," Denis admitted, "but I wasn't very old at the time—about nine or ten."

Rusk waited a moment. "Where is the house?" he then asked. "Why did you never show it to me?"

Denis looked up at him, but did not reply till the tutor had repeated his question. Then he said in a low level voice: "This is the house."

Rusk stared. "This?"

"Yes. Papa bought it and had it repaired and altered—almost rebuilt. Another roof was put on and everything was set right; though the basement, I suppose, must still be there. We used to live over beyond the Birches'."

A silence followed, till Rusk broke it by saying, "I thought you had been living here much longer than that."

"No." Denis glanced at him. "What are you thinking about? Why are you so grave? You've hardly smiled all evening."

Rusk smiled now. "I was only admiring the dramatic way in which you ended your tale."

"Was it dramatic? I didn't intend it to be. I wouldn't have told you it was this house if you hadn't asked me."

"Why? Did you think I'd be frightened?"

"No; but it isn't particularly pleasant, is it? I once asked papa about it, and he got quite angry. Probably he bought the house cheap on account of what had happened. Mamma, too, said I wasn't to talk about it—especially before the servants, because they might want to leave."

"I see."

Denis half closed his eyes. "I suppose you think I must have been a very morbid kid?"

Rusk blew out a cloud of smoke and watched it dissolve before he answered. "No; I shouldn't exactly call it morbid," he said. "At any rate most people seem to enjoy frightening themselves, though I've never been able to understand why. Still, they must, or they wouldn't do a lot of the things they do do. Of course I don't expect many of them would take quite such drastic measures to get a thrill as you appear to have done. The majority, I fancy, content themselves with milder experiments."

"I'm not such a fool now, you know," Denis reminded him.

"I wonder?"

"You aren't very polite?"

"I suppose not. But——"

"But what?"

"Well, as I've told you, I've always felt a strong dislike for—for all that kind of thing."

"And you think I'm just the other way?"

Rusk did not reply.

"I don't *really* like such things," Denis protested. "If I could, I'd never think of them again.... I won't think of them when we're away," he went on softly; "they simply won't be there. We'll be too happy. I'm very happy now."

Rusk smiled as he turned to him. "I don't expect you'll be disappointed."

"I was very *un*happy this afternoon, when I thought perhaps I'd never see you again. I tried to put it out of my mind until after I'd said good-bye, for I knew you wouldn't leave me unless it was absolutely necessary."

"You're a good boy," said Rusk, laying his hand on his shoulder. "That's what one means by friendship, I imagine—at any rate it's my idea of it."

Denis made no answer: he had begun to ponder. There were things happening all round him which he did not perfectly comprehend. He could weave them together in a kind of pattern, yet there were threads missing, and the pattern was incomplete. Meanwhile they sat on in silence, while from the glow of the fire a delightful atmosphere of homeliness poured out into the room, filling it, making it beautiful with a rare and peaceful beauty existing more for the spirit than the sense. He felt himself bathed in it. It washed up about him like a great warm sunny sea. He felt happier than he had ever yet felt, and he wondered a little how it had all come about? Why was he to be allowed to go away with Rusk? Why was it that Rusk himself had been going away? Why was it that all had been changed at the last moment? He guessed, of course, that it had something to do with his sister—she was a part of his woven pattern, a vivid thread coming and going more frequently than any other, and he remembered her in their room last night. Why had she come and why had she been so angry when he had awakened and recognized her? She had wanted to see Rusk alone—to talk to him privately—but there were surely other times and places when they could have talked! It was all very strange, and there had been something strange in the air when he had come into the study yesterday evening and found them together. He had disturbed something; he had interrupted something; Rusk had been very much embarrassed; but again why? Unless there was by chance something between them—something which Amy at all events wished to bring about. He knew more concerning his sister than anyone imagined; more of the moving forces of life; he had intuitions which covered more ground than the asking and answering of questions. He rarely asked questions. Fortunately it was none of his business—not even the pressure which he felt must have been brought to bear upon Rusk, and which so suddenly had been removed. His business now was to taste life for himself as he had never tasted it, to develop a capacity for happiness which he felt springing up in every part of his being. It was as if he were emerging from dusk into sunlight; the strange shadows of his world—its darkness, its mists and dreams—were melting into something brighter and more healthy. He felt his hold on existence growing stronger, tremendously stronger. There had been a few hours that afternoon when it had died down, when it had almost flickered out altogether; but the afternoon seemed by this time infinitely remote. . . .

And then he wondered if he should live long? The thought came to him without any apparent cause. He knew he had already been near death—a year—nearly two years ago. At the time it had not frightened him, had not even greatly interested him; but he remembered someone coming into a hushed and dim room where he had been lying very ill for days—someone talking to him kindly and soothingly—a clergyman—and then the same figure quite unexpectedly kneeling down beside the bed to pray for him. At the time it had stirred nothing deeper than a languid acceptance; it had been unreal, faint, remote. All he had been conscious of was a sense of weakness that had wrapped him round like a vast tepid bath in which he floated without effort, without pain. He had got better, but only very slowly, because he had not cared whether he got better or not, because he made no struggle to return to life. Yet he had always had the idea that life might be delightful—

if—if everything were different. An immense capacity for caring for people had constituted, though he did not know it, his great stumbling-block. There was in the spirit of this boy a quality of unselfishness, of loyalty and affection, which no one, even of those who cared most for him—his mother, May, Rusk—had really fathomed. They had seen a part of it, but not all. They had seen a part of it, because it would have been impossible to live with him and be wholly blind to it; but they had not seen it all, because they had been incapable of comprehending fully the nature of his mind.

The fire slumbered and flickered in the grate. There was something intimate, something almost caressing, in the quiet of the room. A strange idea came to Denis, that he had reached a definite crisis in his life—the last pages of a chapter, the last act of a drama. Yet what could be less dramatic than merely to be sitting here with his tutor, following the wandering flight of his own fancies, in this stillness which was built up of their friendship, of their trust and esteem? Only, oddly, unaccountably, he felt it to be dramatic. Rusk's pipe could not rob it of this quality, nor his leaning forward to strike a match against the top bar of the grate. It amused him to wonder how these thoughts would strike his tutor were he to put them into words; but they were not the kind of thoughts one ever puts into words; they were hardly thoughts at all.

The fire broke and fell in with a slight noise; a tongue of flame shot up and quivered and danced like a spirit dancing on a mountain top; while the reflection quivered and danced upon the ceiling.

Rusk moved again in his chair, sinking lower into it and propping up his feet against a narrow ledge above the grate. He took his pipe from his mouth. "Suppose you read something to me," he said.

"I'll have to light the lamp if I do."

"Well—repeat something then—you know lots of poetry."

"Just anything that comes into my head?"

"Yes; whatever you like."

31

Shortly before five o'clock on the afternoon of the next day Mr. Bracknel, who had still several hours' work before him, was shut up in his private office with two other persons, one of whom was John Brooke. The other was a small meagre middle-aged man of unhealthy and unprepossessing appearance, called Davis. Davis was a despatch-clerk. He was dressed neatly in dark clothes, but his hands and nails were dirty. A straw-coloured beard, whiskers, and moustache grew weakly on his wax-pale face; and his mouth twitched nervously as he watched every movement made by the other two with large round protuberant eyes—eyes of a uniform yellow-blue tint, without any visible iris, and of a curiously opaque, glaucous appearance, like those of a dead fish. There was something cringing, obsequious, yet uncertain about Davis—a hint of latent malignancy perhaps, which might flash out at any moment, though at present his state of mind obviously was that of a person very much frightened.

John Brooke stood slightly to one side, with an air of holding himself more or less aloof, and on his face a calm, self-confident expression.

"Remember, Davis, you'll go to jail for this," Mr. Bracknel was saying. "There need be no last-moment remorse, no sentiment about your wife and children: you've only confessed because you couldn't help yourself; I give you no credit for it whatever."

After this encouraging speech he turned to Brooke. "When did you first suspect anything of this sort was going on?" he asked.

"I can't quite say that I *suspected*," John answered cautiously, as if determined that no matter what happened he would never be guilty of either an over- or an understatement. His manner, indeed, in this respect, contrasted comically with Mr. Bracknel's.

"Nobody knew anything about it but me and Mr. Alfred," the clerk interrupted in a whining voice.

"Keep quiet," said Mr. Bracknel savagely. "You suspected *something*, didn't you?"—he had turned again to John.

"I suspected to this extent," John answered slowly, "that I knew there must have been unusual slackness somewhere, and I spoke to Davis about it."

"Why didn't you come to me?"

John was silent till Mr. Bracknel repeated his question more peremptorily.

"I wasn't sure."

"But you had a suspicion. It was your duty to inform me at once. Why didn't you do so?"

"I had an idea that Davis wasn't primarily to blame. He could have done nothing by himself." These words were spoken quite dispassionately, and hearing them the despatch-clerk, who had begun to edge nearer the door, paused.

"You mean you thought he must have been acting with Mr. Alfred?"

"I thought so."

Mr. Bracknel began to pace up and down the room. Presently he stopped once more in front of Brooke. "I don't see how that made it any less proper for you to tell me."

John met his eyes calmly. "It seemed to be fairer to give Davis a chance," he said.

"A chance! A chance to do what?" Mr. Bracknel snapped irritably. "A chance to rob me, do you mean?"

"A chance to give in his notice and leave in the ordinary way. As I say, I didn't think he could be primarily responsible."

Mr. Bracknel grunted. "Well, I'll have him arrested now at all events"—and he made a motion to lift the telephone receiver, but John touched him on the arm. "Remember Mr. Alfred, sir," he said in a low voice. "You can't very well make the thing public."

Mr. Bracknel paused. Then he turned again to the despatch-clerk, who was standing in the corner, watching them furtively yet viciously. "Who is it got these goods?" he asked roughly.

Davis gave him the name and address he already knew.

"Anyone else?"

"No, sir."

"Have you a note of all he got?"

Davis, who was evidently prepared, took a paper from his pocket and handed it over.

Mr. Bracknel just glanced at it. "You can go," he then said abruptly, and the despatch-clerk glided away.

There was a brief silence after the door had closed, during which Mr. Bracknel studied the paper Davis had given him. "You kept very quiet about all this," he said at last, looking up.

"I kept quiet because I didn't know about it," John answered. "I hadn't inquired into it. I wasn't sure."

"Would you ever have told me?"

"I can't say, sir. I don't suppose I'd have told you if there had been any other way of dealing with it and if Davis hadn't been a fool."

"You mean if he had given in his notice? But if you don't tell me things how am I ever to get to know them? It was a mere chance remark let drop by Irwin that made me look into this."

"I'd have kept a better watch in future," John said.

Mr. Bracknel shrugged his shoulders. His whole bearing, nevertheless, had perceptibly altered, its aggressive pugnacity giving place to despondency. "Well, what are we going to do now?" he asked in a melancholy voice.

"I don't see, sir, that there's very much you *can* do," John made answer. "The goods have been paid for, or we might have been able to get them back; but as it is——"

"We can get back the money received for them," said Mr. Bracknel, who at the moment was thinking more of the total lack of sympathy in the young man's manner than of any pecuniary loss he had suffered.

"I very much doubt it," John returned impassively. "People don't do that sort of thing to put the money in the bank."

"You mean it will have been spent? This is very bad, John—very painful for me." There was an almost appealing note in his voice.

"I can quite understand that, sir," was John's reply.

Mr. Bracknel sighed. "What do you advise? Tell me what you think," he went on in a tone of unusual mildness.

But John was silent, and his stolid face was extremely unresponsive. He seemed, in fact, to be trying hard to stare through the wall above Mr. Bracknel's head. "I'm afraid I can't advise you, sir," he said at length. "I know nothing about Mr. Alfred's affairs. I suppose his salary isn't sufficient."

The—to Mr. Bracknel—atrocious cynicism of this remark was really shocking; it was like a sudden slap in the face administered by one from whom he had every right to expect gratitude. He started angrily. "Not sufficient!" he cried. "Are you asking me to raise it? I may tell you that from to-day he ceases to be a member of this firm."

John Brooke looked unimpressed. "He'll have to live somehow," he said with a shrug. "Especially now he's married. Of course it's unfortunate that he should have acted in this way, but at the same time it's extremely unlikely anything of the sort will occur again, and I dare say he was in debt. Not that I mean he was justified——"

"Justified!" Mr. Bracknel broke in angrily. "Good God—what kind of talk is that! Do you *approve* of what he has done?" His eyes rested indignantly on the young man facing him. Then: "That will do," he pronounced curtly, turning away. "Send Mr. Alfred to me when he comes in."

"Yes, sir," John answered, leaving him alone with his thoughts.

These were more numerous than cheerful. The revelation of Alfred's behaviour threw into the background even Amy's conduct in regard to Rusk. Mr. Bracknel had long been conscious of a bitter resentment against his elder son—for whom at no time had he felt much affection—and now he decided that he had had enough of him. There was no use giving him any more chances. John Brooke's hinted scheme of bribing him into good behaviour he found particularly repugnant, for of course it had only been suggested on account of Rhoda. But there were other ways of meeting the difficulty than that, and the simplest would be to wash his hands of him once and for all. It would have to be done some day, and it might as well be done to-day. He was a fool, a liar, a profligate, and now a thief. . . .

He had reached this point in his summing up when Alfred himself slouched in. "They say you want me," he said.

"Sit down there," Mr. Bracknel answered, pointing to a chair opposite the table at which he himself was seated.

Alfred took another, which appeared to him more comfortable. With his hands in his pockets, he did not, in spite of his father's black looks, show signs of any great perturbation.

"So you've turned thief!" Mr. Bracknel began sombrely.

Alfred shrugged his shoulders. "Did Davis tell you?" he asked.

"It doesn't matter who told me."

"Not a bit," Alfred agreed.

"What have you to say for yourself?" Mr. Bracknel went on, his face growing darker still.

"Nothing."

"Nothing?"

"Nothing you would admit," Alfred amended.

"Oh! . . . You could defend yourself then, if you wanted to?"

"If you'd behaved decently to me I'd have behaved decently to you. That's all. I don't believe in making a lot of jaw about things. As you preferred to be mean, I had to get the money some way. I told you at the time I was in need of it. I don't profess to be a saint, but so far as this affair goes I can't see that there's much to choose between us. At any rate you left nothing else open to me."

"I see." It was odd how the primary effect of Alfred's callousness was to restore his father's self-control, so that when he next spoke it was much less angrily than contemptuously.

"Well, I'll leave something else open for you now: I'll leave the door open for you. You'll get very little more out of me either honestly or dishonestly: can you understand that? You've counted once too often on my softness. There's an end to all things, and you've reached the end of that. . . . And now we can get down to business. I'm not going to waste much time on you, so you'd better attend to what I'm saying. If you consent to emigrate I'll give you a thousand pounds. If not, you'll get nothing. I suppose you're sober enough to follow me, though you smell like a public house? I need not tell you that I no longer look upon you as a son of mine, and that this thousand pounds is the last money you'll get—during my lifetime at all events—and I'll probably last some years yet. The question for you to decide is whether you want the money or not. Will you, or will you not, leave the country?"

Alfred looked up, his small eyes gleaming with hatred. "I don't want your dirty money," he said, rising to his feet.

"Remember," Mr. Bracknel told him grimly, "to-morrow it will be too late. You needn't count on any relenting on my part. From the moment you leave this office I have nothing more to do with you. It's not a matter of much importance to me whether you accept or refuse; only I'm weak enough, for the sake of your mother, to give you a last chance."

"You always were indulgent," Alfred sneered heavily. Nevertheless he hesitated, gazing sullenly down at the carpet. "Make it five thousand and I'll go."

His father laughed unpleasantly. "You're an interesting case," he observed. "It's a pity your field is so limited. With a fair share of brains you might have made quite a passable criminal. However, I take what you say as a refusal. And now you'd better go. I've more important things than this to attend to."

Alfred hesitated again. "Give it me," he said.

"Give you what?"

"The thousand."

"You consent to the conditions, then?"

"Yes. . . . Damn you." The last words were added under his breath.

Mr. Bracknel wrote out a cheque and handed it across the table. With another grunt Alfred almost snatched it from him, and was walking to the door when his glance fell on the strip of paper he held. "This is only for fifty," he snarled, wheeling round.

"You don't imagine I'm going to give it all to you at once," his father returned, "and before you actually go! You must remember that yours is hardly a word to be trusted implicitly. The balance will be paid to you in instalments when you reach your destination, which we will settle later."

Alfred still did not move. "It'll take a good deal more than this to get me away," he said in a low hoarse voice.

"You must do what you can with it, I'm afraid. If you refer your creditors to me I can arrange with them—deducting the amount from the nine hundred and fifty pounds I still hold for you."

He turned back to his desk, and Alfred walked out of the office. In the distance he saw John Brooke, and a sudden idea of vengeance flashed through his mind. He would tell Brooke who his real father was: he would tell them all. Then he thought he had better not risk the rest of the money. The revelation of John's birth would keep. Besides, he didn't believe the old man would really care a straw if everybody knew; and under his breath he called him by a filthy name as he stepped into the street.

32

Alfred walked slowly along the moist, greasy pavement in the November evening. A slight drizzle was falling and he turned up the collar of his overcoat. The streets were slimy and dirty. The gas-lamps threw out golden haloes on the damp air, their yellow light splashing on wet roads and flagstones. It was past six o'clock and the traffic was considerable. Alfred made his way to an hotel in a back street, a place he had only once or twice visited before and where there was little chance of his meeting anyone he knew. He wanted to think things over before he took his next step. He dined most indifferently, and after dinner sat down on a leather-covered sofa at the back of the bar. At first he had the place to himself, but presently two or three commercial travellers entered, and stood about the counter drinking and talking. Their flamboyant vulgarity filled the air, exasperating, amazing; and Alfred watched them with a sombre face. He felt depressed, and the whiskies and sodas he had drunk at dinner had done nothing to make him more cheerful. He ordered another now, but it did not dispel his gloom. The thing was ridiculous, absurd—what could *he* do in the colonies? Yet he knew there would be little use in making an appeal to his father: his father was obstinate to the verge of idiocy, and Alfred had never yet seen him draw back from any decision he had once made. In the present instance, he felt, Mr. Bracknel would be especially mulish: he was probably only too glad of an excuse to be rid of him; he had wanted to get rid of him for some time back; he had always hated him. As he brooded over this, becoming more and more certain of it, Alfred felt like catching his father by the throat. His thoughts travelled round and round the dreary circle of the wrongs that had been done him and the injustices he had suffered till they began to torture him like a probed sore. Yes, he was perfectly sure his father would keep his word. It was not as if he were the only child, or even the only son. There was Denis, and still more there was John Brooke. Alfred's whole soul rose up in hatred of the bastard. The old man would very likely leave the business to John, who was just such a creature as he would wish to have it. In the meantime he might even take him into partnership; things had been shaping in that direction all along. If only his father would die—meet with some accident! Quite apart from accidents, moreover, he had a suspicion that Mr. Bracknel was not at all so well as he pretended to be: there was something he kept secret, but of which nevertheless he was afraid. Alfred had gathered this a long time ago from many little things; but of course such speculations were in the present crisis futile, the idlest dreams.

A few more stragglers had by now drifted in, their incursion being highly resented by Alfred. There was one man in particular, one of the original group of commercial travellers, who irritated him to fury; a person with a fatuous perpetual laugh, a pale face, a waxed moustache, and a signet ring. Alfred felt an increasing longing to bring his pleasant evening to a close. One good straight knock would do it. He stretched out his powerful arms and stiffened its muscles. Finally he got up and strolled over towards his victim. That innocent, leaning languidly against the counter, gave a twist to his moustache as Alfred approached. He eyed him a moment indifferently, and then turned to the barmaid. "Upon my word we did: we thought nothing of a thing like that. I remember once in Manchester—some of us were going the pace a bit—and——"

Alfred brushed up against him and turned round slowly. "Why the devil don't you get out of the way?" he said, with a stare that showed the whites of his eyes. There was perhaps something strange in his expression, for the man with the waxed moustache apologized, and the tale he had begun to tell died into silence. Alfred still lingered beside him, and a curious hush came over the entire group. In a minute or two one of them discovered he would be late for an appointment. He announced the fact with a nervous air of taking the company at large into his confidence. The others glanced at watches and were astonished; nobody had had any idea it was so late! They hastily swallowed their drinks and made for the door, while Alfred, the triumphant male, feeling a little better, returned to his former seat, indifferent to the encouraging glances of the impressionable barmaid.

But this improvement in his spirits was very transient. He opened the evening paper and flung it away. He lit a cigar from mere force of habit, and pulled at it mechanically, with his brows knit and his eyes on the floor. Finally he had another drink—a pretty stiff one this time—before taking his departure. Outside, it was now raining heavily, and as he walked down the street Alfred was uncertain what to do next. Should he go home? Should he go to a music-hall? Should he have a game of cards? Suddenly it occurred to him to go back to the office. He had some things there he must get. He had not thought of them before, and he would rather get them now than return in the morning. The fumes of the drinks he had taken had begun, once he was in the open air, to cloud his brain a little, but Alfred could hold a good deal of liquor and was far from drunk. He paced sullenly on till he reached the tall dark building which at present turned a blank face to the murky night. The few people he met were hurrying by, bent on their own business, or bent on getting as soon as possible into shelter. Alfred paid no attention to them. He fitted a key in the outer door and turned it. Only a single lock was fastened, therefore there must be somebody inside. But the place was in darkness; the only light there was streamed out through the half-open door of the private office, and Alfred at once concluded that his father must be working late—working alone, as very often happened.

His first impulse was to get away without Mr. Bracknel's knowledge, and he wondered that he had not already come out to see who was there. Surely he must have heard the opening of the door! But he did not make his appearance, and presently, and as if by instinct silently, Alfred stole past the open door and on into the rear of the building. Here he suddenly stood still, for he had heard a step overhead—someone was coming downstairs.

Alfred remained motionless as a statue. He had forgotten why he had come back to the place; his slightly muddled thoughts were now wholly occupied with Mr. Bracknel—with the amazing possibilities sometimes dependent on absurdly small things. Perfectly hidden himself, he watched his father descend the stairs. He saw him go on into his office, the door of which he left wide open, as if he did not intend to work much longer. He had probably been up to the lavatory and was going home. But as Alfred watched him he sat down in front of the fire and began to turn over some papers. The sight of this seemed to affect his son powerfully. It was as if it brought home to him in a single swift bright vision the clear intolerable realization of all he was losing, and he felt a sudden recklessness which blotted out everything else. He marched straight to the office and entered without ceremony. He had at least the satisfaction of startling Mr. Bracknel, who jumped to his feet, scattering his papers into the fender and over the floor. Wheeling round, he recognized the intruder, and his fat sallow face grew black as thunder. Next instant his momentary alarm turned to an extraordinary rage.

"What are you doing here?" he asked, speaking below his breath.

Alfred smiled unpleasantly. "I came to say that it isn't good enough," he replied.

"What isn't good enough?"

"Your miserable thousand. It's too thin—the whole idea." He sat down on the leather-covered table and eyed his father disagreeably.

Mr. Bracknel took a step towards him. "Get out of this," he threatened, in the same low husky voice. "Drunken blackguard!" It was visible that he was making an immense effort to control himself. "Go—or I'll call a policeman."

But Alfred only laughed. "I can make it damned awkward for you, you know," he remarked expressively. "If I tell the mater about your bastard, for instance—and in a good many other ways too. No; you'll really have to do something a lot better if you want to get rid of me." Even in the present dubious state of his fortunes he was capable of deriving a genuine pleasure from his father's agitation. The situation, in fact, struck him as extremely piquant, and he produced his cigarette case.

Mr. Bracknel made another movement towards him. His face was now purple, and the veins of his forehead and neck were swollen alarmingly. A flake of froth actually appeared at the corner of his mouth. For a moment he stood quite still, his hand raised as if he were about to strike his son, while his lips twitched and his whole face was drawn as if with a sudden sharp pain. Then he grasped at the table, missed it, and fell to the floor.

Alfred gazed down at him, callously, curiously, watching the colour ebb from his face and leave it a pale waxy yellow. Mr. Bracknel lay almost upon his back. His eyes were wide open and he breathed slowly and noisily, a phenomenon which appeared to interest Alfred keenly, so that he made no attempt whatever to interrupt it. A good many thoughts, suggested possibly by this strange breathing, passed through his mind. He seemed to have become miraculously sober. He gazed down at his father lying there; the odd foolish noise he was making becoming fainter, and his lips turning blue; but he saw something far different, something that shone out extraordinarily brightly, the vision of a life perfectly free and delightful, with plenty of money, more than enough, all that he might ever have expected. And without waiting—that was the great thing—without waiting! A swift train of desires flitted by him and he saw them one by one gratified. He saw, too, justice being done, the humbling of John Brooke. He tasted in anticipation the joy of a long-deferred revenge, the payment of a double grudge. And the only thing that prevented all this from coming true was one paltry little life that was perhaps even now dying out. It certainly appeared to be. It was amazing! A life no one would regret, a life that must be a burden to itself! And all he had to do was simply not to interfere, simply to leave it to Providence. Alfred's prophetic vision seemed to materialize in the air before him, and he stared at it with hard intent eyes in which was no shadow of compunction. It fascinated him, it whispered in his ears: and all this time (the hands of the clock had travelled quite a considerable distance!) he remained absolutely still—as still as if he too had ceased to breathe.

For no sound came now from the dark limp heap upon the floor. Moved by a morbid curiosity Alfred bent lower over that heap. Mr. Bracknel was not a pleasant object to look upon. His face had turned an ash-grey colour and his bulging eyes were fixed and glazed. His jaw, too, had dropped, leaving the tongue slightly visible between the false teeth.

Alfred sat down on a chair and began to think. If his father were to show any serious signs of reviving it might be more prudent to get him some medical assistance: if he did not show such signs—well, then it might be better to slip away from the office unseen. At present Mr. Bracknel looked as if, were he left undisturbed, he would behave perfectly sensibly. Alfred resolved to wait.

He glanced at the clock on the chimney-piece. The hands pointed to twenty minutes past nine. He waited for what appeared to be a very long time before he heard the hour strike. Then he got down on his knees and examined his father more closely. He unfastened his waistcoat, his shirt, his vest, and slipped in his hand: he put his ear close: he could neither feel nor hear the faintest beating of the heart: he could hear no faintest sound of breathing. He lifted one of the arms and let it drop. It fell dead, and the hand he had touched was very cold. So was the face—cold as ice, and covered with a clammy sweat. Alfred decided that it was all over. He rearranged his father's clothes and sat down once more in his chair. It would not do to ring up a doctor even now: a doctor might drag Mr. Bracknel back to life again. This was most improbable of course, but still you never knew. He glanced about the office. Should he let himself out at once, or wait till later? He came to no decision, but merely sat there, though he had begun instinctively to avoid looking at the dark heap lying on the floor, with its upturned face and wide staring eyes. The heavy seals of its watch-chain glittered in the gas-light; there was something gruesomely fascinating about it; and Alfred, though he tried to keep his gaze averted, could not do so, and in the end retired to the darkness of the outer office. He had a strange feeling now that everything was much quieter than it ought to be—except the ticking of the clock, which sounded unnaturally loud. He had begun to wonder how many thousands a year he was worth when suddenly he heard the clear, high ring of the telephone bell. The unexpected noise in that dark still place gave him a most disagreeable shock. His nerves could not be so well under control as he had imagined! The bell rang twice again, and then was silent. Alfred still sat on in the darkness.

One—two—three—eleven strokes. The striking of the hour seemed to come to him from all sides. The traffic in the street had by this time perceptibly diminished; only very seldom could he hear a passing footfall. He went to the front office and peered out from behind the blind. It was raining more heavily than ever; the atmosphere was thick as soup; but there was a street-lamp immediately in front of the door, and Alfred could see nobody. He resolved to run a slight risk, and going to the door, opened it cautiously; then stood listening. Nothing but the rain. Next moment he was outside and had turned the key in the lock: a moment later and he was safe. A feeling of extraordinary exultation took possession of him. He was a rich man: his own master: all life lay before him.

That night, when he went upstairs to bed, his wife asked him sleepily what time it was; but for answer Alfred only kissed her.

33

"Where is papa?" May asked her mother as they sat down to breakfast. "Did he not come home last night?"

"No."

"He must have been very busy, surely!"

Mrs. Bracknel sighed. "I knew he was going to be late; he told me he would be. I rang him up again before I went to bed, but could get no answer. I hope his room was all right—it's so long since he slept there. You and Denis must be very careful about getting good rooms, Mr. Rusk. From all one hears foreigners can't be trusted in such matters. Your best plan, if you have the slightest suspicion that the sheets are damp, is to sleep between the blankets. But Denis is so absent-minded he'd never think of looking whether they were damp or not."

Rusk hastened to reassure her on this point; he would see to the matter himself: but Denis said nothing. He appeared at that moment to be even more absent-minded than usual. His face was pale, and there were dusky shadows beneath his eyes. He looked as if he had not slept, or as if sleep had brought him little refreshment. He seemed nervous, too, and dejected. His mother, noticing these things, questioned him, but her questions elicited little information: he was all right, he told her, and then lapsed once more into silence.

They sat over breakfast longer than usual. May had an atlas open on the table beside her—she had been looking out some of the places the travellers would be visiting—and Rusk had described for the twentieth time all he knew—which wasn't much—of various routes and trains. He was just beginning for the twenty-first when they heard a car driving up to the door.

"Who can it be?" May wondered. "It isn't papa, is it?" And Denis answered in a strange dull voice, as if he were speaking in a dream: "It's Alfred."

Rusk looked at him, but the others were listening to a low murmur of voices coming from the hall. The boy's face had grown whiter, and there was a most peculiar expression in his eyes, a look of suspense, of shrinking, which deepened to one almost of dread as the door opened and Alfred stood there, very grave and decorous, ready to deliver his tidings.

He hesitated before coming on into the room, and his voice was hushed as he wished them all good-morning. Everyone had turned towards him except Rusk, whose attention was still held by the extraordinary gaze with which Denis was watching his brother.

"I've very bad news," Alfred began in a low voice; and then he paused.

Mrs. Bracknel had risen to her feet. She stood trembling beside her chair, her face turned to her son.

"Papa is dead," Alfred continued in the same solemn tone, avoiding his mother's half-terrified gaze. "He died suddenly last night. He was found this morning lying on the floor of his office. John Brooke found him, and of course rang me up at once."

Mrs. Bracknel sank back into her chair, but when May hurried to her assistance she waved her away. "It's nothing," she said. "Tell Alfred to go on."

"There's very little more to say," Alfred continued. "Where's Denis going to?"

For Denis had got out through the window and they could see him running across the lawn. "What's the matter with *him*, anyway?" Alfred grunted, relapsing unconsciously into his ordinary manner.

"Oh, Alfred!" May murmured reproachfully.

But the tone of this remark hurt her brother's feelings, and he turned on her indignantly. "What are you 'Oh, Alfreding' about? What have *I* done?" he exclaimed.

May, however, was occupied with her mother, trying to persuade her to go to her room and lie down.

Presently she succeeded in doing so, and left together, Alfred and Rusk stood confronting each other uneasily and almost hostilely. For Rusk had been struck by a lack of correspondence between the solemn tone in which Alfred had announced his news and a strange expression—very like one of suppressed excitement—which had passed across his face a moment later. Rusk had never seen him look like that before, and, though he could not have told why, he watched him with a vague repugnance.

"They'll be bringing him up here," Alfred remarked, glancing towards the door. "I think I'd better push along." He had already made one or two tentative movements of imperfectly concealed restlessness, and Rusk could see he was impatient to be gone. He did not help him, however, and Alfred went on, as if excusing himself: "There's a lot to see about and there's nothing I can do here. Tell them if they want anything to ring me up at the office, and that I'll be back as soon as I can. I suppose some of the relations will have to be wired to, but May or Amy can look after that."

"Miss Amy isn't here," Rusk said, following him out into the hall.

Alfred turned quickly. "Not here! Why? Where is she?"

"She went yesterday to stay with one of her aunts."

"Then *she'll* have to be wired to. . . . Well, good-bye for the present."

He made his escape at last, and the hall-door had hardly closed behind him before May reappeared. "Where's Alfred?" she asked in surprise. "Mamma wants him to go up to her."

"I'm afraid he's gone back to town," Rusk said: and he delivered Alfred's messages.

"I can hardly realize it," May murmured in an awed voice. "I never even knew there was anything the matter with papa. Nobody knew except mamma and the doctor. She has just been telling me."

Rusk tried hard to think of some way in which he could express his sympathy, and had not yet discovered one when the girl said: "I must go back to mamma.... Alfred might have waited, I think: it's very strange his running off like that."

Rusk thought so too. He knew Mr. Bracknel had not been greatly beloved by his children, but he was sure his death would be a tremendous blow to his wife, and the old problem of that mysterious attachment once again flitted through his mind. His ponderings were interrupted by the reappearance of May. "Has Denis not come back yet?" she asked from the door.

"No, I don't think so. I haven't seen him, at any rate."

May joined him where he stood by the window, and together they gazed out across the lawn. "I wish you'd both got safely away before this happened," the girl said, "especially Denis.... When you're not close to a thing it makes it so much less real.... I wonder if I ought to bring Amy home, or to tell her not to come. I must send her a telegram in any case; and there are other people who must be told."

"Can't I help you?" Rusk said.

She accepted his offer at once. "Thanks, if you will. I feel as if I were dreaming a bad dream. I've telephoned to Doctor Birch to come to see mamma. I'm afraid she isn't at all well—Alfred told us so abruptly."

"It's never easy to tell such news," Rusk said. "I dare say it's better to get it over quickly."

"You won't mind putting off your arrangements for a little, will you?" May continued. "I mean about going abroad. Wouldn't it be better if Denis met you in London? I should think he might go in a few days—when everything is settled. That is, unless you yourself wish to stay for the funeral. But it isn't at all necessary, you know.... You don't mind my speaking so plainly, I hope? It's only because I feel we are old enough friends to understand each other."

"I'll do whatever you think best," Rusk answered. "I suppose there will be some people coming."

"I expect so. I'll tell you later. But it wasn't of that I was thinking—it was of the whole thing—the house will be very uncomfortable."

"Well, I'll do whatever you say."

"I think I'll get mamma to ask the Birches to take Denis for a day or two: he'll be better out of all the fuss."

"That's certainly a good idea," Rusk agreed; "I'm glad you thought of it."

"I'm sure they won't mind.... I wonder what's become of him?"

Rusk helped her to send off the telegrams: then he went out in search of his pupil, but could not find him anywhere. On coming back to the house, however, he met Doctor Birch, who was just leaving, and turned to walk a short distance with him, drawn by that mysterious fascination which lies in the discussion of death and misfortune when they are not too intimately tragic.

"This is a very sudden affair," Rusk began, and the Doctor answered, "Very." They both derived a faint, inexplicable satisfaction from the exchange of even these remarks.

"I hope Mrs. Bracknel is feeling better," Rusk presently added. "It must have been a great shock to her."

"I'm afraid so, though she's keeping up wonderfully. My sisters will be over some time in the afternoon to see her. I may be back myself; but something has gone wrong with the car, which is why I'm on foot now."

There was a brief silence, and then Rusk reverted to the real subject. "I never thought he looked a very healthy man. He even seemed to me slightly—what shall I call it?—hysterical, neurotic."

"It was partly due to the life he led," Doctor Birch answered, "absolutely killing. Besides, what he suffered from often makes people irritable.... I've told them not to talk about it before the boy. Worst possible thing for him: but of course they *will* talk, and the house already has been transformed into a kind of tomb—all the blinds down and everybody speaking in whispers. I suggested that you should take him away at once—I suppose you'll hardly want to wait?—but they've some idiotic idea that he ought to be there for his father's funeral, that people would consider it strange if he wasn't."

"So, very probably, they would," Rusk replied. "But I think I'll cross to-night; there are sure to be relations coming, and anyhow I'm only in the way at a time like this."

"Well—can't you persuade them to let you take Denis with you?"

Rusk promised to do his best, though without much hope of success, and when he returned to the house he found it just as the Doctor had described—wrapped in gloom and silence. Denis had not come back; Mrs. Bracknel was lying down; Alfred had again come and gone.

Rusk and May, in the darkened dining-room, sat down to lunch alone. He told her then of his decision to cross to England that night, adding that if they didn't wish Denis to come with him he would meet him in London on any day they arranged. But *would* they let him come?

May shook her head. She was sure her mother would want both her sons to be present at their father's funeral, and Rusk himself, for that matter, didn't see how a few days one way or another could make much difference—certainly didn't think it worth while worrying Mrs. Bracknel about it.

In the afternoon he went to his own room to pack his things. He had nearly finished and it was growing dusk when his pupil came in. The boy looked pale and dishevelled, with a wild expression in his eyes. At a single glance he took in the situation.

"You're going away," he said.

"Yes, I'm going to-night. You're to join me in a few days."

"But why are you going? If you go I'll go too," Denis cried, in sudden excitement.

Rusk paused in his packing. He did not quite know what to say.

"Your mother wants you to be here," he began. "You'll come over after the funeral, and I'll meet you then."

Denis looked at him piteously. "I can't stay," he said. "I can't—I can't. I only came in now to look for you." He flung himself down on the bed and hid his face in the pillow.

Rusk tried to soothe him. He spoke to him, and stroked his dark coarse hair. Suddenly Denis sat up. He put his hand on his tutor's. "I know what happened," he whispered, staring at the opposite wall. "I knew it before I came down to breakfast this morning. I knew papa was dead. I had a horrible dream about him—that he was struggling against something, or somebody."

Rusk looked at him in consternation, but the boy went on: "I saw him struggling. . . . That was all I *could* see, but it was enough. And when I woke up you were asleep. . . . And then—when I looked at the window—staring in at me——" His voice broke, and he sat trembling.

"But all that is only a dream," Rusk said, trying to speak confidently, though the horror in the boy's voice had impressed him in spite of himself. That horror, indeed, seemed in the gathering darkness to be floating very near them, and he felt a strain upon his nerves he could not shake off.

"I saw it—I saw it," Denis repeated, with an intensity that might have sprung from hallucination. "I saw it last night; and when Alfred came into the room this morning there was something strange about him. . . ."

Denis was clinging to him now, and Rusk held him close, and closer still—held him as if to shield him for ever from all harm. They sat there in the darkness. He could feel the boy's face cold and damp—the sweat broken out upon his forehead, though he was shivering.

"I'll not go to-night," Rusk said, making up his mind. "Denis, you mustn't think of this any more. It was only a bad dream—a nightmare. It's only the coincidence that makes it seem so terrible. You must forget it; you must be a man; you must put it from you."

"I can't—I can't," the boy moaned. "Why are we like this? Why are we different from other people? We are—we are. There's something wrong with Alfred—with me—with all of us. You must go away: you can do nothing. Why should you stay among us? This house is haunted: it's not meant for you: for us it's different."

"My dear boy—dear Denis," Rusk murmured, seeking to comfort him; "you mustn't think such things. In a week or two—when we are far away—do you hear me?—far, far away—all this will be different. Just now you're tired and everything seems wrong: but there is more good in the world than evil. You can trust me, can't you? If you've ever trusted me, trust me now."

"I'll never go away," said the boy wretchedly, with a desolating conviction in his voice. "Something will prevent me, something will hold me back. I can feel it near me now. It will take some form—it will keep me—I'll never go away."

A clock downstairs struck the hour, and Rusk listened to the sound, and then to the following silence. "Will you promise me not to tell your dream to anyone else?" he said. "I don't mean by that, that I attach the slightest importance to it in the way you do; but it would be very painful to whoever you told it to."

"I haven't told it," Denis said. "But I can't bear to see Alfred. I couldn't stay in the room with him this morning. I've been walking for miles. I don't know where I've been: I don't know how I found my way back."

"Remember, if you were to say to anyone else what you've said to me, it would be very wrong," Rusk persisted. "What can I do to prevent you?"

"I won't say it," the boy promised.

"You promise faithfully?"

"Yes—yes. Why should I want to tell anyone! It's bad enough for *me* to know. I wish I could forget it."

"You *will* forget it," Rusk assured him. "If you try to you will; but you must try."

Denis had turned to the window, and suddenly his whole body stiffened.

"What is it? What is it?" Rusk asked, rising hastily to his feet.

"There! It's there at the window now, looking in." He gave a little cry in his throat and fell back on the bed.

He lay there, in a kind of swoon or fit, and it was some minutes before Rusk could revive him. Presently, however, he half opened his eyes; and then he opened them altogether, and smiled a strange dim little smile at his tutor bending over him.

"Are you better?" Rusk asked anxiously, raising him in his arms.

"Yes. . . . I'm sorry for frightening you." He sighed, and his eyes once more closed. "It will always come back now," he said hopelessly. "I thought it mightn't: I got out of bed last night and prayed not to see it again: but it's no use: it will come back always." He spoke quietly, yet the simple despair in his voice to Rusk was worse than anything else.

"There was nothing there," he said very slowly, his own conviction amounting almost to a solemn promise, "absolutely nothing. I swear it. There was nothing but the curtain. I too looked. It was only your imagination."

34

On going downstairs they found Miss Birch and Miss Anna in the drawing-room. The two ladies had come over to convey their sympathies to their old friend, who, with May, was talking to them now.

Rusk had not seen Mrs. Bracknel since the morning. She was seated with her hands folded in her lap, in profile against a dark-green curtain, and her thin sallow face, hollow-cheeked, the skin drawn close over the delicate skull, seemed already altered by the shock she had received. He heard Miss Birch offering to put Denis up, and Mrs. Bracknel thanking her; she would be very glad if they would; the funeral had been arranged for an early hour on Thursday morning; Alfred had been very thoughtful and was looking after everything.

Rusk had sent off a telegram telling his people that they might expect him on the following day, but he would now have to send another, mentioning his altered plans. He crossed the room and sat down beside Miss Anna, and began to talk to her in a low voice. He asked her if she could put him up as well as Denis. The boy was in a very nervous state, he told her, and if she could take them both he would feel much more comfortable about him. Of course Miss Anna declared it would be no trouble at all; and it was decided—Rusk himself proposed it—that they both should go back with her and her sister when they left. Having settled this much, and asking Miss Anna to settle the rest, he went upstairs and packed a bag with such things as they would need.

On coming down again he found the Miss Birches already saying good-bye, and he felt at least a temporary relief when, a minute or two later, they were all walking down the avenue together under the dark bare trees. Yet he still had a dim sense of something evil—something malign though very indefinite—floating in the air, which he hoped to shake from him when he had left the house behind. It was a house he now wished never again to enter: too much that was unpleasant had happened there: it was for him, as well as for Denis, beginning to be haunted. . . .

How long had he been living there? he pondered. A few months only, yet into that brief time so much had been crowded that months were almost like years. Once he had Denis safely away, he told himself, all would be different: the very hour they embarked on the steamer would mark the commencement of a new life. And he now wondered if, when the time had come, he could ever really have gone away leaving the boy behind, as in those first moments of bewildered indignation with Amy he had determined to do.

Meanwhile he was walking beside Miss Harriet Birch, with Denis and Miss Anna some forty or fifty yards ahead; and they had not yet reached the lodge. When they passed out of the grounds, however, and on to the open road, he made an effort to shake off the mood which oppressed him, and to talk a little of his plan for taking the boy abroad. Then, without his noticing it, this topic also dropped away, and he relapsed into a silence which lasted until they reached their destination. . . .

Nevertheless the evening passed off better than might have been expected. Denis looked brighter, and Rusk had begun to feel less anxious about him when they retired to the room they were to share. Here, safely in bed, the boy seemed to fall asleep almost at once, but Rusk himself lay awake for a long time before sinking into a kind of broken slumber. Every few minutes he would open his eyes with a sudden start, and an unaccountable impression that something was trying to get into the room. Then he would reassure himself that he had been only dreaming, and doze off again, to find no sounder rest than before.

Finally he gave it up altogether, and putting on his dressing-gown went down to the library to get a book. On coming up, he paused beside Denis's bed and looked down at the sleeping boy. Denis lay on his side, his brown face strikingly dark against the white pillow. His eyes were shut, yet as Rusk watched him he got the impression that he was not really sleeping. "Denis," he said very softly, and Denis immediately opened his eyes. But he said nothing, and quite suddenly it flashed upon Rusk that the boy was in a state of terror. He felt a deep, an immense compassion for him. He wondered for how long he had been lying like this—perhaps for hours! Truly the ways of Providence were strange!

"Come into my bed," he said simply, and when Denis made no movement, "Come," he repeated. This time his pupil got up, and still without a word, crossed over to the other bed. "I'm going to read," Rusk told him. "Be a good boy and try to go to sleep."

Denis turned on his side with a faint sigh, and almost at once, it seemed to Rusk, fell into a heavy slumber that was like the unconsciousness following upon exhaustion. He slept far on into the morning—even Rusk getting up and dressing, even the fire being lit, failing to awaken him—and when the tutor returned to their room after breakfast he was still asleep. Rusk sat down at a table near the fire and began to write a letter home, explaining his change of plan. He had finished it and was addressing the envelope when Denis at last awoke. The boy sat up, but for a minute or two he did not speak. Then: "Is it very late?" was all he said.

Rusk looked at his watch. "No. At least, it's going on for twelve, but that doesn't matter. I'll ring and get them to bring you up some breakfast."

"Hadn't I better go down?" Denis asked.

"No: it's all right: I told them you would have it up here." He smiled and approached the bed. "How are you?" he asked cheerfully, patting his pupil on the shoulder.

"Very well, thanks."

It was the conventional response, but in spite of that Rusk was sure the long sleep must really have done him good. Denis looked better, too. So he sat down on the side of the bed and talked to him about what he had said in his letter home till the breakfast-tray was brought up.

Then he returned to his chair by the fire and unfolded the morning paper. Nearly the first thing that caught his eye was an obituary notice, half a column in length. He was glad he had seen it: he would be able to keep the paper out of Denis's way. He began to read.

In half a column there was plenty of room to touch upon all Mr. Bracknel's virtues, and the notice did so. It pointed out that in his commercial career the deceased gentleman had set an example of high principles and integrity it would be difficult to exaggerate; it enumerated the various services he had rendered the city in his capacities of Councillor and Member of the Harbour Board; it mentioned that he had been invited to stand for West Belfast on the occasion of the last general election; it dwelt on the deep regret experienced throughout the city at the news of his premature death; and expressed the universal sympathy felt with the widow and the bereaved family in their great loss. Finally it stated that he had left behind him two sons and two daughters, and that the elder son, Mr. Alfred Bracknel, for several years past had occupied a responsible position in the firm, the fine old traditions of which he would doubtless carry on in a manner worthy of his father's name.

Rusk folded up the paper, and putting it in his pocket sat thinking. If only the next forty-eight hours could be safely got over, he decided, all would be well; but till then he knew he should not feel really easy in his mind. Fortunately the funeral would take place to-morrow, and to-night he would get Doctor Birch to give the boy a sleeping-draught.

35

On the morning of the day after the funeral Rusk was seated alone before the fire in the Birches' library. By-and-by he got up and looked out of the window at the bare, wind-swept garden. It was a boisterous and dirty day. A high wind drove the clouds in banks and masses without clearing the sky—drove, too, the rain, with a sharp continuous rattle against the streaming panes. Rusk, looking out, could see the trees bending and dripping, their black naked boughs creaking and straining as they battled with the storm. Nevertheless in spite of the weather, he presently put on his boots and went in search of Denis to persuade him to come for a walk. With their overcoats buttoned up round their throats they sallied forth, splashing through the rain that streamed down the incline of the road. Everything was soaking wet; once or twice they met some bedraggled pedestrian beating up like a battered ship against the wind, with soaking clothes and limp melancholy hat that would have flapped away like a bird but for the hand that retained it; yet they trudged on for a couple of hours, during which very few words passed between them, though at the end of their excursion Rusk, at least, felt much better for the exercise and imagined, rightly or wrongly, that his pupil had benefited too.

In the afternoon he suggested that they should repeat the experiment. He had an idea that if the boy were thoroughly tired out he would sleep all the sounder when bedtime came; but Denis preferred sitting by the fire with a book, leaving Rusk and Miss Anna to depart alone. He watched them walk down the garden path, and as soon as they were out of sight half regretted that he had not gone with them. For the rain had ceased and a faint glimmer of watery sunshine now made its appearance. Nor had his brighter mood of the morning been wholly the creation of Rusk's fancy. Such as it was, it still persisted, and he even began to hope a little that he might keep other things at a distance. The fact of the burial—might not that have made a difference? He grew drowsy as he sat by the fire; his book slipped from his hand; and presently he dropped asleep.

He opened his eyes abruptly in the thickening dusk, and it was as if all the horror of the world had awakened him. It was there!—outside, invisible, but drawing closer. . . .

He tried to banish all consciousness from his mind, but from the beginning the struggle was hopeless. The thing grew and grew with a dreadful intensity, till he could feel its presence in the air about him like a dense cold mist. *It* was there outside—there, floating in the darkness—drawing nearer. It had followed him from the other house: it would follow him to the ends of the earth. He tried to reason with himself. He was here in the library. Outside was the garden, dim and shadowy in the cold November greyness, and the noise he heard was the rustling and sighing of the wind—nothing more. . . .

The last light faded as he sat there, his head leaning back against the cushion of his chair, his face pale and still, his eyes closed. He heard the sound of a coal falling into the fender. He opened his eyes and watched the coming of the darkness. He was afraid—wretchedly, abjectly afraid—and his fear grew with the passing of each moment. At last he slipped down on his knees with a little moan and buried his face in the seat of the chair. He tried to pray: he repeated over and over a few words, begging that what he dreaded might not be allowed to come.

He had prayed and prayed again, yet still he feared to look up. He waited on and on, his face hidden in his hands, while he heard the clock strike the quarter, and then the half hour. With that at last he lifted his head, knowing very well what he was going to see. His eyes turned to the window, gazing out, fixed and dilated, while his hands opened and shut on the chair before him.

When the thing had gone he turned to leave the room. A look of despair had come into his face, and though he could hear Miss Birch moving about upstairs he did not go to her, but went out, bare-headed, just as he was, and hurried down the garden path. It was not absolutely dark. A faint ghostly pallor fell from the sky, and through this misty veil the trees and shrubs showed dim and blurred: it would rain again soon. He walked down the road and took the path that led into the grounds of his own home. He walked quickly and surely, as if he were bent on some definite errand, and paused only when he reached his old haunt by the hawthorn.

36

Rusk and Miss Anna returned a good deal later than they had first intended to, and just in time for dinner. They found Doctor Birch in the drawing-room with Miss Harriet, but Denis was not there, and the tutor immediately inquired for him.

"Was he not with you and Anna?" Miss Birch asked, glancing up from her work. "I've been in the house all afternoon and I haven't seen a sign of him. Perhaps he's in the library."

"I'll go and look," Rusk said at once. In point of fact he felt rather guilty at having left his pupil at all, and his uneasiness increased when he passed from one empty room to another where he thought Denis might possibly be. But he could not find him, and returned to announce his lack of success.

"Could he have gone home for anything?" Miss Birch suggested. "I somehow took it for granted that he was with you and never thought of looking."

The effect of this remark was to make Rusk feel more guilty still, and he had a suspicion that the Doctor was not pleased. But it would be futile to offer excuses now, so he merely said: "I'm sure he wouldn't go home. Why should he? He was only too glad to get away." Then he added, taking a step towards the door: "I'm going out to look for him."

"But won't you wait for him here? Won't you have dinner first?" Miss Birch asked in some surprise. "I don't suppose he has gone very far, and at any rate you aren't in the least likely to find him in the dark."

"I think I'll go all the same," Rusk replied. "I oughtn't to have left him this afternoon. It was a stupid thing to do."

"But why? Surely he doesn't need so much looking after as all that!"

"And you left him in the safest place in the world," Miss Anna pointed out. "You left him reading in the library. What harm could possibly come to him there?"

But Rusk knew they did not understand, and had already reached the door, though he still hesitated on the threshold.

"I may as well come with you," Doctor Birch remarked quietly. "Better go on with dinner without us."

The two men put on their overcoats and left the house together. It was very dark and they knew they were bound on a somewhat hopeless errand. "Which way shall we take?" Doctor Birch asked. "I suppose it doesn't greatly matter. Perhaps we ought to go in different directions."

"There is a place where I think he may be," Rusk replied in a tone of sombre self-reproach. "If he's not there I don't know where he is."

They walked on for some minutes side by side through the darkness. There might seem, on the face of it, little reason for anxiety, yet both were conscious of an undefined foreboding, which grew heavier and heavier as they proceeded. A cutting wind, cold as if laden with snow, blew out of the black starless sky, sweeping across their path and dying away on a desolate note. Rusk was haunted by a vision of Denis wandering alone in the darkness and listening to that dreary sound. He tried to persuade himself that all would be well, but he would have given everything he possessed to have seen the boy coming down the road at that moment. He had a sickening knowledge that if he had stayed with him instead of going out with Miss Anna, all would have been well. His suspense, indeed, gradually became unbearable, and unconsciously he increased his pace till the Doctor found it difficult to keep up with him.

"You think he has gone home after all?" the latter asked in some surprise, for Rusk had turned in at the back gate.

"No. Along here."

He led the way to the edge of the plantation, but among the trees everything was black as pitch and they found it very hard to make their way. Rusk had imagined that by now he knew exactly the whereabouts of the spot he was in search of, yet in the darkness he lost his bearings, and it was some time before he managed to hit on the right place. They could see no one there when they did discover it, and when they called aloud they got no answer.

"I wish we'd brought a lantern!" Rusk exclaimed.

"But what makes you think he would come here?" the Doctor asked uneasily. He had approached the edge of the pool, and in silence both men stared down at the black still water.

"He used to come here very often," Rusk answered. "I never told you about it: I see now I was wrong. I can't explain at present, but when I found he had gone out I thought he might——" He turned to his companion, but though he was almost touching him the Doctor's face was visible only as something pale and indistinct in the surrounding gloom. "Do you think there is any chance of his—his——" He did not finish the sentence.

"Of his what?" Doctor Birch asked, frowning.

"Of his being down there?" And Rusk made an invisible motion towards the water.

The Doctor hesitated, though evidently not altogether surprised by the suggestion. "Why should he be? What put such an idea into your head?"

"He's not well. There's been something troubling him. I didn't tell you about that either."

"But surely——! Is it deep?"

"Deep enough for that. Of course he can swim: but if it should have been intentional!"

Doctor Birch laid a would-be-reassuring hand on the younger man's arm. "I think you might have been a little more explicit earlier," he said, "but aren't you alarming yourself unnecessarily now? It seems to me much more probable that we'll find him comfortably seated at home when we get there."

In spite of these words Rusk remained gazing down at the pool. "I'm going to see," he answered briefly.

The Doctor grasped him by the arm. "See! How can you see? Do you mean you're going to dive?"

"Yes: there's no other way."

"But the water must be like ice! If he's there he's not alive now. Time enough when we really know that he's missing."

"Why should he have gone out at all? He told me he didn't want to."

"And later he changed his mind. I see nothing extraordinary in that."

Doctor Birch had stepped aside towards the edge of the trees, and now he struck a match. Rusk heard him give a sharp exclamation: "He's here. He's—— Quick—strike a light." The Doctor was cutting at something with his knife and Rusk sprang to his assistance.

"Is he—— Is he dead?" he gasped out, sick with the horror of it.

"I don't know. Make a blaze, can't you—with paper, with anything!" The Doctor was bending over the slight prostrate form. "How could he do it?" he murmured to himself. There followed a silence, which to Rusk seemed to last interminably. The Doctor was still kneeling beside the body.

"Is he dead?" Rusk asked again, as the small fire he had kindled flared for a moment and went out.

"Yes . . . poor little chap. It must have been done at least an hour ago. . . . He did it with his braces."

Rusk did not speak.

"Is there a shorter way out? Can we carry him?" the Doctor inquired mechanically.

There was another silence, while Rusk stooped down and lifted his pupil's body in his arms. Doctor Birch helped him, and bearing their burden between them they made their way through the trees. "Who is to tell his mother?" the Doctor murmured, speaking perhaps more to himself than to Rusk. "It's most unfortunate. I don't know how we are to tell her."

APPENDIX

I

Letter from Forrest Reid to Theodore Bartholomew.[1]

9 South Parade.
April 1909

My dear Theo,

I should have written to you ages ago, & I don't know what excuse I can find, that you will very much believe in, for not having done so. I suppose I have been busy, at anyrate I have been taken up with the planning of a new tale which has very much interested me. But first as to the other, it is still in the hands of Mess^r Heinemann. I believe publishers are getting more & more 'difficult'. These $7½^d$ editions etc. are the very devil for anyone who has'nt [sic] huge sales. People won't pay $4^s/6^d$ when they can get something that will do quite as well at an eighth of the price—especially when the 4/6 is a leap in the dark.

However I have got what seems a ripping thing on [my] hands. I have never had so much material—so much plot—for any single effort before. The whole thing came to me one evening after a week of dullness & I have blocked it out in 37 chapters besides writing a rough draft of the first ten. It is my moon tale but transformed beyond recognition. It is really a family history—& a considerable part of it is done very closely from the reality—so closely that I may have to lay the scene of it somewhere else—the thing in it I find perhaps most interesting is the relations between a young tutor & a boy & his two sisters. But there are also other members of the family, & outsiders. It is all very closely woven & I do not

---

[1] Special Collections, Queen's University Belfast, MS44/1/6/33.

believe there is anything in it that could be left out without weakening the whole. I feel that it is excellently strong if I can only do it. You would probably think it morbid, but I am going to please myself in it. It has altogether put me off the last thing I did. It has made me wonder if it isn't really very much in the air. I am quite sure my tutor & my boy are going to be much better than Katherine & Tony—I have almost forgotten their names.

I had written to you a note asking you to send me, if you could find it, something on moon-worship, but the professor of Greek here has told be [sic] that there is no book on the subject in English tho there are several in German. I fancy I can do without, tho if you came across anything I should like to see it. With love, yours always Forrest.

II

Letter from E. M. Forster to Forrest Reid.[1]

31/1/12.
Harnham
Monument Green
Weybridge.

Dear Sir,

I have read The Bracknels, and wish to thank you for it. Most books give us less than can be got from people, but yours gives more, for it has a quality that can only be described as 'helpful'. I do not use the word in the vulgar sense; Denis is no more likely to be prosperous after death than before it; but it does help one to distinguish between the superficial and the real, and to some minds there is something exhilerating [sic] in this. You show so very clearly that intelligence and even sympathy are superficial—good enough things in their way—they do what they can and would gladly do more; but the real thing is 'being there'; and the

---

1 Special Collections, Queen's University Belfast, MS44/1/22/1.

worst of it is that no two human beings can be in the same place. The book has moved me a good deal; it is what a friend ought to be but isn't; I suppose I am saying in a very round about and clumsy way that it is art.

The only point where I do not follow you spiritually, is in your introduction of visions of evil, but perhaps I am trying to define too much; at all events Denis escapes into a confusion that is not of this world.

The other qualities of your work—realism, character drawing, construction &^{ct}—seem to me admirable, but I have dwelt upon the one that interested me most. I hope that you will excuse me for having written to you.

Believe me
Yours truly
E. M. Forster.

III

Letter from Stephen Gilbert to Geoffrey Faber.[1]

Springhill,
Ballyhanwood Road,
Gilnahirk.
20th Feb. '47.

My dear Faber,

I don't like *Denis* alone and I am not quite sure why. If I saw a book with that title by a writer whom I did not know I would think that it was aimed at the Christopher-Robin public. I have the impression that the name Denis with one N has become a rather

---

[1] Geoffrey Faber had met with Reid's friends John Sparrow and John Bryson in Oxford, both of whom had suggested that *Denis* would be a preferable title to *Denis Bracknel*. In his letter to Stephen Gilbert dated 18 February 1947, Faber had expressed his agreement, specifically noting that as a "name" title, *Denis Bracknel* would be too similar to Reid's novels *Brian Westby* and *Peter Waring*. The following is Gilbert's reply. (Letter courtesy of Tom Gilbert.)

fancy Christian name and to put it alone would be to emphasise this, which would be unfortunate.

Do you think that the existence of the titles *Brian Westby* and *Peter Waring* really matters? I don't believe Forrest would have thought so.

I know he intended to let the original title stand—at least I think he did. I think also that he would have consented to *Denis Bracknel*. I haven't the faintest notion whether he would have approved of *Denis* alone or not; but I can very well imagine him saying to me, "What on earth did you let them do that for? Well, I think you might have had a bit more sense."

There at any rate you have my rather muddled thoughts on the subject. My aim, I suppose, is to play for safety, to avoid doing anything of which Forrest could possibly disapprove.

Yours very sincerely,
Stephen Gilbert

IV

Letter from George Buchanan to Stephen Gilbert.[1]

ROE PARK, LIMAVADY
Co. LONDONDERRY
Limavady 55

March 19 1947

Dear Stephen:
Hold out for *The Bracknells* [sic], if you can.

This changing of titles, I think, should be avoided. *The Bracknels* is Forrest's title: it is the same book revised and re-issued. Why *should* it be changed? If it's for the sake of misleading the public —or trying to get more reviews out of the critics—these seem

---

[1] Courtesy of Tom Gilbert.

poor reasons, and really not necessary, for the book will sell well, anyhow.

Strongest point of all, any other title than *The Bracknels* would not be Forrest's title.

There, for what it is worth, you have my view. But I suppose the publishers will have the last word.

All good wishes
George

ALSO AVAILABLE FROM VALANCOURT BOOKS

MICHAEL ARLEN	Hell! said the Duchess
R. C. ASHBY (RUBY FERGUSON)	He Arrived at Dusk
FRANK BAKER	The Birds
WALTER BAXTER	Look Down in Mercy
CHARLES BEAUMONT	The Hunger and Other Stories
DAVID BENEDICTUS	The Fourth of June
PAUL BINDING	Harmonica's Bridegroom
CHARLES BIRKIN	The Smell of Evil
JOHN BLACKBURN	A Scent of New-Mown Hay
THOMAS BLACKBURN	A Clip of Steel
	The Feast of the Wolf
JOHN BRAINE	Room at the Top
	The Vodi
MICHAEL CAMPBELL	Lord Dismiss Us
R. CHETWYND-HAYES	The Monster Club
BASIL COPPER	The Great White Space
	Necropolis
HUNTER DAVIES	Body Charge
JENNIFER DAWSON	The Ha-Ha
BARRY ENGLAND	Figures in a Landscape
RONALD FRASER	Flower Phantoms
GILLIAN FREEMAN	The Liberty Man
	The Leather Boys
	The Leader
STEPHEN GILBERT	The Landslide
	The Burnaby Experiments
	Ratman's Notebooks
MARTYN GOFF	The Youngest Director
STEPHEN GREGORY	The Cormorant
JOHN HAMPSON	Saturday Night at the Greyhound
THOMAS HINDE	The Day the Call Came
CLAUDE HOUGHTON	I Am Jonathan Scrivener
	This Was Ivor Trent
JAMES KENNAWAY	The Mind Benders
CYRIL KERSH	The Aggravations of Minnie Ashe
GERALD KERSH	Fowlers End
	Nightshade and Damnations
FRANCIS KING	Never Again

Francis King	An Air That Kills
	The Dividing Stream
	The Dark Glasses
C.H.B. Kitchin	Ten Pollitt Place
	The Book of Life
Hilda Lewis	The Witch and the Priest
John Lodwick	Brother Death
Kenneth Martin	Aubade
Michael Nelson	Knock or Ring
	A Room in Chelsea Square
Beverley Nichols	Crazy Pavements
Oliver Onions	The Hand of Kornelius Voyt
J.B. Priestley	Benighted
	The Other Place
	The Magicians
	Saturn Over the Water
	The Shapes of Sleep
Peter Prince	Play Things
Piers Paul Read	Monk Dawson
Forrest Reid	Following Darkness
	The Spring Song
	Brian Westby
	The Tom Barber Trilogy
Andrew Sinclair	The Facts in the Case of E.A. Poe
	The Raker
Colin Spencer	Panic
David Storey	Radcliffe
	Pasmore
	Saville
Russell Thorndike	The Slype
	The Master of the Macabre
John Wain	Hurry on Down
	The Smaller Sky
	A Winter in the Hills
Hugh Walpole	The Killer and the Slain
Keith Waterhouse	There is a Happy Land
	Billy Liar
Colin Wilson	Ritual in the Dark
	Man Without a Shadow
	The Philosopher's Stone
	The God of the Labyrinth

WHAT CRITICS ARE SAYING ABOUT VALANCOURT BOOKS

"[W]e owe a debt of gratitude to the publisher Valancourt, whose aim is to resurrect some neglected works of literature, especially those incorporating a supernatural strand, and make them available to a new readership."

Times Literary Supplement (London)

"Valancourt Books champions neglected but important works of fantastic, occult, decadent and gay literature. The press's Web site not only lists scores of titles but also explains why these often obscure books are still worth reading. . . . So if you're a real reader, one who looks beyond the bestseller list and the touted books of the moment, Valancourt's publications may be just what you're searching for."

MICHAEL DIRDA, *Washington Post*

"Valancourt Books are fast becoming my favourite publisher. They have made it their business, with considerable taste and integrity, to put back into print a considerable amount of work which has been in serious need of republication. If you ever felt there were gaps in your reading experience or are simply frustrated that you can't find enough good, substantial fiction in the shops or even online, then this is the publisher for you."

MICHAEL MOORCOCK

TO LEARN MORE AND TO SEE A COMPLETE LIST OF AVAILABLE TITLES, VISIT US AT VALANCOURTBOOKS.COM

Milton Keynes UK
Ingram Content Group UK Ltd.
UKHW042247110924
448191UK00009B/51